Death Rite

Death Rite

Kerry Watts

hera

First published in the United Kingdom in 2021 by

Hera Books
Unit 9 (Canelo), 5th Floor
Cargo Works, 1-2 Hatfields
London, SE1 9PG
United Kingdom

A CIP catalogue record for this book is available from the British Library.

Print ISBN 978 1 80032 614 9
Ebook ISBN 978 1 91297 381 1

Look for more great books at www.herabooks.com

Printed and bound in Great Britain by Clays Ltd, Elcograf S.p.A.

Mum – wish you were here to meet DCI Hazel Todd. I think you two would have got on like a house on fire x

They say it's the number of people I killed

I say it's the principle.

Aileen Wuornos

Prologue

Watching them breathe their last never gets old. He's not quite there yet, but soon, yes, soon his existence will be extinguished. As it should be. If he hadn't been so arrogant, so aggressive, he might have lived. We all make choices every day, every minute. Crossing the road, buying those groceries, stopping to talk to friends. They're all decisions every person makes to survive. One wrong move could be your last.

She understood that. She didn't grieve their loss. Why should I?

Chapter One

Then

The blood spilling from his mouth trickled from under the plastic bag and she frowned because she was sure she'd taped it tight. That was a new idea she'd heard someone talking about. She couldn't remember who. Carrier bag over his head. Watch him squirm. Might as well put the fun into what was fundamentally functional.

His breathing was slowing now, the rise and fall of his chest diminishing now that he'd stopped panicking. Didn't he know it was the rapid, shallow breaths of panic that used up air? It wasn't personal. She'd told him that. Or had she? She couldn't remember. She had definitely told the last one. She knew that because he'd used that to appeal to her compassionate side. Compassion. Rachel didn't have the time nor the inclination for compassion. Nobody had ever shown her an ounce of it. Rachel was so deep in a state of trance that she never heard the footsteps approach the car. She was startled by the door being dragged open and an armed officer holding his weapon close to her.

'Put your hands in front of you and get out of the vehicle slowly. Keep your hands where I can see them.'

All that shouting. The blinking lights from the vehicles surrounding her. Rachel couldn't think. She took a last glance at her meal ticket, panting to attract the officer's attention. A second officer threw the passenger door open and leaned in to assess her victim.

'He's alive,' she heard the huge officer call behind him while he ripped the plastic from the man's head. 'I need a paramedic here now. Secure her.'

'I said, get out of the car!' They were screaming in her ear.

Rachel had no choice. It looked like it was all over. They were so loud, and her head was hurting.

'OK, OK.' Rachel did as she was told, keeping her hands in full view.

'Get her in the van and don't let her out of your sight. I want two officers with her at all times.'

She felt her body slam against the cold metal of the BMW she'd got into an hour before, a price and service agreed with *him*. He was alive. Pity, she thought, as she watched paramedics racing to save his life. Five more minutes, that was all she'd needed. Five minutes would have seen that piece of trash off this planet forever. If only they knew what kind of monster they were saving.

Chapter Two

Such a handsome young man, DCI Hazel Todd thought when she stared into the red 2010 Fiesta. What a waste. Knowing this was a regular spot where sex workers picked men up, she couldn't rule out a connection. The man, who looked barely into his twenties, if that, was slumped back in the driver's seat, his head tilted just a fraction onto his left shoulder, a gaping hole where his stomach should be. She wondered if he'd brought a girlfriend here for some 'alone time'. Somewhere they could be away from prying eyes. Had something gone terribly wrong? An argument perhaps. Hadn't Hazel and Rick spent many nights up Kinnoull Hill looking for 'alone time'? At fifty-two now though that was a distant memory, a very distant memory. That and the fact they were divorced.

The contradiction of the scene was stark. Although his abdomen was blood-soaked, barely a hair looked out of place and Hazel could smell the sweet scent of his hair gel a little over the stench of the dried blood that was staining his blue T-shirt. He looked smart. His jeans and trainers certainly weren't Primark, and the car looked and smelled clean, not like a young lad's car at all. No empty crisp bags or drinks cans. If it weren't for the huge hole in his body he could easily be mistaken for being asleep.

The sunrise over the water of the harbour added to the bitter-sweet atmosphere. The crisp, clear chill of the October morning meant that when Hazel's warm breath hit the air, it left streaks of condensation behind. The sound of the heavy door to a garage being hauled open rattled into the air, scattering a flock of seagulls that had gathered for scraps outside the café where tables were normally set up for breakfast diners. Mainly warehouse workers and the men who worked in the units closer to the Friarton waste depot which was a quarter of a mile further along the road. She wasn't surprised none of the workers had found their victim with the Fiesta being tucked along the track. Far enough away from the main road that ran alongside the river until it stopped at the harbour's edge to be away from sight. The rarely used slipway being just a few hundred metres away. Had the harbour café not been located where it was, Hazel feared it might have been days before the lad's body was found. She wondered if their killer had requested this secluded location deliberately.

'Keep them back, will you,' Hazel shouted to her DC, unwilling to have a bunch of nosy mechanics trampling over her crime scene. 'In fact, Andrea,' she added. 'Get the road shut off.'

The body may have been found deeper along the track that ran alongside the river, but she wasn't taking any chances.

'Sure, boss,' DC Andrea Graham called back.

'Good morning DCI Todd.' The unusually feminine man's voice came from behind her.

'Jack.' Hazel screwed up her face against the morning chill, relieved to see the short, slender pathologist walk towards her. She'd been surprised on meeting the man to see he stood a mere five feet six with an unusually feminine voice to go with the short stature. That didn't stop him being good at his job. What he lacked in stature he more than made up for in other ways. His IQ for one, which Hazel had heard scored 135 but she had never had the nerve to ask him directly. She peeled the paper mask down a touch. 'He looks young. Single stab wound, I think, it's hard to tell. No defensive wounds, from what I can see.'

'Let me be the judge of that,' Jack Blair said tartly and tugged up his hood.

'It's pretty isolated at this end of the harbour,' Hazel suggested and waved to her DI, Tom Newton, as he joined them. 'Seems nobody heard anything.'

'Late night?' she asked Tom, the hint of a smirk on her lips. She only teased him out of affection. Hazel had been delighted to hear that Tom had finally met someone. The two seemed to still be in that loved-up, inseparable phase of their relationship. Something that she hadn't felt for a considerable number of years.

'Maybe.' The slight flush of pink on Tom's cheeks made her smile. 'There's been an accident on the Inveralmond roundabout. Traffic was backed up. It took me ages to get through.'

'Aye, well, you're here now, DI Newton,' Jack Blair said as he snapped on a pair of gloves before opening the car door and leaning close to the dead man's clean-shaven face.

Hazel watched him smell the air around the body. A peculiar thing Jack always did, even at the most gruesome of scenes.

'What have we got?' Tom asked.

'White male found dead by the owner of the harbour café about an hour ago,' Hazel began. 'Poor woman said she knocked on the window because she thought he was waiting for her to open up.'

Tom peered in the passenger window. 'He looks young. Early twenties, maybe.'

'If that,' Hazel agreed. 'Big unit, too. Must have taken some force to overpower him.' She stared at his lifeless body and figured his height to be well over six feet, taller even than Tom who was six foot two. 'A surprise attack perhaps. By someone he trusted.'

'Have we got a statement from the woman who found him yet?' Tom asked, without taking his eyes off their victim.

'Not yet, one of the uniforms is with her. She's still in a right state.'

Jack Blair stood back up on the driver's side.

'Well?' Hazel asked.

'He's been dead no more than twelve hours. You were right, not much in the way of defensive wounds. A couple of broken nails from what I can see. I'll know more when I've been able to have a proper look at him.'

'Do we know who he is yet?' Tom walked round to the back of the Fiesta and typed the registration number into his phone.

'Car is registered to an address at Bertha Park,' Hazel told him.

'Very nice,' Tom commented. 'We've looked at buying one of those apartments.' Then he stopped, seemingly realising he'd said too much.

Hazel shot a quick glance at Jack, who was smiling at her.

'What?'

'It's "we" already, is it? Sounds like things are getting pretty serious,' Hazel said.

'I'm very happy for you,' Jack told him and started to head back to his own silver Mercedes that he'd parked outside the café entrance. 'I'll be in touch, DCI Todd.'

'Yes, I'll speak to you later.'

Hazel opened the passenger door of their victim's Fiesta and started to rummage inside the glove box where she found a packet of condoms and a brown leather wallet next to a small, pocket-sized packet of baby wipes and a multi pack of Polos. Perhaps he was there to pick up a sex worker after all. It took all sorts, she supposed, perhaps even young, good-looking lads. She lifted out the wallet and searched for some kind of identification. The DVLA check indicated the car was registered to Lisa Kennedy. Definitely not the person sat slumped in the driver's seat. Her eyes were drawn to a single hair, which was longer than their victim's, on the mat in the passenger footwell. She placed the hair into an evidence bag.

Tom had moved to the back of the vehicle and opened the car boot where he found a sports bag, a tennis racket and a brown cardboard box filled with various medical textbooks. As he lifted the top book out and flicked through the pages, a piece of paper fell out. He picked it up and found it was a letter from what appeared to be a girlfriend. Someone who looked like she was now an ex-girlfriend. Ouch. The author of the letter was clearly angry when they'd written this. Perhaps angry enough to do something terrible to him. Tom bagged up the letter then unzipped the sports bag where he found what he had expected to see: a crumpled kit comprising a pair of navy tracksuit bottoms, a wrinkled T-shirt and a huge pair of trainers. He peered at the sole to find they were a size thirteen. The side pocket held a reusable drinks bottle, containing the remnants of some kind of isotonic energy drink. He dropped that into an evidence bag. It could be useful for potential DNA and fingerprint evidence too.

'Bingo,' Hazel chirped, and Tom joined her at the passenger door. She held a student ID card she'd found in the wallet up for him to see.

'Sam Kennedy,' Tom read aloud. 'Only just turned twenty. He was a medical student at Ninewells.'

'What did you find?' Hazel asked while she dropped the wallet into an evidence bag and followed him back to the boot.

'A Dear John letter and this stuff.' Tom pointed.

'Angry ex-girlfriend, do you think?' Hazel suggested. 'Angry enough to do that?' She nodded back in the direction of the driver's seat.

'Maybe.' Tom showed her the letter.

Hazel narrowed her eyes at the contents of the letter, telling herself she'd need to get one of those necklaces for her glasses. Something she'd sworn she'd never do but practicality might have to beat pride soon.

'It's just signed "Kirsty".' Hazel's eyes met Tom's. 'Kirsty who, I wonder?'

The sound of tyres on gravel came from behind them and Hazel pressed the bagged letter into Tom's chest and turned round. The canine team. 'Good: the dogs are here.'

Hazel nodded to the female officer who was holding tight to the lead of a stunning black and white springer spaniel whose wagging tail seemed to be defying the laws of physics with its intensity. A memory of a childhood pet hit her mind, but she pushed it away immediately.

'I want the whole bank covered – the trees, the derelict buildings, lock-ups, the lot. I'm waiting on confirmation to go on board the tug vessel as well.' She glanced across at the small boat named *The Fair Maid of Perth*, tied up until she was needed. She doubted it would hold anything of use, but it was here so couldn't be ignored. A lonely sight on the few occasions Hazel had to use the harbour road as a shortcut when the Edinburgh Road, which ran parallel as it wound its way into Perth City centre, was busy. She just wished permission would hurry up and arrive. Any evidence it held could be important. As it turned out, a cargo vessel had been due to dock last night but had been held up because of the weather. It would have been a rare arrival in the once-thriving harbour, now scarcely used. 'Go over and speak to them at the garage will you,' she instructed Tom and walked on ahead, peeling off the gloves and suit as she moved. 'Give Andrea a hand. See if they saw or heard anything. I'm going in to talk to the woman who found our victim.'

–

'Mrs Dean, my name is DCI Hazel Todd.' Hazel held up her identification for the startled woman to see, nodding to acknowledge the retreating uniformed officer who left them. 'I know this is difficult, but I was wondering if you could go over again for me what happened this morning.'

The whites of the middle-aged woman's blue eyes were red from crying and she blew her nose loudly as Hazel approached one of the café tables that had an ashtray with the remnants of two smoked cigarettes in it. The woman pushed the half-drunk cup of tea to the side and damped down her greying blonde hair.

'Yes, of course, anything to help that poor boy.' Her voice trembled almost as much as her hands.

'Can you tell me exactly what happened when you got here this morning?' Hazel asked. 'Was there anybody else around?'

The woman shook her head. 'No, Gary from the garage wasn't even here yet. If he's in, he usually leaves the doors open for me. That's how I know he wasn't here yet. I take a roll and sliced sausage over for him, you see.' She clasped her hands together to stop them trembling. 'I'm sorry, I don't seem to be able to stop them shaking.'

'It's fine, that's perfectly normal, it must have been a terrible shock for you.'

'I imagine you've seen things like that lots of times,' she said.

'Not too many, thankfully,' Hazel told her. 'It's rarer than TV shows lead you to believe.'

The thinnest of smiles landed on the woman's face. 'That's good, then.'

'Did you recognise the victim?' Hazel pressed her. 'Or his car, perhaps?'

Her witness shook her head. 'No, neither, I'm sorry. I honestly thought the lad was waiting for me to open up. I thought he was after an early morning bacon roll or something.'

'Is that something that happens often?'

'Not like it used to. This place is a ghost of its former self. Wouldn't surprise me if they sell the land and put up fancy new apartments.'

Hazel couldn't disagree. You couldn't halt progress and the place was in desperate need of regeneration. This and a lot of Perth, which had not much left in the high street but Primark and M&S. Even the city's hospital had been stripped of many services, meaning most people had to make the thirty-minute drive to Ninewells instead.

'Do you know who he is?' the woman continued.

'Not yet,' Hazel lied, because telling his family had to be her priority and it was becoming clear this witness had nothing much else to offer her. She took one of her cards out of her long grey cardigan pocket and slid it across the table. 'If you think of anything else, please give this number a call.'

Hazel stood.

'When can I open up?'

'Not for a while yet, I'm afraid. We still have some forensic examinations to carry out,' Hazel informed her. 'I have your details, so I'll be in touch if I need to ask you anything else.'

'OK.' The woman sounded defeated, and Hazel didn't blame her. Losing a day's takings wasn't something she'd planned for when she got up that morning.

Hazel hoped Tom was having more luck across the road.

–

'Yes, I've worked on that Fiesta.' The mechanic rubbed at the thick stubble on his face.

'What can you tell me about the owner?' Tom pushed him.

'Beautiful woman,' the mechanic went on, narrowing his eyes, obviously thinking about the car's owner. 'That car's cost her a fortune this year. I keep telling her it's time to get a new one, but she won't listen.'

'Is that right?' Tom asked, glancing briefly over his shoulder at DC Andrea Graham who was deep in conversation with the garage owner, a bespectacled, wiry man in his fifties.

'It's not her over there, is it?' His eyes widened, and his fingers seemed to rub faster over his chin the more concerned he got.

'It's not a woman,' Tom told him.

'It's her son then, is it?'

Tom frowned at him, quietly sizing him up. 'How well do you know her son?'

'I don't, really.' He snatched a dirty rag from the table behind him and rubbed his hands. 'He came to collect his mum's car a couple of times. Nice enough lad. Which was why I was surprised to see him picking up a tart.'

'Do you mean you saw a prostitute getting into his car?' Tom pointed across the road to where the Fiesta was parked. 'In that car?'

The man nodded. 'Yes. It was a while ago, mind.'

'Exactly how long is a while?' Tom pressed him. 'Last week, last year,' he suggested.

'Jesus now you're asking,' he answered, frowning, seemingly searching for a memory. 'It was about a month ago,' he said after much deliberation.

'About a month or exactly a month?' Tom was growing increasingly frustrated.

'It was the beginning of last month.'

'What did she look like?' Tom pushed for more, disturbed by the smirk growing on the man's face.

'What do they all look like?' he shrugged 'They all look like tarts, don't they?'

Chapter Three

Then

RUC Detective Inspector Iain McGill pulled out a chair and sat himself opposite Rachel McMahon. He struggled to square the scenes of horror with the sight of the thin, pale and quite frankly pathetic woman his team had finally arrested on suspicion of murder. But not before she'd brought chaos and carnage to the lives of four men. As if West Belfast didn't have enough on its plate. A recent car bomb had ripped apart a safe house, killing two officers and an informant who had placed his life in their hands. They didn't need a seemingly random multiple murder case too. Intelligence on the ground couldn't prove any connection between the four men, stabbed and suffocated in their cars, leaving three dead and one fighting for his life, which made the case all the more puzzling. She'd stolen fathers and sons from their loved ones for what appeared to be no apparent reason.

The veteran detective sat and quietly sipped from the cup of water he'd brought to the interview with him. He slid another paper cup closer to Rachel.

'Do you understand why you've been arrested?' he began once the formal introductions for the tape were over.

She nodded, just once, then stared back at the floor. A shiver started at her feet and travelled up her body. She was freezing. Her fingers seemed to be so numb she couldn't feel them. 'I don't feel well,' she whispered.

'I need you to confirm you understand,' McGill added. 'For the tape.'

'Yes, I understand,' Rachel responded, obviously irritated.

'And you can confirm you understand you have a right to remain silent if you wish to do so. Has this been fully explained to you?' McGill glanced between Rachel and her solicitor.

'Yes,' Rachel snapped. 'I really don't feel well,' she repeated and clutched her stomach.

'Missing your fix, I expect,' DI McGill said bluntly as he opened the file in front of him. 'You must be well overdue by now, aren't you?' He took a pair of glasses from his suit jacket pocket and put them on while he spoke.

'Fucking prick. You think you're so fecking smart don't you?' Rachel spat in his direction, startling her solicitor briefly into looking up from his notepad, but barely a drop landed on the table in front of him, her mouth was so dry.

McGill tutted and quickly dried the few specks. 'There's no need for that, Rachel.' He turned over the first photo in the folder. 'You've been examined by the doctor, haven't you? Here, drink some water.'

Rachel scratched her cheek then nibbled her thumbnail while he laid the selection of chilling, gruesome crime scene photos in front of her. Her stomach hurt so badly. She picked up the cup of water and lashed it at the wall to her left, narrowly missing the uniformed constable who was nearby. McGill waved away the officer, who had moved forward to restrain her.

'He's doing well, by the way, in case you wondered. That last one,' McGill informed her. 'A bit battered round the edges after three hours of surgery to fix the damage you caused, but the doctors expect he'll make a good recovery, eventually, physically anyway. Minus his spleen, but he'll manage without it, they say. I imagine the mental scars might last a lot longer.' The detective spoke without looking up from the photos.

Rachel shrugged as she shivered. 'What is it you're expecting me to say?'

'An explanation of why you did those things would be nice.' McGill pointed his fingers slowly and deliberately to each of the photos in turn, the sound of his finger contacting the table making her already throbbing head worse. A ringing had started in her ears, and she felt dizzy. She lurched herself forward and banged her palm hard on the table, startling her solicitor.

'These men aren't the innocent victims you've painted them as, I can assure you,' Rachel said. 'It was self-defence, and you can't prove otherwise.'

McGill sighed. 'Did they threaten you? Is that what you're trying to tell me?'

'They were trying to rape me.'

'Were they?'

'Yes they were, so if I killed them, I killed them in self-defence.' Rachel turned to face her solicitor. 'I'm entitled to take reasonable measures to protect myself, aren't I?'

'Murder isn't a reasonable measure, Rachel,' McGill pointed out. 'Putting a carrier bag over someone's head goes way beyond the self-defence argument.'

Rachel huffed and looked away in disgust.

'You don't have to say anything. In fact, my advice is to say nothing more,' her solicitor piped up and wrote something on his pad.

'You've been charged with soliciting in the past.' McGill stared briefly at the young man then thumbed through some of his own notes. 'Last year, I believe. Were you out working last night, Rachel?'

'I've got to eat, haven't I?' she answered plainly. 'Not everybody has a hot meal to go home to every night.'

McGill sat back in the black plastic chair and tried to maintain eye contact with her. 'Did you arrange to provide Mr Lamont with sexual services last night?'

'Yes I did. What are you going to do, arrest me for that now too?' Rachel scoffed, her venom palpable in the tense atmosphere of the small interview room.

'Don't tempt me, Rachel.' DI McGill looked straight at her this time. The pair stared at each other in silence until Rachel's gaze flicked sideways first. 'So you're admitting you killed them?'

'No I'm not.'

'But you've said you killed them in self-defence,' McGill pointed out.

'I was confused then, I'm not now,' she quickly corrected herself, scratching her head aggressively. 'It wasn't me. You've twisted my words.'

McGill's eyebrows stretched up, almost meeting his wispy brown fringe. He exhaled loudly and shook his head. 'Interview terminat—' He reached for the tape, but Rachel laid her hand on his arm.

'That's it, is it, Detective McGill? Or is it Iain? Can I call you Iain?'

Iain McGill pulled his arm back and held her gaze. He noticed the dark circles underneath her eyes like black moons enveloping them. She might have been pretty before the drugs and alcohol had taken their vice-like grip on her.

'Did you kill those men, Rachel? I need you to say it for the tape.' He didn't take his eyes off hers, holding up two of the crime scene pictures, close enough for her to get a good look. 'Look, if you confess maybe I can help you. Get you the help you need.'

Rachel glanced to her solicitor then back at McGill, her eyes briefly skirting the images.

'No comment,' she said, before dropping her gaze to the patch of sticky vinyl on the floor.

Chapter Four

Now

Lisa Kennedy opened the door and lifted the cardboard box from under the hall table.

'Here you go, I didn't think you were coming until this afternoon,' she said and tried to hand the box to Tom. 'The woman on the phone said after two—' She stopped talking immediately on seeing the two ID badges and the expression on her face darkened. 'What's happened?'

'Mrs Kennedy, can we come in?' Hazel asked gently, glancing briefly at the elderly man holding tightly to a lead with a small black terrier on the other end, walking up the path to the next door property, his beady eyes staring at the activity next door.

Lisa Kennedy's face filled with confusion. 'Wh-what…' She stumbled over her words and put the box back down before holding the door wide open for them. 'Yes, yes, come in. Just go through, the last door on the right.' She closed the door and followed them in.

'Please sit down,' she added and lifted a pile of books from the flowery green armchair immediately inside the immaculately decorated room.

Hazel spotted the painting above the fireplace. She recognised it as a Jack Vettriano print immediately, the man and woman dancing on the beach. A classic. A school photo on the mantelpiece below she knew straight away was Sam, smiling next to an older man and his mother. The lad in the picture towered above them. It looked like a holiday snap, given the sunlit ocean view behind them.

'Thank you,' Hazel answered and unzipped her cardigan before lowering herself onto a matching green sofa. The grey cat sleeping on the other end lifted his head, miaowed once and curled back up before going back to sleep.

'For God's sake, just tell me.' Lisa was clearly rattled.

'Please have a seat, Mrs Kennedy.' Tom spoke quietly but firmly enough to make the petite, blonde woman do as he asked.

Hazel hated moments like these. Any officer who said they'd got used to it was lying.

'I'm sorry to have to tell you that the body of a young man was discovered early this—'

Before she could finish, a noise erupted from Lisa Kennedy's mouth which seemed to come from deep within her soul. A hollow guttural sound like a wounded animal.

'I'm sorry,' Hazel persisted. 'But a student identification card found inside the vehicle matched the description of the deceased. Sam Kennedy.'

Lisa expelled a simple whimper and clutched her stomach then ran from the room.

The sound of vomiting made Hazel wince.

'Shall I go and check on her?' Tom suggested.

'No, give her a minute.'

The rush of water running followed the flushing of the toilet.

'Nice place they've got,' Tom whispered and gazed around the room.

Hazel didn't have a chance to let him know she agreed before Lisa re-joined them.

'I'm sorry,' she murmured, wiping her mouth with a bunch of scrunched up toilet paper and flopped down next to Hazel.

'I'll go and make some tea, shall I?' Tom looked at Hazel for approval then back at Lisa.

'That sounds like a good idea.' Hazel smiled gently before Tom got up and left her to it. The cat that had been snoozing woke and leapt off the sofa to follow him. Hazel gave the shocked woman a moment to collect herself before bombarding her with any more information.

'Are you sure it's Sam?'

'Obviously, we'll need someone to formally identify his body but...' Hazel stopped and watched her face disintegrate into floods of tears. She took Lisa's hand in hers and gave it a gentle squeeze. 'Do you feel up to doing that or is there someone else you'd prefer to identify your son?'

'Erm, I don't know... I... erm...' Lisa's eyes narrowed deeply. 'No, I'll do it.' She made to stand up again. 'Just let me get my bag.'

'No, no, we're not quite there yet,' Hazel began to say as Tom walked in with two mugs of tea in his hands. 'I'll arrange for someone to take you when it's time.'

'Oh OK,' Lisa replied, ignoring Tom's proffered mug of tea.

Hazel took both mugs and laid them on the table. 'Thanks, Tom.' She rested her hand over Lisa's once more, this time noticing how cold it was. 'Listen, would it be OK if my colleague went and took a look at Sam's bedroom?'

'Erm, yes, yes.'

'When did you last see Sam?' Hazel pushed on.

'He told me he was meeting someone last night. He didn't say who, but he asked if he could borrow my car.' Lisa stared into space. 'I can't…' Words appeared hard to find.

'What time did Sam leave last night?'

'What?' Lisa's eyes glazed over.

'What time did he leave?' Hazel repeated.

'I don't know. I was out until late yesterday.' Lisa's body started to tremble.

The phone ringing on the low pine coffee table seemingly startled her out of her trance. She coughed and picked the handset up.

'Can I take this?'

'Of course.' Hazel indicated to the door towards Tom. 'We'll go and have that look then, shall we? Sam's room is upstairs, is it?' She stood and was walking out before Lisa had answered.

'Erm, yes, Sam's is the one at the top of the stairs.'

Hazel and Tom heard her answer the phone and burst into floods of tears. What she said to the caller was barely audible between sobs.

'Poor woman,' Tom whispered as they made their way upstairs.

Hazel's eyes were irresistibly drawn to the gallery of photos hung on the wall which wove a path upstairs. She stopped to take a closer look. Most were of Sam at various ages, from a giggling baby through awkward teenage haircuts to what looked like a more recent photo of him with a pretty young woman. Kirsty, perhaps. They made a handsome couple. Sam with his rugged jawline and twinkling blue eyes with his arm round the waist of a petite blonde, smiling and cuddling close to his chest. The couple were standing on a beach, a stunning sunset behind them. The girl's resemblance to Lisa Kennedy didn't pass Hazel by. She wondered what could have happened to make the happy girl in this photo end their relationship. If indeed she was the Kirsty from the letter Tom had found. She climbed the rest of the stairs while tugging a pair of latex gloves on.

'Wow,' Hazel exclaimed on seeing the room. 'Sam was a very tidy lad.'

She looked over the room from the doorway. First impressions were vital. His bed was made, with matching duvet and pillowcase. The pattern was from a video game that Hazel recognised. *Call of Duty*; that was it. Against Hazel's advice, she knew her cousin allowed his young son to play the game. To the right was a gaming desk and a huge chair clearly designed for comfortable hours in front of the screen. The desk was obviously shared between the two parts of Sam's life, the medical student and the gamer. A large fish tank on the top of a tall pine dresser was a surprise. The contents looked more exotic than the simple goldfish she'd had growing up.

Tom opened the bottom drawer of Sam's bedside cabinet, which had three drawers. He flicked through the contents. Inside were porn mags, but after taking a quick look through the pages, he put them back. Nothing out of the ordinary. Just pretty standard naked women with their legs open to the 'reader'. He found a notebook with one of those four-colour Bic pens clipped to the wire on the side. A tin of sketching pencils was underneath the pad. He flipped through the pages, intrigued to see it was a diary of sorts with some pages filled with drawings of women in various stages of undress. The lad was talented, Tom had to admit. The pictures were detailed and from what Tom could tell, anatomically very accurate. Other pages looked like he'd been writing his deepest secrets. Tom laid it down and slipped his hand towards the back of the drawer, stumbling on nothing else but a packet of tissues and two Mars bars. He couldn't rule out the true crime book on top of the unit being significant and bagged that, too.

'Looks like Sam kept a diary.' Tom held up the notebook.

'Mm,' Hazel mused without looking over.

'That's a bit unusual, wouldn't you say? For a young man to keep a diary,' Tom suggested.

'Bag it,' Hazel instructed him as she opened the top drawer of Sam's dresser where she found neat rows of folded black socks in front of a row of carefully folded men's trunks.

The trunks were a variety of colours, seemingly laid out in terms of colour coordination from white on the left, all the way to navy on the right with all shades of yellows, pinks, reds, greens and blues in between. No black, she noticed, a detail which was probably not significant, but she made a mental note anyway. She pushed the top drawer shut and started to examine the contents of the rest of the unit. The lad really was tidy. Every shirt was perfectly folded and ironed. She wondered if that was Lisa's doing, or Sam's.

'I've found a laptop,' Tom told her. 'It was stuffed down between the bedside cabinet and his bed.'

Hazel turned. 'Is that where you'd keep yours?'

'Yes,' Tom frowned. 'Don't you?' He took a large clear evidence bag out of his pocket and slipped the laptop inside. An expensive MacBook, he noted.

'No, mine stays on the kitchen table,' Hazel informed him then saw him suck in air through his teeth. 'What's wrong with that?'

'You know it'll be the first thing a burglar sees if they come in your kitchen. I thought you'd have known that.'

He had a point. 'Mm,' she replied. 'I'd never thought of that.'

Tom shrugged. 'Well now you know.'

Footsteps on the stairs caught his attention before Lisa Kennedy appeared in the doorway, rubbing her face with the sleeve of a pink sweater she'd not been wearing when Tom and Hazel had been talking to her downstairs.

'I'm sorry about that. That was Sam's best friend, Daniel.'

'Have you told Daniel?' Hazel asked.

Lisa only managed a short nod before she broke down again.

'I'm sorry,' she mumbled and coughed to compose herself.

'Hey,' Tom said. 'It's fine.'

Lisa Kennedy closed her eyes and inhaled a huge breath before expelling it slowly through puffed cheeks. Her eyes snapped open.

'What do you need from me?' she asked, looking straight at Hazel.

'OK.' Hazel appreciated how practical she seemed to be. 'Is this Sam's only device?' She pointed to the laptop in Tom's hand.

'No, he has an iPad here somewhere too.' She started to open and close drawers then slid back the door to his wardrobe. She stepped onto her tiptoes and reached her hand as far back as she could until Tom moved closer, easily finding what they were looking for.

'Here we go,' Tom announced and held up an iPad with a blue cover on it.

'Yes, that's it.' Then her eyes widened, and she rushed out of the room with Hazel in pursuit. 'His phone!' she said, coming to a halt in the bedroom next to Sam's.

Hazel was stunned to see how untidy the room was. Laundry was piled so high in a beige plastic basket that there was a white blouse cascading over the side. A half-drunk mug of tea stood on a table next to an unmade bed. One of the sliding wardrobe doors, like the ones in Sam's room, was open a little, displaying piles of books. This was the room where people found the real Lisa Kennedy, perhaps.

'Here.' Lisa grabbed a phone from a charger on the window ledge. 'I'd told him not to move my charger. I said he could charge his phone in my room yesterday.' Her voice started to tremble, the swell of emotion building once more. 'He must have forgotten to take it with him last night.' She broke down again. 'If he'd had it last night then maybe…' Her voice disappeared into the tears.

Hazel took the phone from her and rubbed her hand gently up and down Lisa's arm. 'Thank you.' She felt awful for the woman as she tried to check for missed calls and messages but was locked out. 'Do you know what his password is?'

Lisa coughed to compose herself again, wiping her face quickly. 'Ted Bundy. All lower case.' She took a long breath to help her focus.

Hazel's eyes immediately caught Tom's. That was a new one on her. Birthdays, pets, yes. Serial killers was a first. As if reading her mind, Lisa commented.

'He changes his password all the time. Usually to something from a book he's reading.'

That was actually quite sensible, Hazel mused. Creepy in this case but practical as well as sensible. She typed the password and the phone's screen lit up. Three missed calls and six messages. All were from his friend Daniel except one unread message from the ex-girlfriend, Kirsty.

'We're going to need addresses for Daniel and Kirsty.'

Hazel told Lisa that she'd be in touch and that if she could think of anything that might help in the meantime she should call straight away. She'd had a cool response to her request for details of Sam's father. It seemed the divorce was not a nice one. Even worse than Hazel's, and that was bad enough. She told them Peter Kennedy was a solicitor in Edinburgh and that he did support them financially including Sam's education.

'I'll catch you up,' Hazel said on hearing her phone ring in her pocket. She took out the handset and screwed up her face at the caller ID. She pressed the call decline option and stuffed her phone back in her pocket. 'I don't think so,' she murmured, angry at the nerve of the caller.

Hazel had asked Tom to talk to the friend and told him she'd talk to the ex-girlfriend. She was grateful that Tom had agreed to walk back to the station, which would only take him ten minutes, from Sam's friend Daniel's city centre flat. She dropped him off and headed off to do something very important before heading to talk to Kirsty, the ex-girlfriend. She needed to find out what had gone so wrong in what looked like the perfect relationship.

Chapter Five

Tom rapped on the letterbox of Daniel's city centre rental flat, reminiscing about his first flat when he'd moved from Glasgow to Perth ten years ago. The memories weren't all bad. It was just the noise, the smell and the cold he wanted to forget. Being able to buy his little ex-council house in Luncarty had been bliss.

Footsteps sounded like they were getting closer from inside. 'Hang on, I'm coming,' a voice called out as Tom readied his ID to show Daniel.

'Daniel Macey? Hi, I'm DI Tom Newton. We spoke on the phone.'

'God, yes, come in.' Daniel pulled the door back and ushered Tom inside. 'I can't believe this is happening.' He exclaimed as he shut the door after them.

Tom stepped deeper inside the property and followed him into the living room to find Sam's tidiness had not rubbed off on his best friend. The stench of stale food seemed to linger on the carpets and curtains. Newspapers lay strewn across the coffee table with empty mugs holding them down. History textbooks were piled on top of them too. The sudden barking startled Tom as a huge black Labrador came at him, surging from the kitchen at speed, jumping up to get his attention, whacking its thick tail against the wall with force.

'Don't worry about Ben, he's harmless.' Loud music blared from inside the kitchen that led off from the living room; Daniel pulled the door shut. 'Sorry, I've got my nephew staying.'

It looked like the lad had a lot on his plate even before Tom's visit.

'I know that Sam's mum told you what happened,' Tom began.

'She said Sam's been murdered.' Daniel's brown eyes glistened until he rubbed them with the back of his hand, coughing to conceal his emotion. 'I can't get my head round it, I really can't. What the hell happened?' he tried to ask but the break in his voice gave away his grief.

'Sam was found in his mum's car early this morning. A post mortem examination is being carried out later today.' Tom spotted a photo of the two smiling friends at Murrayfield.

'Sam was a bloody great rugby player,' Daniel said, following Tom's gaze, the wide smile conveying the warmth he'd felt for his friend. 'He loved it, even when we were at school.'

It figured, Tom thought. Sam was a big unit. He'd have made a great scrum half. Daniel wasn't a small man either, standing at least the same height as Tom. Where Sam was blond and fair-skinned, Daniel's complexion was darker. He could even be described as Mediterranean, if not quite as dark as Tom was, with brown eyes and almost jet black hair. Another good-looking young lad.

'Lisa Kennedy tells us the two of you were close.'

Daniel's face flushed pink. 'What?'

'You and Sam were best friends,' Tom clarified. 'Since you both started secondary school.'

'Yes, that's right. We got put together in registration and just hit it off,' he shrugged. 'Sam was cool, you know, nothing fazed him. Not even some of the asshole teachers at the grammar.'

Daniel flopped down on top of a pile of washing on one of the check-patterned armchairs next to the living room window. A view that Tom didn't envy. Looking out on the back of derelict offices wasn't pretty. Now that the over-friendly Labrador had calmed down and left him alone, Tom sat himself opposite Daniel.

'Have you any idea what Sam was up to last night? Did he have a new girlfriend that you know of?'

Daniel shook his head. 'Nah, not after Kirsty dumped him.'

'Do you know why their relationship ended?' Tom asked, spotting what looked like a small plastic wrap of weed on the floor but ignoring it, for now. The last thing he wanted to do was stop him talking. Daniel shifted uncomfortably in the chair, a sure sign that he was holding something back. 'Daniel?' Tom added. 'If you know something, you need to tell me.'

'Look.' Daniel raised his hands. 'Sam was my best mate. I loved him more than I love my own brother.' He stopped and blew air through puffed cheeks, avoiding Tom's eyes before scratching roughly at his short black hair.

Tom eyed him carefully. It looked like Sam had a secret only they knew. A voice burst through the silence.

'Uncle Danny!'

'I'm sorry, excuse me a sec.' Daniel stood up and headed into the kitchen, followed by his dog and closed the kitchen door after them.

Tom picked up the suspicious little bag with the tip of his pen and sniffed it. Yes, it was weed. He put it back down and shook his head.

'I'm sorry about that,' Daniel said when he returned. 'The iPad had frozen.'

'It's fine,' Tom reassured him. 'You were about to tell me Sam's secret.'

Daniel stared at him then flicked his eyes sideways. 'I'm not sure what you mean.'

'Daniel,' Tom said plainly. 'Sam's dead.' He watched the lad swallow hard then close his eyes tight.

'I was supposed to meet up with Sam last night, but he didn't show. I rang him loads of times, left messages but...' he shrugged. 'He probably never got any of them, did he?'

'Sam left his phone at home last night. Seems he'd forgotten it because it was still in the charger,' Tom told him.

'That doesn't sound like him,' Daniel frowned.

This piqued Tom's interest. 'Had his phone glued to him like most of us these days, did he?'

'Yes, but...' Daniel replied. 'Although I suppose Sam had been a bit distracted recently.'

'Oh yes, in what way? Was it the break-up?' Tom pressed him, irritated by the vibration of his own phone in his trouser pocket. He snatched the handset out and quickly muted it. That could wait. 'Daniel,' he added, on seeing his reluctance to continue. 'How bad did the break-up affect him?'

Daniel scoffed. 'It didn't, not like you might think I mean. Sure he was sad but...' He said it loudly as if to emphasise the point. Then he sighed. 'Kirsty was hitting him and roaring and crying but Sam just didn't seem that bothered. Not that he's a hard-hearted bastard, I'm not saying that. It was just…' He paused again as if working up to something.

Tom waited for whatever bombshell was coming. He didn't know what, but the way Daniel was skirting around things, he knew there was something.

'Kirsty ended things with Sam because she found out he'd been paying for sex.'

'Oh,' Tom replied. That was certainly a bombshell. The location his body had been found made more sense now.

'Yes, oh. The shit totally hit the fan, man.' Daniel was shaking his head. 'I told him. I said he had to stop being so bloody stupid. Not even just about losing Kirsty. Think about your career, I told him. They could kick you off the course. Sam wanted to eventually become a psychiatrist. Did Lisa tell you?' Then he sighed. 'But I was mad at myself as well.'

'Why was that? Did you—'

'God, no, I—' Daniel burst in then stopped. 'Well yes, I did, once, but not here, it was my brother's stag weekend a few months ago and, well, I wasn't proud of it. I hated it if I'm honest.'

'Amsterdam?' Tom suggested, unsurprised to see Daniel nod.

'Yep, God it was awful, I felt sick,' Daniel explained. 'It's just not for me. Strip clubs, lap dancers, that's enough for me, you know. More than that is just sleazy.'

'But Sam liked it,' Tom suggested – it explained why he was found in an area frequented by sex workers.

Daniel dropped his head into his hands and exhaled sharply. 'It was my idea in the first place.' He snapped his head back up to face Tom, his fists clenched. 'We dared each other.'

'You think his interest in paying for sex increased when he got back from that trip?'

'I know it did.' Daniel added. 'Then Kirsty found out.'

'How long had it been going on before she found out?'

'Three months,' Daniel replied without looking at Tom.

'That must have been difficult for her to hear. How did she take it?'

'How do you think? She went nuts! Calling Sam all the bastards under the sun. Threatened to tell the university and everything but I managed to persuade her how much it would hurt Lisa to find out.'

Tom noticed the way his face flushed when he said Lisa's name. It was slight, but it was there. An idea came to him. Unsure whether this was even a thing, he asked anyway.

'Did Sam have a regular girl he liked to see? Like a preferred worker. Did he ever mention any names to you?'

'He mentioned the name Natasha a couple of times, but I doubt that's her real name.'

'I don't know but we'll certainly be following that line of inquiry,' Tom said. 'You said you had arranged to meet Sam last night. What was your arrangement?'

Daniel smiled thinly. 'We were going to watch the game in the pub on Tay street, but he was a no show,' he shrugged. 'No phone call, no nothing.'

'Is that unusual for Sam? To make and then break plans at short notice like that?'

Daniel shook his head, looking at the floor, seemingly trying to avoid letting Tom see the tears that were filling his eyes. He sniffed and took a breath before pinching the bridge of his nose between his finger and thumb. Tom felt sorry for him in that moment. The lad's grief was obvious.

'Take your time,' Tom added quietly. 'I know this is hard for you.'

'I'm sorry.' Daniel rubbed his eyes then tried to smile. 'God if Sam was here he'd be ripping the piss out of me for being so soft.'

'Sam clearly meant a lot to you.'

'He was my best friend.'

'So would you say it was unusual for him to stand you up like that last night?' Tom rephrased his question.

'Until a couple of months ago, yes but…' Daniel stopped to take a breath then became distracted by a text. Tom glanced down at the phone on the table to see the ID read *Lisa* and a gentle pink hue grew on Daniel's cheeks.

'Erm, but…' Daniel was flustered now. 'Lately, like I said, he'd been distracted so, yes he'd left me hanging a couple of times.'

'What reasons did he give for not turning up?' Tom asked.

'Och just the usual. He forgot. He lost track of time.'

A thought occurred to Tom, and he went with it.

'Was Sam involved with drugs? Could that have accounted for his poor timekeeping or forgetfulness?'

Daniel shook his head vigorously. 'Absolutely not, no way.' He raised a hand in Tom's direction. 'I would have noticed if he was.' He exhaled loudly. 'Sam was a fitness freak. He would never have touched shit like that.'

Tom had to agree given the great shape Sam appeared to be in. Well-muscled with good skin. He had obviously looked after himself. The gym bag in the boot of the car was also a testament to that. Which made risking his health associating with sex workers seem strange. Was it the thrill? Was it enough to risk catching something from them?

Tom felt he had enough for now, so he left his number with Daniel and asked him to get in touch if he thought of anything else. As he walked back towards the Dunkeld road he saw a familiar car pulling up into a parking space outside the entrance to Daniel's block of flats. Lisa Kennedy. It seemed their shared grief had sent her to him. Tom stepped across the road to get a better view into Daniel's window. Sure enough, the two people who seemed to care most for Sam were comforting each other. Very closely. The reason for his flushed cheeks when her text arrived became clear. He wondered whether Sam knew how close his best friend and his mum were.

Chapter Six

'Sorry I couldn't get here first thing, Mum.'

Hazel cleared a bunch of dead lilies from the vase. She tipped in water from a plastic bottle and replaced them with a spray of pink and yellow carnations, careful to display them nicely.

'I hadn't forgotten,' she continued. 'Work's been busy as usual.'

She wiped the marble headstone with a cloth she'd taken from her bag, taking extra care around the lettering, careful to remove the soil spots that got splashed up onto the surface. Blowing the loose, dried patches away. Then she pulled the back of her cardigan over her bottom and sat. She leaned her head back onto the headstone and closed her eyes, listening to the chatter of council maintenance workers at the other end of the cemetery. A train rumbled in the distance and a chill October wind whistled past her, blowing the autumn leaves from the trees. Switching her phone to silent for fifteen minutes today didn't seem too much to ask. This anniversary deserved that, at least.

'Forty years, eh?' A man's voice broke into Hazel's thoughts. She peeled her eyes open and looked up to see her Uncle Brian standing there, leaning heavily on his walking stick. He had a bunch of carnations in his other hand which he leaned down to give her. 'Great minds think alike, eh?'

'Hey,' Hazel greeted him. 'How are you doing, Brian?'

'You see it all,' he replied, as he had done every time she'd asked him for as long as she could remember. 'Forty years,' he repeated and then tutted loudly. 'Just feels like yesterday your dad phoned me and...' He stopped as emotion choked his throat. 'Aye, well,' he shrugged.

'Aye, forty years,' Hazel said, tugging her cardigan tighter against the increasing wind, sure that there were spots of rain in it. The black clouds speeding across the sky looked ominous. 'Are you using the stick all the time now then?' She nodded towards it.

Her uncle patted his left hip. 'Aye,' he sighed. 'Age doesn't come by itself, does it?'

'No I don't suppose it does.'

'How are you doing?' he asked. 'You need to come over for your tea soon. Your auntie Margaret would love to see you.'

'Have you still got those two mad dogs running wild out there?' Hazel smiled.

'Aye,' he laughed. 'They're still there, alright. They'll outlive all of us.'

'Aye, I'll give you a ring then. Sort something out soon,' she lied. Hazel would never get round to going for tea. But it was what people said in these circumstances.

She looked up to see a blue Renault pull up at the entrance to the cemetery.

'That's my lift,' Brian announced. 'Come and say hello. Your cousin Jenny will be glad to see you.'

Hazel scrunched up her nose at his invitation. 'Maybe next time. You take care of yourself.'

'Aye, it was good to see you, Hazel,' Brian told her. 'I mean that. You look after yourself.'

'I will,' she replied, becoming aware of an unwelcome swell of emotion as she watched her mum's big brother kiss two fingers before touching the headstone. She had to look away.

He was right. Forty years had passed since that day. As the rain grew heavier, Hazel got up and wiped soil from herself and stood for a moment, kissing her own fingertips and laying them gently on her mum's grave.

She checked her phone for messages as she walked back to her car. One from Tom was interesting. He suggested that Lisa Kennedy was closer to Sam's friend Daniel than either of them had said openly. Perhaps Kirsty could shed some light on that for them. That and the bombshell about Sam's new interest, which was a startling revelation to say the least.

–

Hazel lifted a hand to wave to a young woman who looked like the happy, smiling girl in the photos at Sam's house. Only now, she wasn't smiling; she seemed anxious. She appreciated that the girl had agreed to talk to her while she was still at work and waited until Kirsty had handed a tray of empty cups to her colleague then approached her.

'Kirsty, I'm DCI Todd, we spoke on the phone. Is there somewhere we can go to talk in private?' Hazel held up her ID then tucked it away inside her pocket.

'Yes sure, come through.' Kirsty led Hazel through to the back of Willow's café, filling up with the lunchtime rush, and into the staff room. A man who had just finished a cup of coffee nodded once at them and said he'd leave them to it.

'What can I help you with? You sounded serious on the phone.'

'I'm afraid to have to tell you that the body of a young man was found early this morning. I'm sorry but we have reason to believe it was someone you knew, a man by the name of Sam Kennedy.'

Kirsty's face crumpled and the colour drained out of it before her body fell back onto a plastic chair which Hazel was grateful to see catch her. It looked like the girl was trying to say something, but the words wouldn't come. Hazel sat opposite her and allowed her a moment to process what she'd been told.

'What happened to him?' Kirsty eventually asked.

'A post mortem will be carried out later today, but it looks like he was stabbed.'

'Stabbed!' Kirsty exclaimed. 'That's horrible. How? I mean, where?' she corrected herself. 'When did it happen?'

'Last night. His body was found early this morning in his mum's car on Shore Road.'

Kirsty immediately shuffled uncomfortably on her chair. 'Shore Road,' she whispered.

'You don't look surprised,' Hazel suggested.

'I'm not,' Kirsty sighed.

'Daniel told us what happened between you – how the relationship ended, I mean.'

A look of disdain crossed Kirsty's face on hearing that name. 'He did, did he? Did Daniel also say it was him that got Sam into…' she hesitated, seemingly struggling with the conversation. 'Into that!'

'Sam upset you a great deal, didn't he?' Hazel put it to her gently. 'He embarrassed you, made you angry.'

'Of course he did!' Kirsty looked humiliated just talking about it, Hazel thought, wondering what she was capable of doing about those feelings. The hurt and the shame he'd brought into her life.

'When did you last see or speak to Sam?'

Kirsty's eyes narrowed and she fiddled with the cuff of her blouse sleeve. 'I sent him a message last night, but he didn't reply.'

'And before last night?'

'A couple of weeks ago,' Kirsty told her. 'We spoke on the phone because we had booked a holiday together for later this month. He said he wanted me to have it.'

'That was generous of him,' Hazel said. 'As a student, he couldn't have had much money to spare.'

'Have you met his parents?' Kirsty retorted sarcastically. 'Sam was never short of cash.'

'What can you tell me about Sam's dad?'

'I only met Peter Kennedy a couple of times. Neither were very comfortable experiences.'

'How so?' Hazel asked.

'Well the first was Sam's grandmother's funeral so it was understandable he'd not be in the best of moods, but the second time was a dinner, just me, Sam and him.' Kirsty shuddered. 'Something about the way he looked at me made me feel uncomfortable but that wasn't the worst part. The more he drank, the more vitriol he spewed about Lisa. It was horrible. In the end I faked a headache and asked Sam if we could leave.'

'Have you got any idea what happened between his mum and dad?' Hazel was curious.

'That I can help you with. Lisa told me she had to get Sam away from him. She said she had to stop Peter from imprinting his poison on their son. By all accounts he'd

41

made her life a misery and she didn't want Sam ending up like him.' Tears began to roll down her cheeks and she did nothing to stop them pouring off her chin onto the collar of her white blouse.

Hazel reached into her bag and pulled out a couple of tissues. 'Here.'

'Thank you,' Kirsty said. 'I can't believe he's gone.'

'You obviously cared very deeply about him,' Hazel acknowledged the girl's broken heart.

'If you'd met Sam before,' she tried to smile and wiped her soaking wet cheeks. 'You'd have liked him. The thing with the prostitutes, it wasn't him, not the real Sam. He was going to be a doctor. A forensic psychiatrist. That was his goal.'

'Wow, he certainly knew what he wanted out of life,' Hazel said.

Kirsty nodded and dried the rest of her face. 'We talked about getting married. Not for a long time, obviously, but he was the one, I knew that pretty quickly after we met.'

Hazel felt sorry for the poor girl. Kirsty felt she'd been betrayed by Sam but still loved him. She wondered who Kirsty had spoken to about her broken heart. What was their take on the situation?

'What about your family?' She began. 'What did they think about Sam?'

Kirsty was briefly distracted by a middle-aged woman who popped her head round the door before apologising and hastily retreating.

'Mum loved him.' The smile she beamed looked genuine but faded soon after. 'My brother, on the other hand…' She fiddled with the cuff of her blouse again. A nervous tic. 'Mick wasn't so keen. He thought Sam's family were a bit stuck up and that he was arrogant. Didn't like him, especially after I told him what Sam did.'

Hazel's interest was piqued by that. 'What did your brother say when you told him?'

Kirsty gasped and clasped a hand to her mouth. 'No, he wouldn't,' she blurted.

'What did Mick say, Kirsty?'

Kirsty stared straight into Hazel's eyes, her own filled with fear. She stood up and grabbed her jacket from the coat rack behind the door.

'He said he was going to kill him!' She gasped and tried to leave until Hazel stepped in front of the door.

'Wait, woah there, what are you doing?'

'I have to talk to my brother,' Kirsty snapped.

'No,' Hazel stood firm. 'You're not going anywhere. I need you to tell me exactly what your brother said.'

Chapter Seven

Once she'd managed to get Kirsty to calm down, pleased that the girl agreed not to talk to her brother yet, Hazel made the decision to bring the team together before going forward. She wanted to solidify what they'd already learned about their victim. Plus she was starving and gasping for a cup of tea. The sandwich emoji Tom had sent her was his way of pointing out the fact it was lunchtime.

She wanted to check in with DS Billy Flynn, her digital detective, as she called him. There wasn't anything in the wonder of the digital world that this guy couldn't figure out. A great asset to a team headed up by a tech dinosaur like her. She'd set Billy the task of poring over Sam's digital footprint. Bank accounts and social media mainly. Now that they had all of Sam's devices he'd be tasked with tearing into every part of them too. The formal identification was taking place now. Hazel had asked one of the family liaison officers to take Lisa. Such an awful thing, to have to identify the person you love with all your heart and soul, part of yourself. Your only child.

The piping hot cup of tea in her special mug on her desk made Hazel smile. That first sip was glorious.

'Billy Flynn, I think I just might love you,' Hazel teased and swallowed another huge gulp.

He removed the tip of his biro from between his teeth. 'You're welcome,' he grinned.

'I grabbed what was left after the lunchtime rush.' Tom had dashed in and laid a bag of ready-made sandwiches on the desk.

'I bagsy the prawn mayonnaise,' DC Andrea Graham chirped until Tom screwed up his face.

'Sorry Andy, cheese and onion was all they had left.'

'At least we'll all be stinking of onions this afternoon,' Hazel pointed out as she grabbed one of the triangles from the desk, ripping into it. 'Right, let's get started,' she added, with a mouthful of cheese and onion sandwich. 'Tom, how did you get on with the friend, Daniel?'

Tom swallowed down a swig of coffee then wiped his mouth and rubbed crumbs from his shirt. 'Daniel and Sam have been friends since they started secondary school, so, eight years, give or take. Now, Daniel has said that Sam recently developed an interest in using the services of prostitutes, triggered, he thinks by a stag weekend in Amsterdam a few months ago. Given where his body was found, that has to be significant.'

'Did he ever mention any names to Daniel?' DC Andrea Graham piped up, tucking her long, auburn hair behind her ear.

'Yes, someone called Natasha. He said Sam seemed keen on her.'

'Natasha,' Andrea frowned. 'Natasha, Natasha,' she mumbled while she flicked through the pages of a notebook in front of her but shook her head. 'No Natasha but do you think he might have meant Natalie?'

'No, he definitely said Natasha but is that likely to be a real name anyway?' Tom replied. 'I don't know how these things work, though.' His eyes must have drifted towards Billy.

'Why are you looking at me like that?' Billy retorted.

'What? God, no!' Tom protested then laughed.

'Right that's enough the pair of you,' Hazel chastised them. 'Andrea, tell me about this Natalie.'

'Sure, well, she's been living rough for a bit. In and out of the women's shelter over the past couple of years but she can't follow the house rules, you know the kind of thing I mean. She's been addicted to heroin since she was seventeen.'

Andrea's previous experience working with the vulnerable women's team was invaluable to Hazel. Her easy way with the girls was exactly what she'd need.

'Do you reckon you could get her to talk to you?' Hazel asked.

Andrea nodded. 'Aye, I think so.' She glanced at her watch. 'I'll take these with me.'

'Hey, I'm not finished,' Billy tried to protest as Andrea packed the rest of the unopened sandwiches into her bag and laid the carrier bag at her feet.

'Never mind your belly, what have you got for me?' Hazel asked as she bit another chunk off her sandwich, ignoring the crumbs dropping onto her shirt.

Billy shot his wide-eyed glance at Andrea before he flipped open his notebook.

'Right. Our victim, Sam Kennedy, was a young man of substantial means. He has a savings account that contains over one hundred and fifty thousand pounds. Thanks in the main to regular deposits from an account in the name of Peter Kennedy.'

'That's his dad,' Hazel told him.

'A lump sum was withdrawn on the fifth of October. A not insignificant amount, either. Five thousand pounds.'

Tom whistled. 'Wow. What did Sam need that for, I wonder?'

'Yes, but that wasn't the first time that happened,' Billy continued. 'Last month another large sum was withdrawn. Four thousand two hundred, on that occasion.'

'Does he have any other accounts?' Hazel asked.

'I was just getting to that. Sam Kennedy also has a current account that his father also deposits a regular amount into.' He scanned the sheet of paper. 'One thousand on the first of every month. His mum adds to it as well, depositing two hundred and fifty on the fifteenth of the month.'

'Mm, seems he was very well supported,' Hazel said, picking up a photo of a smiling Sam Kennedy. 'Has the father been told yet?'

Tom nodded. 'Yes, Edinburgh sent someone over to his home in Morningside earlier.'

Hazel's phone buzzed on the desk, and she listened to the officer tell her that Lisa had confirmed their victim was indeed Sam Kennedy. The identification process hadn't been pretty by all accounts, but she'd had Daniel there for support, and had immediately collapsed into his arms on seeing her son.

'OK, Lisa Kennedy has confirmed what we already knew: Sam Kennedy is our victim. Billy, have you found anything on his social media to suggest he was having any other kind of problems?'

'Aye, the girlfriend had posted some pretty rough stuff a few weeks ago, calling him all the names under the sun but I found no threats on any of the threads. I couldn't find an Instagram account though which I thought was strange. Just Facebook.'

'I don't have Instagram,' Tom interjected.

'Yes, but you're not a twenty-year-old student, are you?' Andrea insisted. 'Are you even on Facebook, Tom?'

'Of course I am,' he protested and turned to Hazel. 'Are you on Facebook?'

'I am, actually,' Hazel said. Not that she'd been on there much recently. Sure, she'd unfriended both Rick and Cara, but mutual friends meant their cosy new life together kept popping up on her timeline. Hazel wasn't ready for that. As if she'd known Hazel was thinking about them, Cara's number flashed up on her phone. Her instinct to decline the call kicked in and she appreciated the sympathetic glance from Tom who'd obviously seen the number. He'd been a life-saver to Hazel through the divorce in ways she'd never be able to repay. She smiled back just as a text chirped. Cara.

> I remembered it's your mum's anniversary.
> Just wanted to say I am thinking about you
> x

Hazel turned her phone over to hide the screen, a little harder than she intended, she realised, on seeing the reaction on Andrea's face when she looked up again. She was grateful she didn't mention it. How dare Cara think it was OK to send a message like that?

'Billy, so, what about Tinder? We know he'd just split up with Kirsty. Any sign of him on there – or the gay one, what's it called?'

'I doubt he'd be on there, but I'll check. Everyone's got secrets, I suppose.'

Hazel remembered how she'd thought Tom was kidding when he'd suggested she go on Tinder, but he wasn't. Another man was the last thing on Hazel's mind. If she never had sex again she wouldn't care. That was a part of her relationship with Rick she didn't miss. Nearer the end of their marriage, sex had become a chore. Perhaps Cara had offered what she couldn't – or wouldn't.

'Check it anyway, Billy, will you?'

'Sure,' Billy replied and scribbled the word 'Grindr'. 'I'll get the phone looked at as soon as possible, too. There might be photos on there that could be significant.'

'Thanks Billy. You're a star.'

'I try,' he smiled.

'Now, the ex-girlfriend said her brother had threatened to kill Sam but backtracked very quickly. Saw the threats as more of a throwaway remark from a big brother and given the location his body was found, I just don't see him as a suspect. That and the fact the brother sounds more like the type to beat the crap out of someone, rather than stab them. Tom, are you alright to go and talk to him, though?'

'Sure,' Tom replied. 'What's the address?'

Hazel flipped through a pile of paper then slid a sheet across the table. 'It's an address in Tulloch.'

The text that chirped into Hazel's phone was exactly the kind of development she liked.

'Right, we've got a match to a set of prints on the hood of the car and inside on the glove box. Natalie Morrison.' Hazel looked at Andrea. 'Do you know her?'

'I do, do you want me to bring her in?'

'Aye that would be great thanks. There's a set of prints matching Daniel Macey too. I didn't know he was in the system, Tom?'

Tom frowned. 'Hang on.' He opened the lid of his laptop and started typing. 'Mm.' He looked up from the screen. 'Daniel Macey was arrested a year ago on suspicion of sexual assault, but charges were dropped when the girl retracted her statement. The girl had alleged there were

49

two men involved but refused to say who the other man was.'

'Are you thinking what I'm thinking, DI Newton?' Hazel said. 'Could Sam be our *other man?*'

'I'll go and talk to Macey again,' Tom said.

'If he's not at his flat,' Hazel suggested, 'try Lisa Kennedy's place. I have a feeling he'll be there.'

'Sure. What about Kirsty's brother?'

'Michael Morrison, yeah, I'll go and talk to him,' Hazel said. 'Then I'll be looking in on Jack Blair, see how the post mortem is going.' She pursed her lips. 'I'll check out Sam's digs at Ninewells for myself when I'm through there.'

'Do you want some company?' Billy asked.

'No, it's fine, I'd rather you kept on his digital footprint. Keep an eye out for action on his debit card. Did he have a credit card? CCTV as well. Get that watched. Also if forensics get back to us on the hair found in the passenger footwell, give me a shout will you.'

'Of course I will, yes, and he didn't have a credit card that I could see. He didn't really need one, did he?' Billy pointed out. 'And I'll let you know about the council CCTV as soon as.'

'Great, thanks.' Hazel swallowed down the dregs of her lukewarm tea. 'Right; you all know what you're doing, keep in touch, folks.'

Hazel sat back in her chair and opened the text from Cara again. She shook her head. The brass neck of that woman. Was is not enough that she'd stolen Hazel's husband? Couldn't Cara just crawl into a hole somewhere and leave her alone now? Hazel grabbed her cardigan from where she'd slung it across the back of her chair just as another text chirped. This time she picked up her phone and held it close to her lips.

'Piss off!' she growled and grabbed her keys from the desk before heading out.

Chapter Eight

Sam's heart rate increased as he watched Natalie leaving the women's shelter she stayed in sometimes. It was better than that squat she'd shown him. The money she'd said she needed hadn't been hard to get hold of, thanks to his dad's generosity. He knew she'd use some of it for drugs, he wasn't stupid, but if she could pay off the debt as well, he'd be happy with that. Natalie was talking to an older woman who'd been standing outside the building since Sam got there. She stopped all of the younger women as they walked out. Some had ignored her, but Natalie had stopped, seeming happy to see the woman, even.

He'd been thinking about Natalie all day, especially since the blazing row he'd had with Kirsty last night when she'd stormed to his house and thrown a box of his stuff at him. Just some of the crap he'd left at her flat that he didn't really need but he figured she'd wanted to make a point. Fair enough and maybe he'd deserved that slap she gave him. Sam felt bad about the embarrassment he'd caused.

'Who's the old woman?' he asked when Natalie got into the Fiesta.

'Och, I think her name's Rachel or Rebecca or something, I canny mind. She's always trying to talk to me about shit.'

'What, like God?'

Natalie laughed. 'No, not God. Drugs and shit. She says she was addicted to drugs and booze when she was younger. Doesny want to see us going doon that road.'

'Oh right.' Sam indicated into the flow of traffic. 'That's nice.'

'Aye, nice,' Natalie smirked.

Sam pulled a thick brown envelope from his shirt pocket and laid it onto Natalie's knee.

'Here you go.'

'You got me it!' Natalie exclaimed and flipped open the envelope. 'How much is here?'

Sam turned to look at her, enjoying the way she looked. So happy.

'All of it,' he said then laughed at her squeal of delight, almost swerving into the path of an oncoming bus when she grabbed hold of him to hug him. 'Woah,' he said. 'I take it you're pleased.'

'Pull over and I'll show you how pleased I am. This one's on the house.'

Chapter Nine

The pile of black bags and nappies strewn in the front garden repulsed and saddened Hazel in equal measure. A pungent smell hung in the air. Hazel couldn't decide what it was. A possible candidate was cat piss. Her mum had been raised in Wallace Place and if she could see the state of it today she'd be upset too. People didn't have any pride in their neighbourhood any longer. Hazel vaguely remembered a time when the council insisted, as a condition of the tenancy, that tenants took better care of their properties. Including the gardens. A woman used to come and check on communal areas, ensure they were being swept and mopped. Standards had sadly slipped a long way down since then.

Kirsty had informed Hazel that her brother wasn't exactly squeaky clean with his past comprising of an arrest for assault and domestic abuse. All allegations dropped subsequently. She had also told her that he may have made threats, but she didn't believe he would actually have done anything to Sam. He'd been angry and upset that was all. Michael Morrison and Kirsty were half siblings, sharing a father. Ten years older than her, Michael – or Mick, as he preferred to be called – was the product of their father's first marriage. He was protective of his little sister and had said things in the heat of the moment. Hazel noticed through the hall window that he'd seen her walking towards his front door. She lifted her ID up as the door squeaked open to unleash the deafening sound of a large dog barking and scratching from behind a closed door to his left.

'Mick Morrison?' Hazel asked.

'Aye, you're here about Kirsty's boyfriend then,' Mick replied.

'That's right. Is it OK if I come in?'

Mick stood silently for a moment, seemingly weighing up what to do, then stepped aside. He pointed to an open door at the other end of the hall.

'Aye, you'd better come in then. We can talk in the kitchen. My wife's on the night shift. She's sleeping in the living room.'

Hazel doubted that there was any sleeping going on given the racket the dog was making in there.

'Thank you.' Hazel wiped her feet on the threadbare doormat and followed him inside.

The house couldn't be more different to Lisa Kennedy's. The walls were in desperate need of redecoration. More than one of the spindles on the bannister were broken and a selection of mismatched shoes lay strewn in a pile at the bottom of the stairs.

'Are you wanting tea?' Mick offered and sipped from a mug that had two smiling children on it. 'The kettle's just boiled.'

'Nah, I'm fine, thanks,' Hazel said.

'Sit doon.' He lifted a basket of washing from one of the kitchen chairs.

'Thanks.' Hazel sat and laid her bag at her feet, just as the living room door opened allowing a huge, white American bulldog to come rushing in her direction, barking and leaping up on her lap. A thin, bleary-eyed, blue-haired woman with piercings through both eyebrows appeared in the doorway.

'Who was at the door? Oh, hello,' she said and tugged her pink robe tighter round her petite frame, covering the tattoo on her chest. A freshly lit cigarette hung from her lips.

'It's alright Angela, she's wanting to ask me aboot Sam.' Mick grabbed the dog by his collar, more roughly than Hazel was comfortable with, and handed him to the woman. His wife, Hazel assumed. 'Take Dexter, will you? I'll bring you a cup of tea in a minute.'

'Aye, sorry, yes.' His wife smiled at Hazel before guiding the huge canine away, closing the living room door after them.

'Sorry about that,' Mick said.

'It's fine, I didn't realise she'd be sleeping. Listen, Kirsty told me there was no love lost between you and Sam.'

'Aye well, the wee bastard made a fool of her.'

'Did you threaten him as a result?'

Mick started to look uncomfortable and rubbed at his shaved head. Hazel spotted the tattoo on his forearm. A skull with a red rose and black dagger that had something written in it that Hazel couldn't quite make out. He wasn't a tall man but well-muscled, especially his arms. Certainly strong enough to overpower another man. Moisture started to glisten on his head.

'Look,' Mick held his hands up in front of him. 'I did threaten him, but I didn't mean anything by it. I was angry when I saw the state of my wee sister. She was crying her hert oot to me and I saw red.' He paused to sigh. 'She told me what happened to him. Stabbed. That's bad crack, man. That's no' my game and I know what you're thinking. I wouldn't do that. I didn't do that.'

'Where were you last night?' Hazel asked.

Mick stood up and pushed the kitchen door shut quietly, looking sheepish as he sat back down. Hazel had a feeling she knew what was coming.

'I was wi' a lassie last night.' He leaned in closer, close enough that Hazel smelled the stale beer and fags on his breath.

'A lassie I assume your wife doesn't know about.'

Mick nodded. 'I'd prefer to keep it that way.'

That look. Begging her to keep his filthy secret. Hazel hated it. Who had Rick looked at like that?

'I can't make any promises your wife won't ever find out, but I'll need the lassie's name,' Hazel pointed out.

'Come on, surely not,' he begged.

'Mr Morrison, I'm investigating a murder,' Hazel said plainly. 'What you get up to is no concern of mine. I just need her name.'

Mick reached back and disconnected his phone from a charger before scrolling through. He turned it towards Hazel who made a note of the name and number he was showing her.

'When she tells you I was with her, that'll be it, will it?'

Hazel chose to ignore that, grabbed her bag and stood up from the table. 'I'll be in touch if I need to talk to you again.'

From where she'd parked Hazel could see into Mick Morrison's living room window. He was handing a cup of tea and a plate to his wife. The woman happily munching the toast was blissfully unaware of his infidelity. It might not even be the first time, either. She dialled the number he'd given her and spoke to a woman who confirmed that Mick was indeed with her last night. She wouldn't tick him off her list just yet. Not until a cast iron suspect pushed him off.

–

As soon as Hazel's car disappeared round the corner, the thin, red-haired girl staggered up Mick's path and banged on his door, triggering another burst of barking and growling from inside. It was his wife who answered the door, the look on her face one of disdain.

'Is Mick there?' the girl asked. She scratched her arm roughly, staring behind her anxiously.

'Mick,' she shouted behind her but kept the door closed most of the way.

Mick arrived moments later and took the girl inside. He glanced up and down the street before slamming the front door.

Chapter Ten

Rachel Fox was relieved to see the text from Dawn. The rain was coming down in sheets, but she'd not wanted to go yet. She'd been hoping to see Natalie again. She'd planned to ask her if she'd like to go for something to eat. But the only girls who'd come out had blanked her which was sad but not unexpected. Rachel had been there herself. She didn't think she'd have stopped to listen to an old busybody either.

'It's lovely to see you.' Rachel kissed Dawn's cheek and took off her raincoat slowly, careful not to splash the other customers in Willow's coffee shop. She was concerned by the expression on Dawn's face. 'Is everything alright?' she asked as she sat down.

The waitress whose name badge read 'Kirsty' asked if Rachel was ready to order. The young girl looked like she'd been crying, her eyes appeared puffy and sore. Rachel looked at Dawn.

'Just a pot of tea for two thanks,' she said and smiled as the girl left them.

'Molly didn't come home again last night,' Dawn told her while she checked her phone for the umpteenth time, hoping to see a message from her eighteen-year-old daughter.

It broke Rachel's heart to see the worry on her friend's face. She knew Dawn would never blame her for one second, but hadn't they moved from their home in Belfast to Perth to be closer to Rachel? Ever since suffering severe bullying at school, Molly had first turned to booze and now drugs to numb the pain.

'Try not to worry.' Even Rachel knew that sounded ridiculous. Of course Dawn would worry, and Molly was lucky to have people who cared enough to worry about her. 'I assume you've phoned and left messages.'

'Yes, I've left six messages,' Dawn admitted. 'I asked if she was in the shelter, but they said they can't tell me anything because she's an adult. Have you seen her coming and going from there?' Dawn's desperation was palpable.

Rachel wished she could help. 'No, I haven't. Do you think you should call the police this time?'

Dawn scoffed. 'Don't be ridiculous. Molly's just a junkie to them.'

The saddest thing was that Dawn was right, partly. Molly was a vulnerable young woman, but she wasn't a kid.

'There you go.' The waitress laid a tray of tea down for them with a smile, before heading back towards the kitchen.

Rachel knew of a derelict building that the addicts in the local area used. A squat of sorts. But she didn't want Dawn going there looking for Molly. She'd check it out herself because seeing the girls in there was bad enough for Rachel. It would break Dawn's heart to think of her daughter hanging around with girls like them, despite the fact she was one of them.

'Has she been in for a meal lately?' Dawn asked, knowing that Rachel did some shifts in the community kitchen for the homeless. 'Maybe I should come and hang out there. See if she turns up.'

Rachel reached her hand across the table and covered Dawn's. 'I'll call you if I see her. I promise.'

'I know you will,' Dawn replied to her gesture and took Rachel's hand. 'Doesn't stop me worrying.' Her thin smile couldn't hide the pain she was feeling. A tear started to roll from her hazel eyes until she dabbed it away with her fingertips.

As Rachel watched her friend's pain she wondered whether, if she'd had someone to care that much about her when she'd been young, maybe she wouldn't have done the horrifying things she'd done all those years ago. The things that changed her life and the lives of so many others beyond repair.

Chapter Eleven

DC Andrea Graham knocked and waited, listening for movement inside the derelict building. Although in truth, she didn't expect anyone to come to answer the door. It didn't work like that here. She knocked again and clutched the bag of sandwiches tightly as she pushed the door, pieces of the chipping blue paint falling in sheets to the pavement as she shoved her shoulder hard into it. The smell inside made her turn away. The sour stench of piss and vomit. Right inside the doorway lay a stained mattress with a couple of blankets tossed on top. An ashtray next to it was filled with cigarette butts, some spilling onto the green, flowery carpet.

'Hello,' Andrea called out, thinking it was probably better to announce herself now. 'Is there anyone here?'

She pressed a finger against the door to the kitchen area and pushed it gently, the squeal of the hinge leaving her feeling unnerved. Music hit her ears and she realised it was coming from an upstairs room. Andrea laid the bag of food onto the worktop, her stomach churning at the state of the sink which was black with dirt. She dreaded to think what germs were multiplying in there. The perfect breeding ground, for sure.

Andrea crept slowly up the creaking, dark stairs, switching on the torch on her phone.

'Hello,' she called out again as she headed along the hallway. The music was coming from the furthest room, its door ajar. She picked out two women's voices over the music. One sounded like Natalie.

Andrea pushed open the door only to be bowled over by a panicked young girl who'd barrelled into her, in a bid to escape. Natalie snatched a bag of something and tossed it out the window before trying to shove past Andrea.

'Natalie, stop! I don't care about that shit,' Andrea shouted and set off after her. 'Natalie,' she yelled. 'It's about Sam.'

On hearing that, Natalie stopped dead, then turned.

'What about him?' she asked.

Andrea was alarmed to see that Natalie had a black eye as well as a cut lip and she looked much thinner than when they'd last spoken. She was dishevelled and her hair hung lank and thin over her shoulders. Spots around her mouth and nose looked red and sore.

'Can we talk?' Andrea took a ten-pound note out of her pocket and held it out.

A girl with long red hair came bursting into the property and without saying anything to either of them, raced upstairs. Andrea looked at Natalie.

'Well, can we talk?'

'In here,' Natalie nodded and led Andrea into a room next to the kitchen that had an actual bed in it. She shut the door after them and slumped down on it. 'What about Sam?'

'Sam's dead,' Andrea said and watched for her reaction carefully.

Perhaps numbed by the drugs, her response was muted and slow. 'What happened to him?' she asked, without making eye contact.

'He was found in his car early this morning at the other end of Shore Road, next to the café.'

'That sucks,' Natalie replied.

'How well did you know him?'

'I gave him the odd blow job here and there. He didn't always want sex,' she told her. 'Sam liked a lot of different things.' Natalie's eyes began to droop, and Andrea knew she had a very short window to get any sense out of her before the drugs kicked in properly.

'When did you last see him?' Andrea persevered.

'A couple of days ago.'

'How did he seem to you when you spoke to him?' Andrea knew this was a race against time.

'Sam was a good man.' Natalie sniffed and stretched her eyes as if fighting what was trying to drag her down. 'He tried to help me.'

'Help you how?'

'He gave me…' Natalie slurred, ending the sentence with something inaudible.

'Natalie!' Andrea shouted and grasped the girl's chin, shaking it gently to help her focus. 'Wake up, this is important.'

'Just let me…'

Time was up. Andrea lowered Natalie's body down to rest on the bed. Movement upstairs caught her attention. She picked up a tartan blanket that she found on the floor and draped it over Natalie before making her way upstairs, hoping that the other girl could help. She hadn't recognised her when she'd surged past them a few minutes ago but Natalie was barely recognisable either.

Andrea knocked on the room door and walked in to see the red-headed girl slumped against the wall under the filthy window. She checked for a pulse just to be sure and the pulse was strong. Strong and slow. What a waste. Andrea snapped a photo of this new girl in case she had been reported missing. She couldn't be much more than eighteen if that. A man's voice boomed from downstairs, startling Andrea into dropping her phone.

'Shit,' she exclaimed when she picked it up, grateful it was undamaged. She took a last sad look at the passed out girl and crept quietly out of the room.

'Who the hell are you?' a squat, well-muscled man shouted at her, in an accent she didn't recognise.

As Andrea tugged her ID out of her pocket, she could see the man was thinking about making a run for it but his left ankle was in a cast and he seemed to realise any attempt to escape would be futile. He lifted his hands up in front of him instead.

'No, mate, who the hell are *you*?' she asked.

Chapter Twelve

Tom spotted the brand new red Audi parked on Lisa Kennedy's driveway and knew immediately that it had to be Peter Kennedy's because of its distinctive PK10 number plate. Hazel had been right to suggest that Daniel wouldn't be at his own flat so on finding it empty he'd headed straight to Lisa Kennedy's. He noticed a motorbike parked outside the front door and figured that must be Daniel's.

'Yes?' Peter Kennedy answered the front door abruptly.

'Mr Kennedy.' Tom held his ID up and Kennedy took it out of Tom's hand to examine it before thrusting it firmly back into his chest. Then he walked away before Tom had a chance to say anything else leaving the door wide open, which Tom took as an invitation to come inside. Peter Kennedy was short – barely five foot nine, not what Tom had expected. He'd assumed Sam's dad must be at least six foot two or more, given Sam's height.

'Come in, detective,' Lisa greeted him, trying to avoid looking at her ex-husband who was drinking whisky from a crystal glass before refilling it from the bottle of malt in his other hand.

'Yes, come in, detective,' Peter Kennedy growled in Tom's direction.

'Come through, we can talk in here.' Lisa ushered Tom away from the living room and into the kitchen where Daniel was sitting, stroking the cat who had flopped itself down onto his knee at the table. Two cups of half-drunk tea sat on the table. 'I'm sorry about that,' she apologised, a pink hue to her cheeks.

'It's fine, don't worry,' Tom reassured her.

'Is there any news?' she pleaded. 'Because I've been racking my brains and I just can't think who'd want to do something so awful to him.' Tears started to fall from her already red, painful-looking eyes.

Tom shot a brief glance at Daniel who swallowed hard and looked away. He wondered if it was fair to keep Sam's secret life of using sex workers from her under the circumstances but figured Daniel was trying to do what was best by both of them. The thought of shattering Lisa's innocent illusion of her boy must be killing him.

'It's actually Daniel I'd like to speak to,' Tom told them and spotted the lad squirm right away.

'Oh, OK.' Lisa opened the drawer next to the fridge and pulled out a packet of cigarettes and a lighter. She walked towards the double French doors that led out into a modest, immaculate garden. Small in size but well maintained. Typical of the types of homes in the area. 'I'll leave you two to it, then,' she said and pulled both doors shut behind her.

Both men watched her light a cigarette and drop down onto one of the patio chairs before either of them spoke.

'I know why you're looking for me,' Daniel announced and laid the cat onto the floor.

'Why didn't you tell me earlier that you'd been arrested?' Tom came straight to the point. 'You must have known it might come up.'

Daniel sighed, rubbing his eyes before looking at him. 'I was hoping it wasn't relevant.'

'Everything is relevant in a murder investigation,' Tom said. 'Was Sam the other alleged attacker?'

'We did not attack her,' Daniel spat.

'So what did happen?'

Daniel looked out the French doors. Tom followed his line of sight to see Lisa Kennedy leaning over, hunched on the patio chair, talking on her phone in between draws on the cigarette.

'Look; she was willing, I can assure you. Changed her mind, didn't she, that's all. When she sobered up the next morning she felt guilty that she'd done the dirty on her boyfriend.'

'How drunk was she?'

Daniel immediately lifted a hand in protest. 'She was sober enough to be in control of her faculties, if that's what you're getting at.'

'Have you got any idea why it was just you that was arrested?' Tom asked.

Daniel stole another quick glance at Lisa. 'Ask Peter Kennedy.'

Taken aback, Tom considered the idea that Peter had swept away the allegation that was about to be aimed at his son.

'It must have upset you to be the only one in the frame for something so serious,' Tom suggested.

'Not the best moment in my life, I will admit.'

'You must have been upset that Sam didn't own up.'

'Wait a minute,' Daniel protested. 'You can forget that right away. Sam was my best mate.'

'You have to understand that in situations like this we have to consider all possibilities,' Tom informed him. 'Where were you last night?'

Daniel's eyes drifted immediately towards where Lisa Kennedy was sitting. 'With her,' he said quietly.

'Ah,' Tom acknowledged. 'Did Sam know about you and his mum?'

Daniel shook his head. 'No, he didn't.'

'How long has it been going on?' Tom asked.

'A few months,' Daniel admitted. 'Sam's dad was a total shit and Lisa is so…' he seemed to be thinking of the right words.

'How long have they been divorced?'

'God, years. I don't think they were together when I met Sam. So probably about ten years.'

'Was Peter Kennedy abusive to Sam and his mother?'

'Abusive?' Daniel repeated. 'That's an understatement.'

'Physically? Mentally?'

'Both, but it was just Lisa he targeted. Never Sam. Not even when he found out…'

Tom frowned when Daniel stopped and took a quick look at Lisa sitting back, staring into space. 'Found out what?'

'Please don't tell her I told you.' Daniel pointed a finger at Tom.

Tom nodded. 'OK.'

'Peter isn't Sam's dad.'

The height difference made sense now.

'Is that right?'

'Yes, Sam was diagnosed with leukaemia when he was six and when he needed a bone marrow transplant, it all came out then.'

'That couldn't have been easy,' Tom suggested. 'For any of them.'

'Peter was devastated but…' Daniel sighed. 'Fair play to the man. He might be an asshole, but he loved Sam even after he found out.'

'He took it out on Lisa instead, though.'

Daniel nodded. 'Lisa left because she didn't want her son to turn out like him. She didn't want his abuse poisoning Sam against women.' He shrugged. 'Lisa made a mistake and Peter has spent the past few years punishing her for it.'

'But he was still willing to help Sam out of his recent predicament.'

'Yes, like I said, he still loved Sam like he was his own son.'

'Is Peter Kennedy someone who is good at making things go away?'

Daniel scoffed. 'Er, yes. He got some tart off shoplifting charges a couple of months ago too.'

'Is that right? Have you any idea who she was?'

Before he could answer, the two men saw that Lisa was heading back towards the door. Daniel smiled at her.

'Are you OK?' he asked.

Lisa's face crumbled at his question. Tears began to pour down her face.

'I don't think I'll ever be OK again.'

Tom knew that the investigation was an unwelcome guest in their grief. It was the same every time but he was undeterred. He was about to ask Lisa some awkward questions about her son when the front doorbell rang.

'Excuse me a minute,' Lisa said and made her way to answer it. A woman's voice echoed towards them before Peter Kennedy bustled the girl inside. Tom could see that the distraught visitor had fallen into Peter's arms.

'That's Kirsty, Sam's ex,' Daniel told him.

Tom was surprised to hear that after what Hazel had told him about the way Kirsty felt about Peter Kennedy. Lisa looked back at Tom before rushing upstairs.

'I better go and see if she's OK,' Daniel stood.

'Wait a minute,' Tom insisted. 'I need to talk to you about the girl who alleged you assaulted her.'

'Jesus,' Daniel exclaimed. 'I just want to forget about her.'

'Daniel, it could be important. You do want us to find out what happened to your friend, don't you?'

'Of course I do.' The volume of Daniel's voice rose. 'Her name's Katie Sheehan. She's a second-year medical student, lives in the same dorm as Sam and I never want to see her again as long as I live.'

'I get that,' Tom acknowledged. 'But it could be important.' He watched Daniel take a breath, a moment to compose himself.

'OK, what do you want to know?'

Chapter Thirteen

'My name's Craig Douglas.'

Andrea stared at the squat man and pointed to the chair nearby so he could take the weight off his leg. He looked ex-military to her with those tattoos. Not that she knew exactly what tattoos veterans had. He just gave off that vibe.

'Sit down, Craig. What are you doing in a place like this?' she asked because he was obviously not homeless. His clothes looked new, and his face was clean, and it was obvious he'd recently shaved. Andrea could even smell some kind of body spray on the man from where she was standing. He wasn't someone who had planned to doss down there.

Craig did as he was told. 'Listen, I was just checking on the girls, see if they needed anything.'

'Is that right?'

'Yes,' Craig rubbed his leg and winced.

'What happened to your leg?'

'Car accident six weeks ago. Chipped the ankle in three places but it's on the mend. At least I can get about now. Being stuck in that flat was murder.'

'How do you know the girls that come and go from here?' Andrea looked him over, watching for signs of deceit. Body language was a real interest of hers. So far, this guy was telling the truth.

'I live in that block of flats down there.' He pointed further down the road. 'I've seen them coming and going for years but it wasn't until I found one of them unconscious at the side of the road one night last year that I thought I had to do something to help them, so I pop in and out from time to time to see if they're needing anything.'

'Are you married?' Andrea asked.

Craig frowned. 'Sorry, but what on earth does that have to do with anything?'

'Humour me.'

'No, I'm not married,' he said drily. 'Not that it's any of your business.'

'Divorced?' she suggested.

'No.'

'And your relationship with the girls, what's that like?'

'My relationship?' Craig repeated. 'I don't have relationships with them.'

'So why the interest, then?'

'I've just explained that I found one of them in trouble and I helped her, but I can see exactly what you're implying, detective.' Craig made to stand back up. 'I don't have to sit here and take this shit from you.'

'Sit down,' Andrea insisted, more loudly than she intended. 'Please.'

Craig looked at her, glancing briefly at his watch before sitting back down.

'What is all this about?' he asked. 'Why are you here anyway?'

'The body of a young man was found early this morning.'

Craig's eyes stretched wide as he gasped. 'Jesus, that's horrible. I saw a bit of police activity this morning. Was that it?'

'I'm afraid so. His body was found behind the wheel of his car which was parked next to the harbour café. Do you know it?'

Craig nodded. 'I've taken a couple of the girls there for breakfast in the past.'

'When did you last do that?'

'Oh, not for a few weeks.' He patted his leg. 'This has kind of put the kybosh on a lot of stuff lately.'

Andrea scrolled through her phone for a photo of Sam that they'd all been given.

'This lad.' She turned the phone to face him. 'Do you recognise him?'

Craig screwed up his eyes and held his hand out to take the phone from her. 'Do you mind? I haven't got my glasses.'

'Not at all,' she replied and released the phone to him. 'Take all the time you need.'

'Good-looking young lad,' Craig said. 'Is this the guy who was killed?'

Andrea nodded. 'Do you know him?'

Craig pressed his lips together while he shook his head and laid the phone back into her hand.

'I'm sorry, I don't recognise him. Poor lad. What happened to him?'

'All I can tell you at the moment is that we're treating his death as suspicious.'

Andrea glossed over Sam's cause of death because his post mortem hadn't yet been carried out.

'He looks young,' Craig said.

'We have evidence to suggest he used the services of some of the sex workers.'

'What have they said?' Craig asked.

'I haven't been able to talk to any of them yet,' Andrea explained. 'Natalie had started talking then the drugs took over.'

Craig nodded knowingly and sighed. 'Aye, that sounds about right.'

Andrea wondered if Craig would recognise the new girl with the long red hair that she hadn't seen before.

'Look, it might be a long shot but...' she scrolled through the photos for the one she took and showed him it. 'Do you know who this girl is?'

Craig's expression softened. 'Yes, that's Molly. She's originally from Belfast. Her and her mum moved here last year.'

'She told you that?' Andrea's surprise must have been obvious.

'They're not always wasted,' Craig said. 'Sometimes they can hold conversations.'

The sarcastic undertone wasn't missed. 'Did she say what brought them to Perth? Have they got family here?'

'No, Molly said there was an auntie, but not a real auntie, just one of her mum's best friends.' He smiled thinly. 'Molly seems really fond of Auntie Rachel.'

Andrea wondered about the logistics of someone in Belfast having a best friend in Perth.

'I don't think she touched the drugs until she came here though,' Craig added. 'Damn shame.'

'Sounds like a bitter-sweet reunion with this Auntie Rachel, then.'

'Aye, she's a good kid,' Craig said. 'Just mixed up in shit that's going to kill her if she doesn't do something about it.'

Their conversation was interrupted by another visitor. 'It's a busy place some days,' Craig told her.

A petite young woman walked into the kitchen. Seemingly startled to see them, she turned to walk away until Craig called her name.

'It's OK, Kelly, come in.'

The girl stopped and stared. Andrea didn't recognise her, but thought she didn't appear as far down her addiction road as Molly or Natalie. She smiled at her.

'It's OK.' Andrea spoke quietly. 'There's some sandwiches in the bag on the bunker.' She pointed. 'There's a couple of bottles of water as well.'

The expression on Craig's face was filled with concern. Maybe Andrea had been wrong about him.

'Come and have a seat, Kelly.' He stood up and offered his chair to her. 'I'll go and have a quick check on the others.'

'How will you manage the stairs?' Andrea asked.

'Oh I've mastered the stairs by now.' He winked. 'I live on the first floor.'

Andrea liked the way the girl smiled at Craig's comment. He'd been able to put her at ease with little effort. Despite her first impressions, Andrea was quite taken with the man. Once he'd left them, Andrea smiled at Kelly who was munching on one of the sandwiches.

'Are you the police?' Kelly asked.

Andrea knew her answer could make or break this conversation. She obviously couldn't lie, but it was how she delivered the information that mattered. She took her phone back out and scrolled down to Sam's photo before holding it up closer to Kelly's face.

'I'm investigating what happened to this boy,' she said plainly, hoping that she wouldn't flee. Kelly looked closely at his picture.

'What happened to him?' Kelly asked and devoured the last of one sandwich before lifting the second half out of the plastic wrapping.

'He was murdered,' Andrea told her, watching closely for her reaction which, like Natalie's, was muted.

'God,' Kelly replied. 'How?'

'He was found along the road sitting in his car.'

'Yes, but how did he die?' Kelly's persistence struck Andrea as unusual.

Craig's shouts startled both women into running to see what had happened. Andrea feared that one of the women was dead. That was all they needed. An overdose to deal with on top of Sam's murder.

'What is it?' Andrea urged before her eyes stretched wide at what Craig had in his hand. She snatched her phone from her pocket. 'Don't move and don't touch anything else!' she barked as she called it in.

Chapter Fourteen

Hazel was already halfway to Dundee to talk to pathologist Jack Blair when Andrea's call came through. Tom had been sent to take charge of the scene, along with a forensics team to examine the building for other evidence. Craig Douglas had gone up to check on the two girls who had passed out and found a ten-inch, blood-stained knife on the floor not far from where the girl Craig had called Molly lay slumped under the window. Andrea had been so apologetic, saying she couldn't believe she'd missed it. A ten-inch bladed knife would be hard to miss, Hazel had to admit, especially one that was covered in blood but there was no way anyone else could have brought it in. Was there? The girl was passed out on the floor and the other one, Natalie, was in a similar state in another room. If this blood were Sam Kennedy's and it was highly probable given his connection to the sex workers, then the investigation would be narrowed down significantly. For now, all possibilities were still on the table and Hazel's first stop was the lad's post mortem with Jack Blair.

'Hello, DCI Todd,' Jack greeted her from behind the glass in the anteroom. 'Get yourself suited up and we can begin.'

Hazel gave him a wave and tucked her cardigan and bag under the counter before donning the coverall and overshoes. She grabbed a paper mask from the box on the table and pulled up the hood. Those damn hoods. Surely she wasn't the only person whose head itched like a bitch when they wore them.

'I hear you might have found the murder weapon,' Jack began as he held the blade over Sam's chest, ready to make the first incision.

'Good news travels fast,' Hazel replied. 'But we won't know if the blood is Sam's or not until we've had it examined.'

'How long was the blade that was found?'

'Ten inches, they think.'

'Given the depth of the stab wound I think it's very probable that it is indeed the murder weapon. Have they said what type of knife it is?'

'Not yet, it's being examined as we speak,' Hazel said. 'What type caused those injuries, would you say?'

'A boning knife, in my opinion,' Jack told her and pointed to the huge wound in Sam's abdomen. 'See the way it goes right through to the spinal cord.'

Hazel was reluctant to edge forward to take a proper look but did it. For Sam's sake. The thyroid medicine the doctor had put her on was already causing some nausea. Being in this environment was a challenge. Jack was right. The wound really was right from front to back.

'Spinal cord is still intact from what I can see but I'll know more soon,' Jack continued.

'Any results on his bloods yet?' Hazel lifted her eyes up from the huge stab wound to where Jack was now slicing into Sam's chest cavity. That sound. The crunch of the ribs. That was something she'd never got used to.

'Not even a drop of alcohol; that I know for sure. I'm waiting for the rest to come back but his general condition suggests to me we won't find any other illegal substances. He looks like a man who took care of himself.' Jack removed Sam's heart and dropped it gently onto the scales before laying them aside. 'Heart: three hundred and five grams. All good here but I don't think the strength of the boy's heart was ever in doubt, was it? No signs of cardiopulmonary disease.' He turned back to Sam's chest cavity and lifted out his lungs. He looked at Hazel before dropping them onto the scales. 'I've sent a hair sample off to test for any long term drug use though, just in case.'

'Good idea.'

'Lungs: one point three kilos.' Jack looked closer. 'Right bigger than left. Good, good.' When he turned back to Sam's body he stopped to glance up at Hazel. 'Well, his liver, spleen, and intestines are all destroyed. There's blood displaced.' He screwed up his face to get a closer look. 'The knife has torn through all of it, I'm afraid. There are signs of severe internal bleeding.'

'So to be clear, he died as a result of this stab wound.'

Instead of giving her a straight answer Jack hesitated. 'On its own without doubt, yes, this poor lad would have died from this stab wound, however...' He ripped off his gloves and dropped them in the bin next to the cold steel table before standing next to Sam's face. Jack peeled open both eyelids. 'What do you see here?'

Hazel peered over and saw tiny pinprick red marks in both of Sam's eyes.

'Is that petechial haemorrhaging?' she suggested.

'Correct.'

'That's not usual in a stabbing, is it?' she asked, leaning closer to get a better look. Then she spotted red marks on Sam's neck. 'Wait a minute. Was he...' She stared at Jack. 'Was he strangled?'

'No, the hyoid bone is still very much intact.' Jack pointed to Sam's neck and pressed down on his throat to prove his point. 'No, I suggest he was suffocated.' He lifted up Sam's head and showed Hazel the hairline. 'I found traces of tape stuck to his skin here, just between the nape of his neck and the hairline.' Then he rested Sam's head gently back down. 'I've taken swabs and set them off to find out which substance is there but if I were to take a guess…' He paused, 'I would say duct tape.'

'Duct tape,' Hazel repeated. 'So something was taped to his head. Are there traces over his mouth and nose?'

Jack shook his head. 'No, just the neck.'

'So something was taped to—' she stopped to correct herself. 'Over him. Something was taped over his head.' She traced her fingers down his arms and lifted his hands to examine his wrists. 'No restraints.'

'It doesn't appear so,' Jack confirmed.

'Stabbed and suffocated,' Hazel said and went back to look at Sam's face, particularly into his eyes. 'Suffocated,' she whispered.

'The volume of carbon dioxide in his blood doesn't indicate to me that was necessarily the cause of death,' Jack emphasised. 'It was a combination.'

'While you lay dying of major abdominal trauma,' Hazel spoke quietly, directly to Sam's lifeless body, without taking her eyes off the table. 'You would have been weakened by the stabbing, unable to fight back when they put something over your head.' She crouched next to Sam's face. 'They taped it onto your neck but you were losing blood, didn't have the strength to stop them.' A text alert snapped her back into focus. A cursory glance said it could wait. 'Forensics didn't find anything at the scene that could have been used to suffocate him, did they?'

Jack shook his head. 'Not that I'm aware of.'

'Do you have a more precise time of death for me?' she asked, struggling to take her eyes off Sam's lifeless body.

'I'd say you could narrow it down to between nine and ten pm,' Jack told her. 'That's the best I can give you.'

'Thanks Jack,' Hazel said. 'That's a big help.'

'I aim to please,' Jack replied as he pulled on a fresh pair of gloves. 'I'll be in touch with my full report.'

'I appreciate that,' Hazel replied.

'No problem, listen I think I might have met this poor boy before he found his way to my table,' Jack suggested. 'He came to a lecture I gave at the university. Damn shame, he seemed like a nice lad.'

'Aye, it is that,' Hazel agreed.

Before Hazel could leave Jack said the words she'd hoped to avoid.

'How are you doing anyway?' he asked.

'I'm fine Jack,' she said, hoping he would accept her answer. She was to be disappointed.

'Have you heard from either of them recently?'

Hazel sighed. She really did appreciate that he cared. Jack and Tom had both been great. She knew she was lucky to have such a good support network. Finding out your husband of twenty-five years is shacking up with your best friend of more than forty years was a shock to say the least.

'Cara has been texting, but I've not spoken to him.'

'Well you know where I am.' Jack looked at her over the top of his silver framed glasses. 'Anytime.'

'I know.' Her voice wobbled a little at that. She didn't have time for this and made her excuses before leaving, telling him she'd be in touch. Talking about it was still too raw at times. Hazel decided another search of the harbour should be done. She would arrange for it to take place at first light tomorrow. She went straight into the ladies' bathroom where she scrubbed her hands and splashed water on her face. That place always made her feel unclean. She stared at her reflection in the mirror. She was tired but that was hardly surprising. Getting up twice nightly to pee didn't really constitute beauty sleep. The crow's feet that had once bothered her didn't anymore. She wore them as a badge of pride because not every woman gets the privilege of growing old. She ran her hairbrush through her short black hair, now peppered grey and white, particularly round the ears.

Hazel had arranged to be let into Sam's dorm room, hoping something in there would shed light on who wanted to stab and, now it seemed, suffocate him.

'Thanks,' she said to the caretaker who unlocked his door for her as she pulled on a pair of gloves and blue overshoes.

The state of this room was the polar opposite to Sam's room at home. The unmade single bed sat in the corner next to what she supposed passed as a wardrobe which in reality was nothing more than a tiny cupboard. The wardrobe door lay open with a pile of clothes lying on the floor below a row of empty coat hangers. A small desk under a tiny window had a lamp, a thick ring binder and a pencil case left open with pens and pencils spewing out of it, surrounded by a pile of medical textbooks on either side leaving barely any space to work. The floor under the desk had a jumble of trainers next to a pair of brown wool slippers.

In that moment Hazel could picture Sam as a living, breathing man, flopping down to do an assignment, kicking off his shoes to get comfortable. A photo frame on the window ledge which would be directly in his eye line as he sat at the desk held a picture of a smiling Sam cuddling up to Kirsty. The young couple sat round a fire on a beach at sunset. It seemed so sad that their relationship ended so horribly. They looked happy together. Just starting out in life.

She moved to a short, stumpy chest of drawers and with her gloved hands rummaged through the contents which consisted of nothing more than a few T-shirts and some underwear, all stuffed inside like he'd been in a rush to put them away. She tried to picture him running to a lecture, rushing because he'd overslept. Then her fingers stumbled upon a book which she pulled out carefully. Another notebook like the diary Tom had discovered. The drawings inside this one were much more graphic than the ones in the other book. Naked women in chains and handcuffs, their mouths taped and gagged. A hand pressing a knife next to their throats but just the hand, jutting in from the edge of the paper. The most haunting part of it was the look in the women's eyes. Sam had captured their fear perfectly and it leapt from the paper, making the drawings difficult to look at.

Hazel dropped the notebook into an evidence bag and laid it down before reaching inside again, dragging her fingers across the MDF boards of the unit. Another book. This time a true crime book she recognised as one she'd read herself. *Green River Running Red* by Ann Rule. A fascinating insight into the investigation and arrest of Gary Ridgway, the Green River Killer in the US. A man who spent decades murdering prostitutes. She flicked through the pages and found passages marked in what she assumed was Sam's handwriting. Hazel quickly bagged the book and flipped open the folder on the desk to see if the writing matched Sam's, which it did. It seemed Sam Kennedy had two sides to him; a secret side that he kept from the people he loved. Perhaps only sharing it with girls who would do what he wanted for a price. Had he gone too far? Did someone fight back? Or did they plan their revenge in the most brutal way? Hazel decided she needed to speak with someone she knew to have been with Sam. Natalie Morrison. If anyone knew what Sam liked, she did.

Hazel turned on hearing a knock at Sam's dorm room door. The young woman standing in the doorway was tall and slim with long black hair, and the expression on her face was serious.

'Are you Detective Todd?'

'Yes that's me,' Hazel replied.

'Good, good, I'm Katie Sheehan.' She turned and pointed along the corridor. 'My room is just along the hall from Sam's. I heard what happened to him and I saw the activity in here, so I put two and two together.'

'Hello Katie, I was about to come and find you, actually.'

Katie let her gaze drop to the floor before taking a huge breath and returning her focus onto Hazel.

'I thought you might.'

Chapter Fifteen

'Naloxone is wonderful stuff,' Tom said as he stared in through the two-way glass at Molly Barker sipping a glass of water.

'Aye, it must have been a bit of a rude awakening, opening your eyes to us staring at her,' Andrea agreed. 'Same with Natalie, to be honest.'

'Yes, well, they were in the place a possible murder weapon was found.'

'I still don't understand why I didn't see it.' Andrea looked concerned. 'I mean if it had been there I would have, wouldn't I?'

'Don't be so hard on yourself. We don't know what happened yet.'

'Do you reckon we should have had that place searched earlier?' Andrea suggested.

Tom shrugged. 'I'm sure it would have been at some point soon, once we'd found out about Sam's connection to those girls. Are you OK talking to Natalie if I take Molly?'

'Yes, no problem, but she'll not be happy with me ruining her hit like that,' she smirked.

'Tough,' Tom announced, 'and make sure you emphasise the seriousness of the situation.'

Tom and Andrea went their separate ways to talk to the girls. Fingerprint analysis of the knife hadn't shown a match to either of them, but their statements could be invaluable. Kelly Tate had been able to give hers at the scene and had given the address of the women's shelter if they needed to contact her again, adding that she often hung out at the community kitchen where they provided meals and clothes for the homeless. She'd told Andrea that she'd never met Sam and didn't recognise his photo either. She'd not been in Perth for long, having moved there just a couple of months ago, although was reluctant to be persuaded to say more about her life.

'Hello Molly,' Tom said as he took a seat opposite her.

'I haven't done anything so you can't keep me here,' Molly announced in a strong Belfast accent.

'I know,' Tom spoke gently. 'I'd just like to ask you a few questions about something that happened early this morning.'

'I don't know anything about it.' Molly nibbled her thumbnail and avoided Tom's eyes.

'You don't know what it is yet.'

'Yes, well, I still don't know anything,' Molly retorted, her mood becoming more brittle.

'How long have you been living rough, Molly?' he asked.

'Who told you I was living rough?' she barked back.

'Why were you in the squat if you're not homeless?'

'None of your business,' she blasted. 'It's not a crime to be there is it?'

Tom would have to rely on his years of experience to get through to her.

'I can refer you to people who can help you with...'

Molly started laughing. 'Yes, yes, course you can. You're as bad as everyone else. I'm fine as I am, now can I go?'

Tom could see he wasn't going to get anywhere with her and didn't have time to help her as much as he'd like. There was no evidence to suggest she'd touched the knife that had lain feet from where she'd passed out in the squat, let alone used it to murder Sam Kennedy. He hoped Andrea was having better luck with Natalie in the room next door.

Before allowing her to leave, Tom gave Molly a leaflet for the community kitchen so that she could at least get a decent meal every day. He wasn't optimistic when he witnessed her tossing the leaflet onto the floor of the station entrance. Tom understood why Craig Douglas wanted to keep an eye on these women who lived lives that left them so vulnerable, and it was Craig he wanted to speak to next.

–

'How are you doing, Natalie?' Andrea asked and slid a cup of coffee towards her. 'I've put a couple of sugars in it as well.'

'Thanks,' Natalie whispered and took a sip. 'You didn't have to do that.'

'It wasn't a problem. I was having one anyway.'

Natalie nodded. 'I'm sorry about earlier. You just got me at a bad time.'

'I know.'

'I do want to help you,' Natalie admitted. 'Sam was a good guy. Fucking horrible what's happened to him.' She sank another mouthful of the coffee. 'This is nice.' She lifted the cup up slightly and drank more.

'It's not bad, is it?' Andrea smiled. 'Look, you know you're free to leave at any time but whatever you can tell me, no matter how small, might just make all the difference.'

'I'll try but…' she shrugged. 'You know I'm out of it sometimes.'

'I understand that,' Andrea assured her. 'You started to tell me that Sam had helped you. What did you mean?'

Natalie closed her eyes and took a breath. 'I feel a bit sick,' she said and laid a hand on her stomach.

'I'll try not to keep you much longer but please, any information you can give me would be good. It sounds like you knew Sam.'

'I suppose I did kind of know him,' Natalie shrugged.

'How often did you see him? Once a week, a fortnight, how did it work?'

'It started as once a week then…' she stopped to take a breath. 'We clicked, you know. As bizarre as that sounds. Sam was…' she paused. 'He was different.'

'In what way?' Andrea asked, genuinely intrigued.

'He saw me as more than just a fuck,' Natalie answered bluntly. 'He listened to me. I mean actually listened.'

'Not like the other men,' Andrea suggested.

Natalie shook her head. 'Nah, Sam was a one off,' she sighed. 'He gave me money to pay off my debts.'

Andrea recalled the last amounts withdrawn from Sam Kennedy's account.

'How much did he give you?'

'Almost ten grand in total. Like I said, Sam was a one off.'

'That's a lot of money,' Andrea said and considered her next words carefully. 'What did he expect from you in return?'

'Nothing weird if that's what you're suggesting,' Natalie answered her question plainly.

'I wasn't. I was just curious,' Andrea admitted. 'It was a lot of money, that's all.'

'I know but…' Natalie shrugged gently. 'He didn't want me to do anything weird or nasty for it. He choked me a bit, nothing I couldn't handle.'

The calmness in her voice shocked Andrea and she found herself instinctively reaching for her own throat. 'Did you manage to pay off the debts?' she asked. Natalie nodded. 'I did, kind of.' She pressed her fingers against her temple. 'Look, my head is starting to hurt and I think I might be sick in a minute. Can we wrap this up. I honestly don't know who did that to Sam.'

'I know.' Andrea pressed on regardless. 'Have you any idea how the bloodied knife found its way to the upstairs room of that place?'

Natalie shook her head. 'Nah. What has Molly said?'

'My colleague is speaking to her at the moment. I'll find out in a bit. What do you know about her?'

'Nothing, except she's Irish and has a hell of a temper when she's rattling.'

Andrea frowned. 'Is that right?'

'Yes, she's punched walls and smashed plates. She even had somebody by the throat one night. Maybe you should be speaking to her about Sam.'

'Do you know if she had ever met with Sam? Had sex with him.'

Natalie shrugged. 'I've got no idea.'

Chapter Sixteen

Katie Sheehan stared into Sam's room, seemingly saddened by the state of it.

'Sam wasn't always as messy as this,' she said.

'How well did you know him?'

'Better than Kirsty wanted me to,' she said plainly.

Hazel was surprised to hear her talk like this because she'd been under the impression the incident had been a one-off.

'Was Sam sleeping with you behind Kirsty's back?' It was sounding more and more like Kirsty had a lot to be angry at Sam about in the end.

'Not exactly,' she replied and pressed her hands to her cheeks. 'The whole thing is so embarrassing.'

'You mean what happened a year ago,' Hazel suggested.

Katie nodded. 'Yes,' she said in barely a whisper. 'It all got out of hand and...' she sighed, 'I never meant for it to go so far.'

'Do you mean the sex with both lads or the complaint you made afterwards?' Hazel came straight to the point.

'God,' Katie exclaimed. 'Both!'

'I'm curious,' Hazel said. 'Why didn't you name Sam Kennedy?'

'Because I didn't want him to get chucked off his course,' she replied. 'Sam was really clever, and he'd have

91

made a brilliant doctor.' She stopped to sigh. 'That and the fact I knew who his dad was.'

'But it was OK to shove Daniel Macey under the bus, was it?' Hazel said.

'God, no, of course it wasn't, which was why I retracted it.'

'Yes, but not before putting Daniel through quite an ordeal,' Hazel pointed out but could see how much the guilt was weighing on the girl. 'When did you last see Sam Kennedy?'

'Erm… before he went home for the half term break, so a couple of weeks ago.'

'How did he seem to you?'

'Fine,' she told her. 'Under the circumstances.'

Hazel's interest was piqued by that. 'Under what circumstances?'

'Some guy had been here shouting his mouth off at Sam, although Sam didn't look that fazed when I think about it. He held his hands up and said he was sorry. I didn't hear what they were arguing about, but I did hear Kirsty's name a couple of times.'

Hazel figured that must have been Kirsty's brother.

'Sam was fine once he had left,' Hazel suggested. 'Was he?'

Katie nodded. 'He seemed to be.' The ghost of a smile landed on her lips. 'Sam just shrugged and gave me a wink before shutting the door again.' A well of emotion filled Katie's face.

'You were fond of Sam, weren't you?'

'I suppose.'

Hazel got the impression they were closer than Katie was letting on. The two of them lived so close together after all. Late night liaisons weren't impossible to imagine.

'You and Sam were having a relationship weren't you.' Hazel pushed her for the truth. 'And the encounter with both Sam and Daniel, something happened, didn't it.'

'No, no, it wasn't like that,' Katie insisted. 'It was just a stupid mistake. A party game that went too far.'

'But you don't deny you were in a re—'

'Yes OK,' Katie snapped before Hazel could finish. 'Yes, me and Sam,' she sighed. 'We were kind of close. He told me he felt he could be himself when he was with me.'

'What did he mean *he could be himself*?'

Katie looked uncomfortable.

Remembering the graphic nature of the drawings in Sam's notebook, Hazel was curious about the kind of sexual encounter she'd had with the lad.

'Listen Katie, I'm going to ask you something very personal and probably extremely uncomfortable.'

Katie frowned; a hint of a pink flush grew on her cheeks. 'OK.'

'What kind of sexual encounter did you and Sam have?'

Hazel could see she'd hit a nerve; Katie's discomfort was crystal clear. 'I'd rather not talk about it and, to be honest, I've got somewhere I need to be so…'

'Did he hurt you?' Hazel asked before she had the chance to leave.

Katie avoided eye contact as she nodded.

'He liked to choke me,' Katie's face turned bright red when she said it.

The drawings of terrified women in chains. The look of fear in their eyes. Was that what Sam wanted to see in Katie. In Kirsty. In the girls who sold sex to feed their drug addiction. Was that what got him killed? Hazel didn't press the matter further. She had what she needed but told Katie she'd be in touch if she needed to talk to her again and emphasised how grateful she was that the girl had come to talk to her.

Hazel's phone rang as she was walking back to her car.

'Hello,' she said, clicking to unlock it. She frowned when there was silence on the other end. 'Hello,' she repeated while she got in the car. 'Hello!' Hazel raised her voice then, irritated, she hung up as she started the engine.

The unknown number would have to remain a mystery for now. She didn't have time for that now because Billy had texted to say he'd discovered something very interesting on his trawl of the CCTV.

Chapter Seventeen

Craig Douglas stifled a yawn as Tom sat opposite him.

'Sorry we've kept you waiting so long,' Tom said.

'It's fine,' Craig replied. 'Are the girls OK? That stuff doesn't half snap them back to life.'

'Aye it does that alright. Who else, apart from Natalie and Molly have you seen hanging around there recently?' Tom asked and rubbed the stubble that was already growing on his chin. 'Have there been any faces that you don't recognise in the past few days?'

'Nobody new, just Natalie and Molly, as well as Kelly. Your colleague spoke to her earlier. Nice lassie.' He tutted. 'She doesn't seem like the others somehow,' he shrugged. 'I don't know, what do I know?' Craig stifled another yawn. 'God, excuse me, sorry.'

'Late night last night?' Tom said.

'Something like that,' Craig agreed. 'I don't sleep very well. Doc says I've got PTSD.'

Tom hadn't realised. How could he? Why didn't Craig mention this before? 'You should have said; I wouldn't have kept you waiting so long.'

Craig smiled. 'It's OK, it's not like I'm a basket case, don't worry.'

'Were you in the military then?' Tom asked.

'Aye, I was, yes, two tours in Northern Ireland and one in Bosnia before I left.'

'Wow, that must have been tough,' Tom acknowledged.

'It certainly had its moments. Some of that stuff stays with you, you know.' He tapped his temple. 'In here.'

In his late fifties and never having married, Craig Douglas must have been through hell, Tom thought.

'Right I'll try not to keep you much longer.'

'It's my dog I'm needing to get back to more than anything else,' Craig explained.

'Oh yes, what kind?' Tom asked as he took notes.

A wide grin crossed Craig's face. 'I inherited my mum's poodle last year after she went into a care home.'

Tom struggled to get the image of this macho ex-soldier walking a little poodle round the South Inch every day.

'I know,' Craig chuckled. 'I'd have a right good laugh at the thought of me with a little black poodle on a lead as well.'

Tom brought the conversation back to the subject of Sam Kennedy.

'My colleague showed you a picture of our victim and you said you definitely hadn't ever seen him? Not even with Natalie, who seems to have known him very well?'

'No, like I said to her, I'd never seen him at all,' Craig explained. 'Poor lad.'

'What about this Fiesta?' Tom scrolled to find a photo of Lisa Kennedy's car. 'Have you ever seen that before?'

Craig took his phone out of his hand to examine the photo more closely. 'Yes, I do know this car. I've seen it sitting outside Gary's garage. He's done a fair bit of work on an old Land Rover of mine and I saw the Fiesta, at least I think it was this Fiesta, outside one time when I went to pick mine up.'

'Is that the only place you've seen it?'

'Yes, I think so. Was that the guy's car then?'

Tom nodded. 'Well it was his mum's, but he used to drive it.'

'Did he pick the girls up in it?'

Tom was curious. 'Why do you ask that?'

Craig's eyes widened. 'What? I just figured with your interest in the squat, he must have been paying some of them for sex. That'll be how he met Natalie, of course.'

Tom took a moment to try and figure out this man's intentions. An unmarried middle-aged man. Was his interest in the women really as altruistic as it appeared or was Tom adding motivations that just weren't there?

'I really appreciate you being prepared to give your fingerprints, Craig,' Tom said.

'Not at all, anything I can do to help and besides, I quite like the idea of being ruled out of your investigation.'

Tom showed him a photo of the knife Craig had discovered. 'You found this knife close to where Molly was sitting. Have you ever seen it before?'

Craig shook his head. 'No, but to be honest, the place is in such a mess, there could be anything in there. I don't go poking around too much, what with the chances of getting stuck with a needle, you know.'

'Mm, yes, I know what you mean,' Tom agreed. 'So what do you do for the women who come and go from there?'

'Like I told your pal, I take them stuff. Food and money – that kind of thing. Sometimes I just drop in and say hello. I suppose I'm just checking that they're still alive, if I'm honest with you.'

Tom understood that. 'That's incredibly kind of you.'

'Aye, well, some of those lassies…' He stopped to sigh. 'They've already been through hell. If I can offer them a wee bit of kindness then why shouldn't I?'

'I get it, I really do.'

'I'm not the only one, either. There's an older woman who checks in from time to time.'

'Oh is there?' Tom flipped over a new page in his notebook. 'Do you happen to know her name?'

'Yes, she's called Rachel, works in that food kitchen down by the Lade.'

Rachel. Rachel.

It wasn't the first time Tom had heard that name.

'That's great, thanks, Craig. You've been really helpful. Listen, could I take a phone number just in case I need to talk to you again?'

'Aye, no problem.' Craig wrote his mobile number down on the piece of paper Tom gave him. 'I'll give you my work number as well. I'm starting back this week after being off with this.' He patted his leg.

'That would be great.' Tom smiled as he took the paper back from him. 'Where is it you work?'

'The butcher's in the old high street,' Craig said as he got up from the seat.

'You're a butcher,' Tom said, an image of the ten-inch blade of what he knew to be a boning knife flashing in his mind.

'Yes,' Craig smiled. 'That's right.'

–

Craig was glad to be out of there. He wasn't lying about having to get back to the dog but hadn't admitted how elderly the poodle was. Promising his mum he'd not have

Spot put to sleep unless it was the last resort meant regularly cleaning up puddles of pee and he imagined there would be plenty after leaving him for so long.

He thanked the guy behind the counter after taking his change. Popping in for bread and milk would be his last stop. It was turning out to be a milder evening after the heavy chilled rain that day. He'd take Spot for a short walk once he'd something to eat. Let the little man stretch his legs a bit after being in the flat all day.

Craig yawned, looking forward to sinking the last couple of beers in the fridge and considered ordering a curry because he really couldn't be arsed cooking even though he was famished.

The woman standing outside his front door was in a shocking state.

'I thought I'd told you not to come here again,' Craig said, troubled by the state of her as he grabbed his keys from his jacket pocket. 'We agreed that, didn't we?'

'I had nowhere else to go,' the girl explained. 'And can I charge my phone?'

Craig glanced around him, anxious that she might have been seen, and slid the key into the lock.

'Yes, yes, you'd better come in then before somebody sees you.' He sighed and followed the dishevelled girl inside.

Chapter Eighteen

Hazel wondered why the drive from Dundee to Perth always seemed shorter than the journey in the opposite direction. She was grateful to find that the A90 was quiet now that the rush hour traffic was gone. Seeing the covers coming off the soft fruit tunnels that littered the countryside was always a sign that the season was done for another year. She did miss that. Hazel noticed the 'For Sale' sign was still up on the derelict cottage she'd had her eye on. She made a mental note, like she did every time she passed it. One day, she thought. One day. The time on her car clock read 6.45p.m. as she turned into the station car park, glad that the heavy shower that had lashed down in sheets until five minutes ago had stopped.

October had always been a bitter-sweet month for her. The anniversary of the death of her mum arrived alongside the end of the hotter months that she'd never enjoyed. Hearing the geese arrive, squawking overhead always made her heart sing. People seemed to be quieter and more respectful during the winter months when the late night, noisy barbeques that she hated had stopped. Not that they were as much of a problem now that she didn't live in the terraced house she'd shared with Rick for most of their twenty-five-year marriage. Her flat overlooking the North Inch was far quieter. One bonus of his betrayal, at least.

'Alright Billy, how's it going?' Hazel tossed her cardigan across the back of a chair and smiled at the fresh cup of tea waiting for her. The KitKat next to it was a beautiful sight, especially because it was a four-finger, not a two.

'Great, yes.' He yawned and sat back to stretch his arms up then flopped down and sank the dregs of his brew.

'What have you got for me?' Hazel asked.

'Right, I've two bits of what I think are very useful things for you.' He typed some keys and rolled the mouse over an image before pausing. He pointed to the time code. 'See that, it says ten past ten.'

'Yep, do we know who the girl is?' Hazel asked as she watched what looked like a drunk woman weaving on and off the pavement. She snapped her KitKat before offering a stick to Billy which he took and bit into.

'Ta,' he said. 'We don't, it's too grainy but just see what happens next.' He clicked on to the next frame which showed a small woman with long hair approaching the girl who started to gesticulate wildly and pushed the woman away, almost knocking her off her feet.

'Ten past ten,' Hazel announced. 'Jack says time of death was around then or a little before.' She stared at Billy.

'Hang on, there's more,' he said, stuffing the last bit of biscuit in his mouth and clicking play again. 'A Ford Escort pulls up and another woman gets out.'

'The girl is not pleased to see her, is she?' Hazel's eyes widened as she exclaimed. 'Oh ya, boy she is not happy.'

Hazel watched on as the two women tried to load the seemingly angry girl into the car but, failing, watched as she staggered away from them. The woman with the long hair hugged the one who had arrived in the Escort and they both drove away without the girl.

'I've sent a copy to see if it can be sharpened up a bit for us but this one image…' he froze the screen on the long-haired woman who'd first tried to reason with the girl. 'This is the clearest we've got so I've downloaded it to facial recognition. Hopefully, we'll get a hit on her soon.'

'I know that girl,' Andrea's voice piped up from behind them. 'That's Molly Barker. She's one of the girls from the squat.'

'Are you sure?' Hazel asked, pleased to see Andrea nod. 'Do you recognise the other two?' She tapped Billy's shoulder. 'Rewind a bit, Billy, play it for Andrea.'

'Sure thing,' Billy rolled over the mouse then clicked play.

Hazel watched Andrea narrow her eyes as she concentrated. Her shaking head was disappointing.

'No, I can't say I know them but I'm positive that's Molly.'

'Positive or almost positive?'

Andrea stared at the screen again. 'Positive. It's the hair. The slight curls and she looks the right height. Natalie says she's got a bit of a temper on her and by the looks of it, she's not wrong.'

Tom arrived just as they were examining the footage and Andrea turned.

'Tell me you have an address for Molly Barker,' she called out as he walked towards where the team was gathered by Billy's laptop screen.

'Well, I've got as much as I'm going to get. She's registered as staying at the night shelter. She was as much use as a chocolate fireguard, though. What's this?' He pointed to the screen.

'CCTV,' Hazel told him. 'Have you seen either of these two before, Tom?'

Tom narrowed his eyes at the screen but shook his head. 'You can't even make out that number plate. What camera is this from?' He turned to Billy.

'The garage one.'

'What about the harbour café one?' Tom suggested.

Billy smiled and typed the keys which brought another image onto the screen. He smiled triumphantly at Hazel.

'Is that…' she asked.

The detectives stared at the footage of what appeared to be a homeless man raking in the commercial wheelie bin at the side of the café, picking stuff up and tossing some back. Hazel stared at Tom.

'A witness,' she said with a smile and excitedly tapped her fists on Tom's chest. 'It's only a bloody witness.'

Hazel's phone rang before she could get too excited by the development. As it was getting late she asked for a couple of night shift uniform patrols to search for the man in the image and sent the rest of the team home. They'd try and pick Molly Barker up first thing in the morning. Talk to her again and ask her what she was doing last night and who she'd been having a disagreement with.

'Hello,' she said anxiously on recognising the number. It was very unusual for them to call her because they knew what she did for a living. Her heart raced on hearing what she'd been told. 'I'm on my way,' she said and grabbed her bag and keys.

Chapter Nineteen

The burst of raucous laughter outside the living room window of her ground-floor Canal Street flat made Rachel jump. She checked her phone again but there still wasn't a message from Molly. After the disagreement last night she had hoped she'd get in touch. The pain on Dawn's face when they watched Molly walk away from them was still fresh in her mind. They couldn't force her into the car and make her accept help. She'd screamed whenever they tried, and the last thing Rachel needed was someone calling the police. Drawing attention to herself was something she avoided at all costs.

The knock on the door made her smile. She'd come round instead.

'Hang on, I'm coming.' Rachel took a quick glance in the hall mirror then frowned on seeing the envelope lying on the doormat. She picked it up and stuffed it into her pocket and opened the door.

'Kelly, what a surprise,' she said, disappointed not to find Molly standing outside her front door. Instead, it was a girl she'd met a handful of times at the community kitchen whom she'd invited to come round anytime if she needed anything.

'Have you got a minute?' Kelly asked.

'Of course, yes, come in.'

'Thank you.' Kelly stepped inside and headed straight for the open-plan living area. She took her rucksack off and dropped it at her feet.

'Is everything OK?' Rachel asked as she closed and locked the door and followed her guest inside.

'Erm, it's a bit embarrassing...' Kelly nibbled her lip.

'What is it? Is it something I can help with?' Rachel filled the kettle and switched it on. 'I was about to make something to eat. Can I get you anything?'

She smiled but felt sad for the poor girl who was shivering in the cold, standing there in just a light jacket over a thin T-shirt and leggings. Rachel had been exactly where Kelly was and felt desperate to help. She knew the squat wasn't perfect but staying there was sometimes better than the shelter. The hard truth was that although the shelter provided the women with a roof over their heads, it didn't mean they were safe. Some of the other residents could be violent and the constant state of tension was horrible. Now that the squat had been sealed off with police tape and had a patrol car parked outside, she knew Kelly wouldn't even try and go there. Rachel didn't know what had happened in there but had turned right back when she'd seen all the activity.

'I've...' Kelly avoided Rachel's eyes. 'I've got my period and I've not got anything.'

'Sweetheart, just wait there. I'll go and get you some clean things.'

Rachel flipped open a suitcase that she kept under her bed. From inside she pulled out clean underwear and sanitary towels. At sixty, she might be finished with all that, but Rachel knew that period poverty was a real issue for some of these young women. She kept a supply on hand for these situations because this wasn't the first time, and it wouldn't be the last.

Rachel's phone rang before she could get back to Kelly and she snatched it up when she saw that it was Dawn.

'Have you heard from her?' she said before Dawn had a chance to say anything but had to listen to her old friend tell her she'd heard nothing. 'No, she's not been here either,' she replied.

'Have you heard about the body that was found on Shore Road last night?' Dawn asked.

Rachel hadn't heard and the thought sent shivers through her whole body. Suddenly she felt so cold. 'No, was it a man or a woman?'

'A man, I think,' Dawn replied. 'I'm not exactly sure, to be honest. My head is so all over the place. You will call if Molly gets in touch with you,' Dawn urged. 'I know she talks to you. Trusts you.'

Dawn was right. Molly did trust her 'Auntie Rachel.' At least she did until recently. The teenager had changed, and Rachel didn't know whether she would come to her for help now. The drugs seemed to have scrambled her mind to a frightening degree. One that Rachel knew all too well.

'I'll call if I hear anything, I promise,' Rachel assured her as Kelly's concerned expression greeted her from the hall. 'I'll call you later, Dawn. Keep in touch.' Rachel ended the call and pressed her phone into her trouser pocket.

'Is everything OK? I haven't come at a bad time, have I? Because I can go.' Kelly snatched her bag up. 'I'll go, I can see you're busy.' She made to leave until Rachel stepped in front of her.

'Not before having a shower and something to eat, you won't,' Rachel smiled at her.

'Are you sure?'

'Very sure. Now, there's a towel in the cupboard outside the bathroom. Take as long as you like. I've got a couple of shower gels in the basket on the counter. Help yourself.'

Kelly reached forward and gave Rachel a long, tight hug.

'Thank you,' Kelly beamed.

'Don't be daft.' Rachel held her tight then patted her back. 'Go on, get cleaned up and I'll make us something to eat.'

'Will it be OK to use your phone too? I'm out of credit.'

'Of course it is,' Rachel smiled. 'Whatever you need.'

She hoped Kelly would want to stay for a chat after freshening up because Rachel was keen to find out what she knew about the murder on Shore Road, hoping that it had nothing to do with Molly. But given the volatile personality the drugs gave her, anything was possible. Rachel knew from experience just what drugs made a person capable of.

Chapter Twenty

Cara's text, which landed on her phone right before Hazel rushed into the care home, was ignored just like all the others. That woman had the cheek of the Devil in her.

'Dad!' Hazel exclaimed on seeing the bruises on her dad's cheek. The cut lip looked angry and sore too where he'd bitten down on it when he fell. 'What have you been doing, huh?' She hugged him tight and kissed the cheek that wasn't bruised.

She turned on hearing footsteps approaching. 'What the hell happened?' she asked Rena, the care assistant, a woman in her fifties that Hazel had known from her days at the grammar, who'd been caring for him since Hazel had made the decision to find him full-time care five years ago.

'Och, he tried to go for a wander by himself and tripped.' She squeezed Hazel's shoulder. 'It looks worse than it is because of how fragile their skin is at that age.'

'Are you sure he hasn't broken anything?'

The woman shook her head. 'No, there was an on-call GP in checking on one of the other residents, so he was able to come and examine him. Says he's just bruised but if he seems worse in the morning he'll see him again.'

Hazel dropped her hand over her dad's, struggling to fight the urge to cry at the state of him. She quickly rubbed her face.

'Surely he needs an x-ray or something,' she said anxiously.

Rena pulled up a chair and sat down. 'You know how confusing that would be for your dad in his condition.' She spoke gently and slowly. 'He's better off here, with people he's familiar with.'

Hazel considered that. She trusted that Rena, who'd been caring for the elderly all her working life, was right. Knowing Hazel's father as she did, she knew what was best for him tonight. Perhaps it was Hazel's guilt that bothered her the most. Guilt that she wasn't there to protect him. Guilt that she'd brought him there in the first place after the sacrifices he'd made for her, especially after her mum died. Neither of them had been prepared for that.

'You're right, I'm sorry.' Hazel softened and searched her bag for a tissue until she was handed one. 'Thanks.'

'Doc has suggested a sedative.' The woman lifted her hand when she could see Hazel open her mouth to protest. 'I know, I know,' she continued. 'But he thinks it's time your dad got something to help with some of the agitation he feels.'

'Suggested means prescribed,' Hazel scoffed. 'That's what that means, doesn't it?'

The woman nodded. 'Yes, but it's not a heavy dose and it can be adjusted easily if it's too much. I explained how strongly you feel about it.'

Hazel appreciated that. The thought of her dad sitting in a chair all day, doped up to the eyeballs like a zombie had been Hazel's worst nightmare when she'd decided to put him into a home. But his dementia diagnosis had meant sedatives were inevitable at some point. The weird thing was, Rick had been great at first when his father-in-law had become ill. Now Hazel was losing both of them.

An unknown number called again.

'I'll leave you to it,' the woman said, squeezing Hazel's shoulder again before bustling away.

'Aye, thanks,' Hazel replied simply and frowned at the screen as she clicked the 'Answer Call' button. 'Hello, DCI Todd,' she said into the handset and waited. 'Hello,' she raised her voice this time, irritated by the silent treatment. 'Oh piss off,' she muttered under her breath as she hung up and tossed the iPhone back into her bag.

She picked her dad's comb up from his dresser, her eyes drifting over the collection of framed photos. Her parents wedding photo always made her smile. A heavy rain shower had just stopped long enough for the wedding photographer to get the shots before pouring down in torrents again. It was coming down in sheets apparently, so the story had been told to her. They were so happy that day, her mum in her mini skirt and beehive and her dad in his best suit with his best man in matching outfit, both men with sideburns that could easily terrify children. Hazel's maternal grandmother's face was severe, and she had a tongue so sharp it could cut metal, her dad always said. The other end of the dresser had a picture of Hazel and Rick on their wedding day. Hazel's dress looked like a literal meringue with matching veil and headdress. How wedding fashions had changed in a relatively short time.

The picture of her dad as a boy standing next to one of the Clydesdale horses the farm had for working the field, made him seem tiny. Hazel lifted that one up. She loved that picture of his smiling face.

'Right, let's see if we can make you a bit more presentable,' she murmured and began to tidy what little hair the old man had left until his frail hand touched hers.

He peered into Hazel's eyes and mumbled something. She smiled.

'I know,' she whispered.

It had gone ten by the time Hazel left, grateful that the night shift had allowed her that extra time, but her dad needed his bed. The old man appeared tired and thin these days. She told herself she would make more time to see him.

—

The figure standing outside the security door into her block irritated Hazel but didn't surprise her.

'Hello, Hazel.'

'I have absolutely nothing to say to you,' Hazel blasted. 'Or him, so if you don't mind, it's been a very long day...'

Hazel lifted her key to the external door lock but her path was blocked. She had neither the time nor the energy for this. She wasn't lying when she'd said it had been a long day.

'I remembered your mum's anniversary was today.'

'Good for you. What do you want, a medal?' Hazel spat.

'But that's not why I'm here.'

Hazel stared into the turquoise blue eyes she knew so well, squeezing her keys tightly in a bid to displace the anger she wanted to take out on that perfect face. What was her damn secret? Why didn't she have crow's feet yet?

'Well?' Hazel growled. 'What do you want, then?'

'Rick hasn't come home.'

Hazel laughed sarcastically and shrugged, wishing she could think of a jibe about karma, but her mind went blank.

'Well, you reap what you sow, Cara,' Hazel finally said and pushed forward to slip the key into the lock, causing her oldest friend to reluctantly move back.

'I've not been able to get hold of him for three days,' she explained. 'I totally get it, I do, I'm the last person you want to see but—'

'You *think*?' Hazel blasted and started to open the security door. 'Go away, Cara,' she said more politely than she wanted to – she didn't want her neighbour twitching his net curtain on hearing raised voices and by God she wanted to shout right then. How dare she have the nerve to come here!

Hazel began to close the door but Cara stepped inside the doorway to stop her. It was then that Hazel spotted the redness in her eyes and what appeared to be genuine worry etched on her face.

'Please, Hazel,' Cara begged. 'He's not answering his phone and the office haven't heard from him either.'

The two old friends stared at each other, and Hazel sighed as she took the key out of the lock.

'You'd better come in then,' she invited reluctantly.

Chapter Twenty-One

Cara had appeared to be in denial when Hazel explained that Rick was probably up to his old tricks. She'd asked if he'd been *working late* recently. Or if he had been to any *conferences* – weekends where he'd be up to his eyeballs in work, couldn't call her, not even between meetings because it was all about networking, even at this stage in his career. The reality was, it was never his eyeballs Rick had been up to. She advised Cara the same as she would anyone else, though: report him missing if she was that concerned.

But the early morning wake-up call to say another body had been found certainly distracted her. This time a dog walker had found a man slumped over the steering wheel of his Vauxhall Astra and had become concerned that he'd had a heart attack. Checking on the man's welfare, the dog walker had been shocked to find a man in his forties with a gaping stab wound in his stomach and a carrier bag hanging loosely from his neck. The victim's hand was clutching his stomach, covered in blood, with his head leaning against the steering wheel.

Kinnoull Hill Woodland Walk, rising sharply from the banks of the River Tay, was an area enjoyed by walkers and wildlife alike, where it wasn't unusual to see roe deer and squirrels. The park also featured grassy paths and marked nature trails through fine mixed woodland.

The car park was a stunning viewpoint, affording vistas across Perth. Dotted along the path were also alternative parking places where a couple could spend time together, privately, unseen by prying eyes. This man was parked in an isolated spot known to be very private and out of view.

As she approached the car, Hazel wished she hadn't devoured the half bottle of chardonnay she'd had in the fridge last night. Nausea churned her guts, clawing into her throat, and she had to fight to stop the urge to vomit from overtaking her.

'Good morning, boss,' Tom greeted her and handed her a pair of gloves. Then he frowned. 'Are you OK?'

'Yes, why do you ask that?'

'Nothing, you just look a bit pale.'

'I'm fine, don't you worry about me,' she told him. 'Is this one the same as Sam Kennedy?'

'Kind of, yes.' Tom followed her as she made her way to the driver's side of the Astra, the distinctive stench of blood and death hitting her nose long before she got close. 'Except—'

'The carrier bag,' Hazel interrupted. 'Stabbed and suffocated. Just like Sam Kennedy.'

'But where's the bag that was used on Sam?' Tom asked.

'There's a search team back at the harbour.' She glanced at her watch. 'Right about now. I'll go and call them, tell them to scan specifically for carrier bags. Bring every one of them in.' The strong autumnal gales that had roared through Perth late last night meant the haul of plastic bags was likely to be large but given this development, it was necessary. In fact she wanted the South Inch scoured for bags as well as the grounds of HMP Perth nearby which she knew would be trickier to organise.

While she waited for her call to be answered she instructed the dog handlers, that had just pulled up, to search the nearby trees along the woodland walk and beyond.

'Thanks,' Hazel said to the lead handler and walked away. 'Hi, it's DCI Todd, can you check the harbour for plastic bags, specifically carrier bags,' she said into her phone when her call was answered and rolled her eyes at the retort that came back at her. 'Yes, yes, I know,' she replied to the officer's argument that his team had already started. She shook her head as she hung up.

Hazel walked back to their victim's car and crouched next to their latest victim. The glove box dropped open easily because it was missing one of the clips that held it shut.

'Have you run a check on the car's registration yet?' She craned her neck round to look up at Tom who was talking on the phone.

He lifted a finger to his lips as he ended his call. 'Sean Cooper is the registered keeper of the Astra. I've texted his name to Billy, see what he can dig up on him, if anything,' he informed her and crouched down next to her. Smelling stale alcohol on her breath he asked, 'Heavy night last night, was it?'

Hazel was taken aback by that. 'What?'

'Nothing, forget I said that, sorry,' he corrected himself.

Hazel reached inside the glove box and found a wallet. 'Right, let's see who you are, shall we?' Before she could examine the wallet, a single hair in the footwell caught her eye. Just like the Sam Kennedy crime scene. Hazel bagged the hair and then concentrated on the wallet.

Inside the tatty old wallet she found several reward cards for what seemed like every shop in Perth. Tesco, The Works, Superdrug and more. He even had a couple of points cards for two coffee shops. A condom was tucked in a zipped pocket next to some loose change. He had a twenty-pound note stuffed in next to a pile of receipts. It wasn't until she flicked through his bank cards, of which he had three, that she found a driver's licence which told her that this man was the registered keeper of the Astra. Sean Cooper was in his mid-forties and lived in one of the new build properties at The Rookery, Muirton, next to St John's Academy.

'I hope you're not contaminating my crime scene, DCI Todd,' Jack Blair's voice echoed along the track.

Hazel stood back up and smiled at him. 'Hello, Jack, nice to see you too.'

'Same as the other lad, I believe,' Jack suggested as Tom nodded a greeting and wandered away to talk to the dog walker, who was talking to a uniformed offer a little further down the track.

'I reckon so,' Hazel agreed. 'Except the two men seem very different. Sam was barely twenty years old, and this guy is well into his forties.'

Hazel stepped aside to let Jack get closer. The pathologist kneeled down and removed his thermometer from his bag.

'Did you have any luck locating a bag at the other crime scene?' he asked.

'Not yet,' she admitted. 'Can you give us a time of death yet?'

'Mm,' Jack mumbled to himself. 'Given the ambient temperature and signs of rigor mortis already gone, I'd say this poor chap has been dead at least forty-eight to seventy-two hours.'

'So he was killed before Sam Kennedy.' Hazel exclaimed.

This revelation was unexpected because despite this track being off the main path it would still have been used, not least by dog walkers like the poor unfortunate man that Tom was talking to. The recent wet weather had perhaps put the less hardy walkers off, given the sloppy mud that would have been underfoot in the past couple of days. She'd not heard of any missing person's reports in Sean Cooper's name. Their conversation was interrupted by a call from Billy Flynn, back at the station.

'Billy.' She answered the call quickly, keen to know what information he had for her. She mouthed the word *sorry* to Jack and stepped away to take the call. The dark clouds gathering above them looked ominous.

'Hey Boss, your man, Sean Cooper, had been arrested several times for domestic abuse and the police had been called numerous other times to the address he shared with his wife, Lynne,' Billy told her. 'Mostly just to warn him.'

'Really?' Hazel replied. 'That's interesting.'

'A sexual assault allegation had been made against him a year ago, by a woman he worked with, but this had been retracted,' Billy added. 'The wife left him suddenly apparently too, in the middle of the night, three months ago according to the last assault report.' This detail intrigued her. Sean's wife upping and fleeing in the middle of the night. Things must have been bad.

Before she hung up she asked Billy to text her the address of the shelter Lynne Cooper was staying in.

'Interesting,' she mumbled under her breath and walked back to where Jack was examining Sean's body.

Tom could see the poor man who had discovered the body was still trembling.

'It must have been quite a shock,' he said. 'I'm sorry you had to see that.'

'Shock?' The middle-aged man exclaimed as he vigorously stroked his collie's head. 'That's an understatement if ever I heard one.'

'Would it be OK to ask you a few questions while things are still fresh in your mind?'

'Fresh? I can't see that ever being anything but fresh.' The man shook his head and tugged his black, woollen beanie tighter on his head.

The wind whipped around them as the dark sky above turned blacker, threatening a downpour any minute. Losing evidence to a deluge was a possibility if they didn't hurry.

'Can you tell me exactly what happened?' Tom asked, clicking his pen, ready to take notes.

'Like I already told your colleague there,' he nodded to the uniformed officer who was chatting to one of the canine handlers, 'me and Biscuit hadn't managed to get out for a few days, so we started up the track, hoping to be back down before it rained again,' he added, running a gloved hand over the back of his neck, the trembling still obvious.

'Take your time,' Tom said.

'I saw the car and I thought the guy was sleeping at first but then I thought, he's awfy still for a man that's sleeping. I mean, he didn't move when I called out to him and even when Biscuit jumped up at the window...' The man seemed to be reliving that first image and closed his eyes as he shook his head. Tom didn't blame him for shuddering. 'So I knocked on the window but nothing.'

'So what did you do then?' Tom asked and indicated to the bench nearby so that the man could sit.

'I thought he'd had a heart attack or something, but then…' He paused to gather himself together, exhaling loudly. 'I saw the blood.' He squeezed his eyes tightly shut, shaking his head. 'So much blood… and he had a carrier bag dangling from his shirt.' The man shivered before his collie jumped onto his lap, licking his face vigorously.

'And then you called the police, is that right?'

The man nodded. 'Of course, yes. I daren't touch anything. I know you're no' supposed to touch anything.' He gently pushed his dog down again. 'I've never seen anything like it in my life. Not in the flesh so to speak, plenty on the telly but…'

'I understand,' Tom said. 'Can you give me a number that I can contact you on in case I need to speak to you again? Would that be OK? And if you could give me your full name, that would be great.'

'Yes, sure.'

Tom gave the man his own details too and urged him to get in touch if he remembered anything else.

He turned to walk back up the track but noticed a figure watching him from deep inside the trees. Screwing up his eyes, he tried to get a better view.

'Hey,' he called out as he walked towards them, until the small figure turned and ran. 'Hey,' he called out again and started running into the trees to find them.

'Tom, where are you going?' Hazel shouted.

'I saw someone in the trees,' he yelled back.

Chapter Twenty-Two

It wasn't too hard to outrun that tall detective. Tom, he was called. He seemed nice. That little woman detective was far too old to be chasing people through trees. She was well past it. Mind you, she had a lot on her plate, what with her husband shacking up with her best friend. Ouch. That had gotta hurt. Betrayal on that scale was too much for anyone to cope with.

There was no real chance of being caught but anger fizzed at being seen like that because that hadn't been part of the plan. Observing from a safe distance for now, that was all it was supposed to be. Seeing all the goings-on, the ins and outs of an investigation. That was intriguing. Fascinating. The game of cat and mouse was thrilling. It must have been like that for *her.* All those years ago. So much time had passed since she'd done those awful things. But had they really been that bad? Really.

The police would have so many questions. Who was their victim? How did he die? Did the pathologist have a time of death for them yet? All fascinating stuff. Talking to the witness, that was vital. What had he seen? What time did he find the body? Had he noticed anything unusual?

DNA. Fingerprints. Examining the victim's phone. Now that would be interesting. Talking to the grieving widow, that would be next. It was doubtful there would be many tears shed over him. Hadn't she wanted to kill him also? How she'd dreamed of stabbing him herself!

The number eleven bus arrived in the nick of time. Five minutes and they'd be long gone. Long before the dogs were sent to follow the trail. Long before either of those detectives had any idea who they were.

The shadowy figure slipped off the bus in Mill Street and was swept along with the crowd heading towards the High Street, just another face in the crowd. A face that wore a smile that grew in the knowledge they were on track to deliver the biggest surprise of all. She was going to love it.

Chapter Twenty-Three

'I'm sorry, Hazel,' Tom said sheepishly as they drove back towards town.

'Don't worry about it,' she replied despite the fact her lungs burned and her thighs were like jelly after chasing off after a mystery person that Tom said he saw watching them.

She'd left a canine team going over every inch of the woodland park. If there had been someone there, they'd find them.

'I was sure I saw someone,' he added. 'Just standing there, watching.'

'What did they look like?' Hazel asked as she accelerated away from the traffic lights at the bottom of Lochie Brae towards the bridge.

'I couldn't see them properly from so far away, to be honest,' Tom admitted, shaking his head. He checked his phone on hearing the text land. 'The search of the harbour has brought in six carrier bags and a gravel sack from a builder's merchants,' he read aloud.

'I don't think it's going to be the gravel sack, but we'll have it all checked for Sam's DNA and prints.'

'What if that was the killer,' Tom suggested drily, 'and I let them get away?'

'That's enough of that. If there's somebody there, you know as well as I do, those dogs will find them,' Hazel chastised her DI. He was a lovely guy but did have a habit of dwelling on the negative.

'I know, you're right,' Tom acknowledged just as Hazel pulled in through the gate of the homeless shelter. 'Lynne Cooper has been staying here for the past three months apparently, while she's waiting on council housing.'

'Poor woman. Sounds like their marriage was pretty turbulent,' Hazel said as she switched off her engine.

'Violent rather than turbulent,' Tom corrected her. 'Sean Cooper sounded like a right nasty piece of work.'

Hazel frowned at her DI, her lips pursing gently, thinking how different Sean Cooper sounded to Sam Kennedy. Did the two men have anything in common apart from how they died?

'Do you think Cooper and Sam knew each other?' she suggested to Tom.

'I doubt it, but hopefully the wife can fill us in on that.'

Hazel buzzed the security bell on the entrance and got her ID ready to show to the camera. She smiled and pushed the door open as the lock buzzed open. 'Hello, my name is DCI Hazel Todd, and this is DI Tom Newton,' she said to the young, blonde girl on the reception desk. 'We're here to speak to Lynne Cooper.'

The girl smiled at Tom and Hazel in turn before typing something into her keyboard.

'Hang on, I'll just check if she's here.'

Hazel glanced around at the posters on the noticeboard behind her. A picture of sad women standing next to their children was a powerful image for a domestic abuse information leaflet. Another promoting mental health had a smiling man on it. Quite the contrast.

'Yes, I'll just go and see if I can get her to come and speak to you,' the girl said and let herself out of the reception area before unlocking another door that led deeper inside the building.

'God, it's like Fort Knox in here,' Tom mumbled just as a petite, fragile-looking woman came back through the door accompanied by the receptionist.

'I'm Lynne Cooper,' she said timidly. 'They said you want to talk to me. Is it about Sean?'

'Is there somewhere more private we can go?' Hazel asked the receptionist.

'Sure, follow me,' she replied and led them through a door to their left into a room that had bean bags and children's toys scattered around and a table and four chairs under a small window.

'That's great, thanks,' Tom said and closed the door after them.

'Shall we have a seat, Lynne,' Hazel suggested and pulled one out for her.

'OK,' Lynne stuttered. 'But if this is about me testifying, I've already said I won't change my mind. I've left him and I'm trying to get my life back together.'

Hazel noticed the three-inch scar across Lynne's neck, then her eyes were drawn to the lines on her upper arms and palms. The woman's nose appeared as if it had previously been broken. More than once. But it was her eyes that really showed the damage. They were so sad, as though every ounce of her soul had been sucked out of them. She was painfully thin and pale. Birdlike, almost.

'I just want to forget about all that,' Lynne continued, fiddling with the zip on her shirt.

Hazel sat and pointed to one of the other chairs. 'Please, have a wee seat, Lynne.' Then she nodded to Tom to leave them.

Hazel was annoyed with herself that she hadn't thought to go in alone. At six foot two, Tom was a huge presence and although Hazel knew what a wonderful, gentle man he was, Lynne didn't. Tom nodded and left quietly. Lynne's eyes traced his every move out of the room and Hazel watched her shoulders drop as a result before she sat opposite her.

'What's this about, then?' Lynne asked, maintaining eye contact this time.

'I'm sorry to have to tell you that the body of a man was found earlier and I'm afraid to say that we think it's Sean.'

Lynne's jaw clenched then relaxed. Her lips parted slightly as a short gasp of air escaped.

'I'm sorry,' Hazel repeated.

'I… I mean…' Lynne's body language loosened. 'What happened to him?'

The absence of tears didn't surprise Hazel. Lynne was numbed by shock on top of the years of abuse.

'His body was found a short time ago. We think he'd been stabbed.'

'You think he'd been stabbed?!'

'We'll know for sure once the post mortem has been carried out.'

'I don't know what to say.' Lynne swallowed hard and slumped back in the seat.

'We still need to have someone come and identify his body officially.'

'I don't want to do that,' Lynne blurted, seemingly panicked at the prospect.

'Hey, it's OK, you don't have to do it,' Hazel tried to reassure her.

'Get his brother to do it.' Lynne pulled at the collar of her shirt. 'God, I can't breathe.'

'It's OK Lynne, look at me.' Hazel inhaled a huge breath and blew it back out slowly. 'Copy me, look, Lynne.' She inhaled again.

'I can't breathe,' Lynne gasped.

Hazel grabbed her hand and held it in hers.

'Look at me, Lynne.' Hazel breathed in and exhaled slowly. Breathed in and exhaled. Breathed in and exhaled.

Lynne finally seemed to be following her instructions. Breathing in and gasping out. Breathing in. Breathing out. Then gasping out more slowly, tears pouring down her cheeks.

'That's good, you're doing great.' Hazel breathed in. Breathed out. 'That's it, again, in… out.'

Hazel poured water from the jug on the table into one of the paper cups and passed it gently into Lynne's trembling hand.

'Thank you,' she whispered and sipped.

Hazel offered her a sympathetic smile and gave the distraught woman a chance to gather herself. No matter how bad her relationship with Sean had been, the news she'd just been given must have been a hell of a shock for an already fragile person.

'OK?' Hazel asked, pleased to see Lynne nod slowly and wipe her face clean.

'Yes, I'm sorry, it was just such a shock.' She sighed. 'The thought of seeing him again…' she shuddered.

'It's fine. Can you give me Sean's brother's details so I can contact him?'

'Yes sure.' Lynne scrolled through the names on her phone and turned to show Hazel.

'Great, thanks.' Hazel made a note of Phil Cooper's number and slipped her phone away. 'Were they close, Sean and his brother?'

'They're as thick as thieves, those two,' Lynne said and the disdain in her voice was obvious. 'Phil's as bad as Sean, if not worse. He put my sister-in-law in hospital last year with two broken ribs and a fractured jaw and cheek.'

Hazel's eyes stretched wide. 'He sounds like a nasty piece of work.'

'Yes, well, she went back to Australia as soon as she could after that. Took the kids with her.' Lynne sighed. 'I still miss her and my nephews but they're safe where they are.'

'You and Sean don't have kids.'

Lynne shook her head. 'Thank God.'

'Things got pretty bad did they?' Hazel pointed to Lynne's neck.

On reflex, Lynne's fingers searched out the scar. 'It was a nightmare that I thought I could never escape until…' She stopped as if she'd said too much.

'What is it? Whatever you tell me will remain confidential, I promise.'

'It's not that; it's embarrassing, that's all.'

'Try me,' Hazel smiled.

'I had to go the foodbank for six months when Sean got laid off at work.'

Hazel could see that pride had made that a horrible prospect for her. 'People use foodbanks for all kinds of reasons. There's nothing to be ashamed of.'

Lynne smiled. 'That's what Rachel said. She's the woman who runs it. She saw me that day and just seemed to know if you know what I mean. She seemed to see me, the me that was desperate, behind all the make-up and stiff upper lip.' She breathed out quickly through puffed cheeks. 'I don't know if it was divine intervention or what but if it hadn't been for Rachel, I think I'd be dead. No, that's not true. I know I'd be dead.'

When Lynne said that last part directly into Hazel's eyes she knew she was deadly serious. She allowed her to talk because it was as if a cork had been released and Hazel didn't want to stop the flow.

'He'd come home one night after the darts with Phil, as usual, and he was pissed, as usual. I hadn't kept him anything to eat, and I knew it would happen. I must have been mad, but I was so angry with him. I hated him so much I wanted to ki—' She stopped as if realising she'd said something she shouldn't and swallowed as if forcing the words back down. 'I'm sorry, I didn't mean that, I was just…'

'It's OK,' Hazel told her. 'But you know I have to ask you.'

Lynne nodded. 'Yes, I know.'

'Lynne, did you kill Sean?'

She shook her head. 'No, I didn't.' She paused, seemingly giving her next words careful consideration. 'But I'm glad he's dead.'

Hazel didn't blame her for feeling like that.

'Do you still have a key for the house?' Hazel asked.

Lynne nodded and pulled a key chain from her pocket before removing one of the keys from it. She slid it towards Hazel. 'There you go, I should have thrown it away really. I nearly did but…' She paused and sighed. 'Anyway, it's just as well I didn't now, isn't it?'

'Thanks for this. I'll make sure you get it back as soon as we're done. Just one more thing. Does the name Sam Kennedy mean anything to you?'

Lynne shook her head. 'No, is he the one who killed Sean?'

'No, no, that's fine, thanks anyway and thanks again for this.' Hazel lifted the key up.

'Keep it,' Lynne said. 'I never want to set foot in there again and anyway, the council will be taking it back soon. I'm sure there are others in need of it.'

'Isn't your name on the tenancy?'

Lynne shook her head and stared down at the table. Everything about that was wrong to Hazel. Lynne had fled that home with just the clothes on her back and he'd still had everything. That didn't seem fair at all.

'It's OK, I don't want to live there,' Lynne told her. 'Too many bad memories.'

Hazel did understand about memories. Ones that lingered, cropping up and slapping you across the face when you least expected them. Except hers were good ones that had been stolen, tainted by Rick's betrayal. She thanked Lynne again and headed, with Tom, over to the home she had shared with Sean.

–

'Jesus, what a tip,' Tom said as he tightened the latex gloves on his hands and stepped over a small pile of post just inside the front door. The rest of the hallway was littered with newspapers and shoes.

Hazel bent down and picked the envelopes up and, after flicking through the pile, laid them on the last available part of the hall table, the rest of it being stuffed with other envelopes, leaflets and magazines that were piled high, next to a selection of dead and dying plants. The dust on the surface she could see was thick and caught in her throat. A layer of dust covered the leaves of what she recognised as a spider plant. A rack of shoes by the door had a pair of slippers, half on, half off it, a pile of mismatched trainers underneath. No signs of any of Lynne's shoes, she noticed. Even the coat hooks held only men's clothes. A fleece and a light waterproof cagoule jacket. She knew Lynne hadn't taken anything with her. He must have chucked all of her stuff out. A navy hoodie hung on the end of the bannister. Hazel considered the floor above.

'I'm going up the stairs,' she called out to Tom. 'Shout if you find anything.'

'Sure,' he called from the kitchen.

Hazel had barely stepped away from the top stair when Tom's voice drifted up to her.

'Boss, I think you need to see this!'

Hazel turned and headed back down to join him in the kitchen. She scanned the photos he'd laid out on the kitchen table. Her eyes widened at the pornographic images.

'Is that who I think it is?' she asked.

'Yes, that's Molly Barker.'

'Do you think he paid her to pose nude for him?' Hazel suggested, allowing her eyes to drift between the snaps which looked like they'd been printed on photo paper from the printer she spotted on the dresser nearby.

'I can't see her doing it for nothing, can you?' Tom said.

Hazel's ringing phone interrupted them.

'Billy,' Hazel said as she answered, and heard with interest that he'd got a result from the facial recognition request. 'OK, that's unusual, I'll be back as soon I'm done here.'

'What's unusual?' Tom asked.

'There was a hit on the facial recognition, but the identity it matched is classified. I have to call a phone number for more details.' She hung up on Billy and started to head outside. 'You keep looking, I'll just be a minute.'

Hazel dialled the phone number Billy had given her, unsure exactly what to expect.

'Oh, is that right,' she replied when the girl on the other end of the line said who she was and that she'd been expecting Hazel's call. Apparently, the facial recognition request had triggered an alert. She'd be more than happy to talk to her after she'd finished with her next appointment.

Chapter Twenty-Four

'Hello Rachel, how are you doing?' Samiera Jordan smiled and held her hand out to offer Rachel a seat.

'I'm OK, and you?' Rachel replied and unzipped her raincoat before sitting opposite her probation officer, a woman barely half of Rachel's age.

'Not too bad, thanks. So, what's been happening with you since we last saw each other?' Samiera glanced down at a folder in front of her. 'You're still helping out at the community kitchen, are you?'

Rachel nodded, the thin smile developing slowly. 'Yes I am, three days a week just now but I might increase it if I can. Would that be OK, do you think?'

'I'll double check but yes, I should think so. Don't do anything until I get back to you, yes?'

'Of course, yes, I mean, no, I won't.'

She gave a short, embarrassed laugh, feeling sweat gather under her collar at the back of her neck. These meetings were still a struggle even though she knew Samiera had her welfare at heart. It wouldn't look good on her department if Rachel ended up back inside for breaching the rules they were supposed to be enforcing. Those journalists who'd stirred up such venom would have a field day, not to mention the social media explosion that would erupt. Thankfully, none of them knew where she was.

'You enjoy it then, I thought you might. I've had a few clients doing voluntary work and they've all, mostly, been successful.'

'Yes, it makes me feel useful after so many years of…' Rachel stammered, searching for the right words, 'Well, so many years of feeling like a burden, I suppose, and helping the girls is so rewarding.' She ended with a shrug.

'You were never a burden, Rachel,' Samiera told her. 'Have you given any thought to the extra counselling sessions I suggested? I can't force you to attend these, but I think it would be a good idea.'

Rachel agreed deep down, if she was honest, but she wanted to look forward to what time she had left. Not go back into the past where the pain was. She didn't need to revisit it to know it was there.

'I'll think about it,' she answered quietly.

Samiera's smile lit up her large brown eyes. 'Have you heard from Steven?'

Rachel was sad that she had to shake her head at that. 'No, not yet. I've written to him again.' She leaned down and pulled an envelope out of her bag, then slid it across the table to Samiera. 'Could you pass this one on for me? I know I'm not allowed his address yet, which I do understand, of course I do.'

Samiera reached over and placed the letter onto a pile on the desk with a nod. 'Of course I will, and I'll be contacting him again on your behalf. Is there anything you want me to say specifically?'

There were so many things Rachel wanted to say to Steven. She wouldn't know where to begin. 'Not really.'

'I'll be telling him about your progress and my thoughts about contact with him and his family but again, it's not something I can force upon him. I can only act as your advocate.'

'I know,' Rachel sighed. 'It's amazing the love you can feel for another human being especially when…' She hesitated, seeming to need strength to continue. 'Considering the way he came into this world.'

'I know,' Samiera agreed.

'Do you think he knows he's a product of rape?' Rachel kept her voice low deliberately.

'I don't know, but he's not asked us to stop contacting him,' Samiera said. 'That's a very positive sign in my opinion.'

Her words made Rachel smile, while a small tear gathered at the corner of her eye which she wiped away quickly, hoping Samiera hadn't spotted it. Of course, she had, and handed Rachel a tissue from the box on the bookcase behind her chair.

'Thank you,' Rachel sniffed and blew her nose.

'This is going to be hard sometimes. Life on the outside is foreign to you still. That's why I'm here to help you.'

Rachel nodded and wiped her eyes dry. 'I'm sorry, I don't know what came over me.'

'Talking about your son is a very emotional subject. I'd have been more surprised and quite frankly worried if you hadn't got upset when we mentioned contact with him.'

'You're right, I know.' Rachel inhaled a long slow breath. 'I'd give anything to see him, to hug him.'

'It'll take time. This is new to him too,' Samiera reminded her. 'He's adjusting to a world with his mum a free woman now which is perhaps something he'd never considered would ever happen until a few months ago.'

'I understand it must be hard for him, I do.'

'Just give Steven time,' Samiera repeated.

Rachel knew she was right but couldn't help thinking it was Steven's wife who was stopping their relationship from being healed. She didn't even really blame her for wanting to protect her husband, her sons? But then, could *she* really blame Rachel for wanting to get to know her grandchildren? But that didn't stop Rachel wanting to have a relationship with the boy she'd given up when he was just a toddler.

'Listen, there's something I have to ask you.' Samiera looked serious.

Rachel didn't like that expression on her face.

'What?' she asked tentatively.

'I've been alerted to a facial recognition match for you during the course of a police investigation.'

Samiera's words made Rachel's heart rate surge. The room started to feel small and hot, and it was a struggle to breathe. Rachel wanted to get up and run, as panic whirled in her chest.

'I don't have much detail at the moment, but I've arranged to talk to DCI Hazel Todd in a little while. I'll gather the information we need then.'

'But will you have to tell her who I am?' Rachel asked, feeling the tears gather behind her eyes, trying to force their way out uninvited. 'That I'm Rachel McMahon?'

Chapter Twenty-Five

'Right, you lot, listen up,' Hazel told her team and pointed to the two grisly photos from each of their crime scenes. 'Sam Kennedy and Sean Cooper. Both men stabbed and suffocated in their cars. Each body found in areas known locally as places people go to have sex. How are we on forensics on the carrier bags?'

'Still waiting,' Billy told her.

Hazel stared between the two men's photos that hung above each crime scene image, snaps that showed them both very much alive and smiling. She would not put those two faces together in a crowd at all.

'Have we found a definitive connection between Cooper and Kennedy?' Tom asked.

'Apart from the sex workers, nothing yet,' Andrea told him.

'Molly Barker in particular,' Tom pointed out.

'Exactly,' Hazel pointed a finger at him.

'Have we got enough to warrant bringing her in?' Billy suggested.

Hazel pursed her lips and nodded to Tom. 'What do you think? You've spent more time with her than any of us. Does she look good for this?'

'She's certainly volatile enough.' He turned to Andrea. 'What do you know about her?'

'Her and her mum came to Perth to be closer to her mum's friend, Rachel. Fell into drugs and prostitution. Has a bit of a temper, by all accounts.'

'Rachel.' Hazel frowned. 'I'm hearing the name Rachel a lot.'

'Yes, she works at the community kitchen,' Tom chirped. 'Craig Douglas mentioned her too.'

'What are we thinking about him?' Hazel asked.

'Nice enough, genuinely seems to care about the girls. Ex-military. Was diagnosed with PTSD. Works in the butcher's in the high street.'

Hazel held a hand up. 'Back up, he's a butcher?'

Tom nodded. 'Aye, I know, I've considered that too, but his prints weren't on the knife so it's not his.'

'The knife, Billy, where are we with that?'

'Still waiting, boss,' he shrugged.

Hazel tutted then sighed. 'OK, Andrea you go and talk to this Rachel at the kitchen. See what she can tell us about Molly and any of the other girls, as well as this Douglas bloke. Get her feelings about him,' Hazel said firmly.

'Sure thing.' Andrea snatched up her jacket and left.

'Tom, chase up the forensics on the squat – in fact, go back there but this time with Molly Barker in mind. And what about the man seen on CCTV raking the bins outside the café, our potential witness?' She was disappointed to see blank faces staring back.

'Sorry,' Billy said. 'Uniform patrols didn't find anyone matching his description last night.'

'Thanks Billy, but I want to keep on him. He could have seen something. What about the two phones, how are you doing with that? And Cooper's finances. Is there anything there we should know about?'

'I'm done with Sam's phone. There's nothing on there that tells us anything. I've only just got hold of Sean Cooper's. I'll let you know as soon as I'm done,' Billy replied. 'As for Sean's finances, there are no large withdrawals if that's what you're meaning.'

'OK good, keep on it.' She patted his shoulder and grabbed her bag. 'I have an appointment with a probation officer. Keep in touch, everyone.'

—

With two victims in such a short space of time, Hazel was grateful she had a team she trusted one hundred per cent. Every one of them, she knew, wouldn't leave a stone unturned. She counted herself very lucky.

'Come in.' The woman's voice came from inside the door.

Hazel got her ID ready and went inside.

Samiera Jordan held out her hand and shook Hazel's.

'Please have a seat,' she offered. 'What can I do for you, detective?'

'Thank you,' Hazel replied. 'You can start by explaining the cloak and dagger with my facial recognition hit for a start.'

'Yes, I appreciate that must have been confusing,' Samiera said with a smile.

'So?' Hazel pushed. 'What's going on?'

'You have to understand something first,' Samiera sighed. 'Confidentiality is incredibly important. There are some identities in the system that need special measures to protect them.'

Hazel frowned, feeling stone-walled, even if this young woman was being polite about it.

'Who is she?' Hazel asked bluntly.

'Before I can decide if I can release the information, I need you to tell me what your investigation is about?'

'Are you saying you're going to decide whether it's important enough?' Hazel was fuming at her attitude.

'To put it bluntly, yes.'

'I'm investigating the murder of two men,' Hazel informed her and produced the still image from the CCTV, holding it up before sliding it across the desk. 'This woman is a person of interest in the investigation. She's talking to a young woman we're very keen to talk to.'

Hazel watched her pick the photo up and examine it carefully, chewing the inside of her cheek, breathing deeply, in and out, several times. She eventually looked up at Hazel.

'Could I please ask you to wait outside while I make a call?'

Who the hell was this woman in the picture? MI5?

'Sure,' Hazel replied and stood up to leave. She glanced at her watch. 'But could you make it quick? Two men have been murdered and I'm keen to find who did that.' Her sarcastic smile was meant to show her disdain for the process.

While Hazel waited on one of the row of blue plastic chairs outside Samiera Jordan's office, she checked her phone for messages. Against her better judgment, she opened the one from Cara.

> I've taken your advice and reported Rick missing. I'll keep you posted and if you hear anything will you let me know.

It seemed Rick was up to his old tricks if he still wasn't home yet. She should feel sorry for Cara but part of her was pleased he'd disappeared. A second text was from her dad's care home.

> Dad's had a settled night. Bruises don't look so bad today Hazel. Don't worry.

That made her feel a little better. She knew in her heart that he was in the right place, but she supposed the guilt would always be there. A third text chirped just as Samiera called her back in. That one would have to wait.

'Come in, DCI Todd, sorry to have kept you hanging around.' Samiera smiled, seemingly lighter after talking to whoever it was she'd called. A superior, Hazel supposed.

Hazel closed the door after them but didn't bother to sit down this time.

'Well, who is she then?' she demanded.

'Her name is Rachel Fox, once known as McMahon,' Samiera began. 'She was released from prison in Belfast twelve months ago and has been living under the name Fox since then.'

Alarm bells started ringing in Hazel's head. What did Rachel have to do with all this?

'Does Rachel work in the community kitchen?'

Samiera nodded.

'What was Rachel in prison for?'

'Murder,' Samiera explained. 'She was released on licence and lives in a flat in Canal Street.'

Hazel took her notebook out and clicked her pen in readiness. 'I'm going to need Rachel's address.' She was disappointed to see Samiera's reluctance.

'I've known Rachel for over a year. She's not the troubled teenager she was all those years ago. She's a sixty-year-old woman who volunteers in a community kitchen.'

'She may be as pure as Mother Teresa these days but that doesn't alter the fact I still need to talk to her,' Hazel said plainly. 'So, please, can you give me Rachel's address?'

Samiera wrote the details down on a piece of paper and ripped the page out of the notepad.

'Here you go,' she said quietly and sat back in her tall, leather chair. 'But for what it's worth, I know Rachel couldn't have done anything. She's just not like that.'

Hazel had ended the meeting by telling Samiera that she'd be the judge of that and was now sitting in her car scrolling through every website she could find, searching Rachel McMahon's name. To say her crimes were similar to the scenes her team had witnessed was an understatement. It seemed Rachel could be very helpful indeed.

Hazel's phone rang just as she prepared to start the engine.

'Tom, what have you got for me?' she said and listened to him fill her in on the development.

A second blood-stained knife. Two victims. Two knives. A recently released serial killer in their midst. She put the gear stick into first and prepared to drive off when another text chirped. This time it was from an unknown number. Hazel pulled in and opened the message.

> You're getting warm, DCI Todd, but you're not quite there yet.

Hazel quickly dialled Billy's number.

'Hey, I'm forwarding you a text. I need you to do everything you can to find out where it came from.'

Hazel didn't allow him time to answer. Instead, she threw her phone onto the passenger seat and indicated into the flow of traffic towards the address she'd been given for Rachel Fox – or whatever she called herself these days.

Chapter Twenty-Six

Calls had started coming into the station from journalists asking them to confirm the rumours circulating about the two dead men. Hazel was relieved to learn they'd all been passed to Superintendent Daly. He would tell them that a press conference would be scheduled. For later today she imagined, tomorrow at the latest. The bad news might be that he'd persuade her to do it. Hazel would cross that bridge if she came to it.

Hazel knocked on the door of the address in Canal Street and listened for movement inside. She was about to leave when she heard footsteps coming to the door.

'Hello,' Hazel said to the young woman who answered the door. 'I'm looking for Rachel, is she in?'

The girl shook her head. 'No, she's at the kitchen but I can tell her you're looking for her.'

Hazel smiled. 'No, it's OK, I'll catch up with her later.'

'OK.' The girl started to close the door until Hazel spoke again. 'I'm sorry, what's your name?'

The girl's eyes narrowed. 'Kelly.'

Hazel recognised that name as one of the girls from the squat that Andrea had told her about. She lifted her ID out of her pocket and showed it to her.

'Do you think you could spare me a few minutes? I'd like to ask you a few questions.'

After hesitating briefly, Kelly opened the door wide enough to allow Hazel inside the immaculately kept flat. It was small but clean and more than big enough for a single woman.

'Rachel let me have a key so I could come and get my washing,' Kelly explained.

'I see,' Hazel said and followed her into the living room.

The room was sparsely decorated with just a few scattered ornaments and a single photo of a smiling toddler on a cherry oak unit next to a pile of books, mainly romantic comedy and science fiction. The books seemed to be from charity shops rather than new.

'Rachel reads a lot,' Kelly said, obviously seeing Hazel's interest in the pile.

'So I see,' Hazel said. 'How well do you know Rachel?'

'Well enough,' Kelly replied. 'She's good to me. She let me come here last night and have a shower and do some washing.'

'She sounds very kind.'

'She is,' Kelly confirmed. 'Why do you want to talk to her?'

'I'm investigating the murder of two men, and I was hoping that she could help clear a few things up for me.'

Kelly looked shocked. 'How on earth can she help you with—' Then she clasped a hand to her mouth. 'Is this about Sam Kennedy's death?'

'Did you know Sam?'

Kelly shook her head. 'No but that other detective asked me about it, showed me his picture. You've got the squat crawling with police and forensics.'

'Where have you been staying?' Hazel frowned, fearing the girl couldn't even be twenty yet.

'Around,' Kelly replied and avoided her eyes.

Hazel decided not to pry and grabbed a photo of Sean Cooper out of her bag. 'Do you recognise this man?'

Kelly's reaction gave away the fact she knew him right away. 'Yes,' she muttered.

'Tell me what you know about him,' Hazel urged then noticed how uncomfortable she seemed. She softened her approach. 'Anything you tell me might be really important.'

Kelly twirled her ponytail in her fingers and bit her nails. 'I only met him once,' she confirmed. 'But that was enough.'

Hazel tried to hold her gaze. 'What happened?'

The discomfort seemingly increased the more Kelly thought about it. 'He was…' she stuttered. 'Just… he's not a nice man.'

'In what way?' Hazel pressed, weaving a fine line between not scaring the girl into silence and getting what she needed. A bloody hard thing to manage.

'I'd rather not talk about it and to be honest, I really need to be going.' Kelly snatched her rucksack up from the floor at her feet and slung it over her shoulder.

'His name is Sean Cooper,' Hazel persisted then added. 'He was murdered just like Sam.'

Kelly stopped. 'Oh.'

'What do you know about Sean Cooper?'

'Nothing, listen, I really do have to go.' She became agitated and fiddled with the strap of her rucksack.

Hazel would have to change tack. 'It was nice of Rachel to let you do your washing.'

'What?' Kelly stopped fussing with her bag. 'Erm, yes, it was.' Her thin smile faded quickly.

Hazel relented, knowing this young girl would rather be anywhere but there. She pulled a card from her pocket and pressed it into Kelly's hand.

'Listen, if you think of anything that might help my investigation, please call.'

Kelly curled her fingers round the card then slipped it into her jacket pocket. 'I will,' she whispered, flicking her gaze sideways as she spoke.

'Call me anytime.' Hazel gently laid a hand on Kelly's arm. 'It doesn't have to be about that. You can call if you're ever needing anything, OK?'

Kelly's thin smile returned before she opened Rachel's front door. 'I better get her keys back to her.'

Hazel stepped back into the street and waited while Kelly locked up. 'Can I drop you anywhere?'

'No thanks.' Kelly yanked up her hood and headed off through the vennel towards the centre of town at speed. Hazel had been horrified to see how scared Kelly had seemed when she'd mentioned Sean Cooper. It appeared it wasn't just Lynne who'd been on the receiving end of his unpleasantness.

'Billy, what's up?' Hazel answered the call on seeing his number ping on the caller ID. She punched the air when she heard what he had to say. This day was getting better after all. 'I'm on my way.'

Chapter Twenty-Seven

'Where did they find him?' Hazel peered through the window into the soft interview suite at the dishevelled man she recognised from the CCTV on the night of Sam Kennedy's murder. His hair was long and thin, in need of a good wash. The jacket he was wearing was not nearly thick enough for the colder evenings that had arrived. His trainers had a gaping hole in one of the toes.

'Poor bugger,' Billy said. 'He was rambling something incoherent in the middle of Poundland in the centre, so the police were called. The uniform that attended recognised him as the homeless man we were looking for and called me.'

'Has he had something to eat?'

Billy nodded. 'Aye, I went to the canteen and brought him a plate of stovies and a custard and sponge. Poor bloke devoured it like he'd not seen a good meal in a long time.'

'So he doesn't use the community kitchen then?' Hazel questioned.

'Doesn't seem so but I can check.'

'Thanks, Billy.' Hazel was pleased to have this man sitting there waiting for her but given his mental state, she feared he might not be as useful to her investigation as she had first thought. 'Has the doctor seen him yet?'

'Not yet, do you want him assessed before you talk to him?' Billy asked.

Hazel pursed her lips and weighed up her options. The man was mumbling to himself; it would be a waste of time to try and talk to him before a doctor had checked him over. She narrowed her eyes.

'Yes get the on-call doc to speak to him. Maybe get him referred to social work as well.'

'Sure,' Billy replied just as his phone rang. 'Hello,' he said into his handset, the caller's words causing his eyes to stretch wide. 'Thanks so much.'

'Good news?'

'Only if you consider a match for the fingerprints we found on the second knife—'

'Who?'

'Craig Douglas.'

'You keep an eye on him, will you?' She nodded to the dishevelled homeless man in the interview room. 'I'll get Tom to meet me at Craig's address.'

Sometimes Hazel felt guilty for leaving Billy behind, but he didn't seem to mind, and he was the best at coordinating forensics and everything digital. She snatched her keys from her bag and headed to her car, tightening her jacket closer to her skin in a bid to keep out the biting cold.

'Tom, where did they find it?' Hazel asked as she locked her car a little way from the block of flats.

'This one wasn't as easy to find. It wasn't just left lying on the floor. A piece of the floor had been disturbed and the knife was concealed underneath.'

'Luckily for us, it wasn't concealed well enough,' Hazel smiled. 'Where are you parked?'

'I left my car on the other side of the Inch like you said. I didn't want him seeing it and doing a runner, although with that stookie on I doubt he'd be able to move very fast.'

Hazel had considered that but wasn't taking any chances. Craig Douglas's fingerprints were on a bloody, concealed knife. Regardless of whose blood it was, it was still suspicious. She wished forensics would hurry up and confirm a blood match.

'In the window, look, he's in the flat at least,' Hazel said and pulled open the outside door to the four-apartment block, surprised to see how well kept the close was. It even smelled clean, like disinfectant.

When they reached Douglas's flat, Tom knocked on the door and rapped the letterbox causing a yapping bark to ring out. Craig Douglas's voice could be heard speaking to the dog before heavy, slow footsteps came closer to the door. Hazel got her ID ready to show him as the door swung open.

'Hello again detective,' he said to Tom then stared at Hazel.

'Hello Craig, I'm DCI Hazel Todd, can we come in?' she said plainly.

'Aye, OK.' Craig stepped aside. 'Go through, excuse the mess.'

Hazel could see right away that he'd recently had a visitor because of the two mugs sitting at opposite ends of the coffee table. She could smell grilled bacon and thought he could do with opening a window. The view from his living room window immediately caught her attention. He had a perfect view towards the squat and in the other direction, in between a gap in the hedge, he had a spectacular view of the River Tay and right across to Moncrieffe Island. On a good day people could even walk across to the island.

'What's this about?' Craig added: 'I've told you everything I know already.'

'I'm going to have to ask you to come with us,' Hazel began.

'Wait a minute,' Craig lifted up his hands. 'Woah there, why do you want me to do that?'

The little black poodle, as if sensing his increased stress, began barking loudly.

'Fingerprints found on a bloody knife have been matched to a sample you voluntarily provided my colleague with.'

Alarm fizzed over Craig's face. 'What?' he snapped. 'I thought you said my prints weren't on that knife I found.' He appealed to Tom. 'What's going on, I don't understand.'

'A second knife has been found, Mr Douglas,' Tom informed him.

'What?'

'We're going to need you to come with us, Craig,' Tom said firmly and stepped forward to take Craig's arm.

'It would be better for you if you came with us of your own accord, otherwise I can arrest you,' Hazel informed him.

Until she had a definitive match on the blood, she wanted to avoid that. Right now, the blood could just as easily be animal. Unlikely, but possible.

'I-I…' Craig gasped. 'I need to organise someone for Spot.'.

Tom shot a concerned glance at Hazel.

'OK,' she said firmly. 'What do you need to do to sort that?'

Craig started to walk away. 'My phone is in the kitchen.'

'Go with him,' Hazel instructed Tom.

'What? Do you really think I'm going to do a runner with this?' He slapped his leg in frustration. 'I've got pills I need to take as well after tea time. Can I bring them?'

'Tom, you take them, will you?' Hazel said before the two men left the room.

She would arrange a full forensic search of the property when she got back to the station. It struck her as a very masculine environment. There wasn't a single woman's item lying around. Not even a photo frame with a picture of what could be his mother or daughter. A pile of magazines were tucked in each side of a magazine rack that had a small glass table on top. Something she'd not seen for many years. It was like the kind they'd had when she was growing up. Somewhere to stuff everything but the kitchen sink and not just newspapers in her house. Knitting needles. Post. Medicine boxes. Not long before her mum's death, it often concealed half bottles of vodka.

'This is ridiculous,' Craig exclaimed as he got in the back of Hazel's car.

'Mind your head,' Tom said gently and closed the door.

The drive to the station from Craig's address only took five minutes and he'd been placed in an interview room and cautioned before Hazel grabbed a chance to go to the bathroom. His first response to their discovery seemed to be genuine shock. Either he was a great actor, or he was telling the truth. He'd asked for a duty solicitor to be present, though. Was that significant? Hazel wouldn't be able to tell until she spoke to him again. Perhaps he wanted to err on the side of caution.

Before going into the interview room, she called Andrea to get an update on her visit to the community kitchen. Andrea said she'd not found out anything useful.

Rachel wasn't there and neither was Molly Barker. As they were talking, she mentioned that Kelly Tate had just walked in, and Hazel asked her to hang round a bit longer. See if she could cut through the girl's defences better than Hazel could.

–

Andrea hung up then smiled at Kelly who was walking towards her with two mugs in her hand.

'I thought you looked like you could use that.' Kelly laid a mug in front of her.

When Hazel told Andrea about her chat with Kelly, she didn't recognise the girl her boss had described. Kelly had seemed relaxed when Andrea had spoken to her, not edgy in the slightest. She would mention Sean Cooper's name in a minute. See what response she got.

'That's really nice of you,' Andrea said and sipped.

'I didn't know if you took sugar or not but...' she reached behind her and grabbed a sugar bowl from the next table, 'you can add your own.'

'It's fine – perfect, in fact,' Andrea grinned. 'I'm gasping.'

'You're welcome,' Kelly replied and sank half of hers without taking her eyes off Andrea.

'So I see that Rachel isn't here,' Andrea pointed out.

'Yes, that's strange, I was sure she said she was working here today.' Kelly scanned the room behind her.

'Does she usually do the same shifts every week?'

Kelly nodded. 'Yes, so it's weird she's not here.'

'Have you got any idea what she gets up to when she's not here?' Andrea said, hoping to nudge her gently into giving her whatever information she had, wondering whether Kelly knew who Rachel was and what she'd done all those years ago – the echo of which couldn't be discounted with what was happening today.

'Not really, except sometimes she tries to talk to the women in the shelter and checks on the girls in the squat.'

A text that hit Kelly's phone seemed to rattle her a little.

'Is everything alright?' Andrea pressed carefully, trying to strike a balance between concern and curiosity.

'Yes,' Kelly said firmly and stuffed her phone into the rucksack she'd dropped at her feet under the table.

Andrea sensed that to be the end of that conversation.

'So, you mentioned the shelter,' Andrea changed the subject. 'Do you stay there too?'

'Sometimes but not always.'

Andrea wanted to ask why but resisted. She was much more interested in the squat and Molly Barker.

'Tell me about the squat,' Andrea said without looking at her. Instead, she sipped from the mug, hoping that a casual approach would remove some of the pressure because Kelly's mood was changing, and she feared she might flee any minute.

'What about it?'

Andrea shrugged. 'Tell me about it.'

'You know as much as I do. It's a place to escape to.'

'Escape what?' Andrea knew she was pushing her luck.

'Life,' Kelly shrugged. 'The streets.'

'I get it,' Andrea said.

'Do you?' Kelly scoffed.

Andrea realised she'd just tried too hard and had probably come off as a cop trying to be street. Of course she couldn't *get it*.

'You're right, I probably don't,' she answered honestly and sank the rest of the mug of tea.

'There's more in the big pot in the kitchen, I'll go and get you a refill.'

Before Andrea could protest, Kelly had snatched both mugs and walked away toward the kitchen door. The fact she'd taken her rucksack meant one of two things. Maybe Kelly didn't trust her not to snoop in her belongings or worse still, steal something, but Andrea knew deep down the more obvious reason was that Kelly was planning to slip out of the kitchen door to avoid more questions. Andrea hoped not as she'd not yet asked her about Sean Cooper.

Raised voices from outside gave her the answer when she saw Kelly being challenged by a heavily tattooed man. It took Andrea a moment to remember where she'd seen him until he grabbed hold of Kelly's arm and pushed her against the wall. Andrea grabbed her bag and raced outside to help but by the time she'd got there Kelly was running and Mick Morrison was driving off in his black Escort. Why was Sam Kennedy's ex-girlfriend's brother harassing Kelly Tate? She called Hazel on a hunch and wanted to know if it was OK to pay him a visit.

Chapter Twenty-Eight

Rachel was shocked to discover that the police had wanted to talk to Craig Douglas, a man she knew cared about some of the girls as much as she did – although admittedly at first she was suspicious of his motives. She'd been sceptical to say the least when he'd said his only interest was in their welfare. Digging deeper had led to the discovery that he'd seen girls trafficked in the Balkans when he'd served there as a soldier and had struggled to get the images out of his head. He hadn't said what the police wanted to talk to him about, but she wondered if it was something to do with the murder she'd heard about. She couldn't imagine Craig having anything to do with it and told him she was sure he'd be home in no time but, of course, she'd check on Spot. He'd leave his spare key where he usually left it, under his wheelie bin.

Rachel liked Craig Douglas. He was a lot like her and not much younger. His past had left him scarred and haunted, but he didn't want to give up on humanity. Nobody could blame him if he did. Not after what he'd been through. Their friendship had grown through their joint concern for the girls.

She'd swapped shifts at the kitchen with one of the other women who'd asked Rachel to do her shift tomorrow as she had a hospital appointment, in return for which she'd taken Rachel's shift today. That wasn't a problem. It left her free to meet Dawn who was still desperately trying to find Molly. Rachel was worried too. Molly's mood was becoming more volatile, and she feared what might happen if she didn't get into a detox programme soon. Only a long period of rehab could help her make any progress in kicking the drugs for good.

'I've ordered a pot of tea for two already.' Dawn kissed Rachel's cheek when she arrived.

'That's grand, thank you.' Rachel offered her oldest friend a gentle smile. She looked dreadful and obviously hadn't slept last night. 'No word from Molly, then?'

Dawn shook her head and checked her phone simultaneously. 'You?'

'No. Do you think it's time to report her missing?'

'Do you think I should?' Dawn asked.

'I think so,' Rachel told her bluntly. 'The squat is off limits. I've asked around and nobody has seen her.'

'Will you come with me? I don't think I could face it alone.'

Sitting in a police station was the last place Rachel wanted to be, but she reached across the table to squeeze Dawn's hand in hers. 'Of course I will.' She'd do it. For Dawn and for Molly.

'They'll want a picture, won't they?' Dawn scrolled through her phone, frowning and nibbling her lip nervously.

'Give it here,' Rachel held out her hand.

Dawn handed it over, anxiously biting her thumbnail as Rachel scanned the photos of Molly. She was struck by how much the teenager had changed in such a short period of time. It took all her strength to not give in to the tears that pressed up behind her eyes.

'Here, this is a nice one.' Rachel smiled and handed the phone back over.

'Yes,' Dawn agreed and wiped away a tear that had escaped and was dripping down the side of her face. 'She looks beautiful in that one.'

-

'Can I help you?' the desk sergeant asked.

'I need to report a missing person,' Dawn said, while Rachel held tight to her hand.

'If you take a seat over there, I'll get someone to come and talk to you.'

'OK, yes thanks.'

The two women sat themselves on the row of black plastic chairs that lined the far wall, above which there was a long, rectangular noticeboard filled with leaflets about knife crime and domestic violence. More than twenty minutes had passed when Rachel left Dawn sitting and returned to ask why it was taking so long. As she opened her mouth to speak, Dawn's voice hit her ears.

'Rachel,' Dawn shouted and leapt up, holding her phone up. 'It's from Molly! I've got a text, look.'

'Thanks officer, but we'll be fine now,' Rachel told him and re-joined Dawn. 'What does it say?'

Dawn handed Rachel the phone and sobbed into her hands.

I'm sorry Mum but I think I've done something terrible. I love you x

'Come on let's go,' Rachel urged and swept Dawn outside before she had a chance to say anything else. She didn't want that officer overhearing them.

'What does she mean?' Dawn cried. 'What has she done?'

'Call her.'

On seeing Dawn's hands tremble, Rachel took the phone from her and hit Molly's number. She listened to her call ring out until it went to voicemail.

'Molly sweetheart, it's Rachel, call me please,' she said. 'It's ok, you're not in any trouble. Just… call us… we're worried about you.'

Chapter Twenty-Nine

Hazel told Andrea to be careful when she spoke to Mick Morrison because it sounded like he was a nasty piece of work and it had angered her to hear how he'd grabbed Kelly. She texted his address to Andrea and said she should keep in touch. She added that if she'd not heard from her in an hour, Hazel would send a couple of uniforms. Overkill perhaps, but she wasn't taking any chances with her young DC, whose initiative had greatly impressed her.

'Mr Douglas, can you explain how your fingerprints came to be on this knife?' Tom asked, glancing between Craig and the smartly dressed duty solicitor. Tom recognised him from a night out a couple of years ago and hoped he hadn't recognised him. He held up an evidence bag so Craig could get a better view of it.

Craig Douglas licked his lips, which felt dry. The stress, he supposed.

'Could I please…' His words tailed off until he coughed to compose himself. 'Could I please have some water?'

Hazel nodded to the uniformed officer who was standing by the interview room door.

'Thank you,' Craig said.

'Do you recognise this knife?' Hazel asked as the water was laid down in front of him.

Craig guzzled the contents in seconds and slid the cup away from him.

'It looks like one of my boning knives,' he said. 'I did tell you I'm a butcher.'

Hazel's heart rate increased a little. 'Can you explain how it came to be under the floorboards of the squat on Shore Road? A house I know you've visited because my colleague has spoken to you there. A place you've already admitted to frequenting?'

'I don't *frequent* it,' Craig snapped and picked up the paper cup again, hoping to find more water. 'I go there, yes, but not by choice.'

'What is your relationship with the girls who frequent it?' Hazel asked.

'I don't have a relationship, not in the way you're implying.' Craig's eyes flicked sideways as he sat back in the chair.

'Where were you two nights ago, Mr Douglas? Between nine p.m. and eleven p.m.'

'Why are you asking me that?' Craig sounded panicked.

'Just answer the question please,' Hazel added.

'I was, erm…' Craig licked his dry lips. 'Erm, I was in my flat.'

'Was anyone with you?' Hazel pressed him.

Craig frowned. 'No, I live alone, you already know that.' Then his eyes widened. 'I had a call at home. On the landline.'

'What time was that?'

'It was erm, ten o'clock, I remember because the news was on.' He looked relieved.

'Who called you?'

'It was Rachel,' he told her.

Hazel shot a knowing glance at Tom.

'Do you mean Rachel Fox?' Hazel asked.

'Yes, that's right. She was asking me to keep an eye out for her friend's daughter, Molly.'

That fitted with their timeline. The CCTV showed the three women together shortly before that. Arguing. Rachel could have called him right after to ask him to look out for Molly. She'd get Billy to check his phone records to be sure, but that alibi was sounding solid. Hazel didn't have an exact time of death for Sean Cooper, but Jack had said he'd been dead for at least forty-eight hours.

'Did you see Molly at all that night?'

'No I didn't,' he shook his head. 'What time is it? I have medication to take.'

Hazel's watch read five o'clock. She had to ensure Craig got access to what he needed so decided it might be time to take a break.

'Interview terminated...'

She'd noticed that Craig's hands had begun to tremble which piqued her curiosity. What motive did he have to kill those men? His experience in the Balkans during the wars in the nineties, was that it? Or was there something else? Something more personal. She didn't think he would be physically able to overpower either of them with his ankle like that – especially not Sam Kennedy, a lad more than half his age and built like an athlete.

Until Hazel had confirmation of whose blood it was on the knives, she did what she felt she had to. The fact that he'd given Rachel Fox as his alibi for both murders did trouble her. Only once Billy had checked that out for her could she be sure but if he was telling the truth then Craig Douglas was miles away from the Sean Cooper murder scene. Sam Kennedy's car may have been closer but with the stookie on Craig's ankle, Hazel couldn't see it. He'd have to be a magician to limp there, brutally stab and suffocate the lad then hobble back in time to talk to Rachel on the phone. But his knife, his fingerprints. The only obvious answer was that the killer had been in his flat and had taken the knife.

'Tom, could you escort Craig to the front desk?'

Craig stood slowly, adjusting his posture carefully because of the heavy boot over his ankle.

'What happens now?' Craig asked.

'You're being released pending further enquiries,' Hazel told him. 'So don't go anywhere without telling us.'

Craig didn't say anything to that. Instead, he followed Tom out along the corridor coming to a stop at the front desk where the homeless man they'd picked up was being processed. The doctor had assessed him and advised that he should be transferred up to Murray Royal hospital for further psychiatric evaluation. The dishevelled man turned and looked right at Craig and for a moment Tom watched them stare at each other in silence until Craig eventually broke away.

'Alright, mate,' he said gently before flicking his gaze sideways.

'Alright,' the man replied then followed the duty social worker out the station door.

'Remember what DCI Todd said,' Tom told him. 'Don't go anywhere.'

'Whatever,' Craig replied and turned to walk in the direction of his flat, pulling his mobile phone from his jeans pocket. He scrolled for the number he needed. 'It's me, we need to talk.' He listened to the person on the other end protest their innocence. 'Yes, yes, just do it!' He growled before hanging up.

It must have been less than five minutes later that the text chirped back.

> I'd be very careful if I were you. I'm sure you wouldn't want everyone knowing your secret.

Chapter Thirty

'Is Mick in?' Andrea held her ID up close so Angela Morrison could see it better.

As Andrea tucked her card away the sound of the back door banging shut echoed along the hallway.

'Er, he's…' Angela stammered. 'Mick's not…'

'Mick Morrison, stop!' Andrea shouted as the panicked man ran behind her, appearing quickly from the back of the house. 'Don't make this any harder for yourself than it already is.' Morrison stopped instantly.

He turned and walked back to where Andrea was standing on his doorstep.

'I think we need to talk, don't you?' Andrea questioned him.

'I'm no' saying anything without a solicitor,' Mick said firmly which confused Andrea until she walked inside and saw the bags of brown powder lined up on the kitchen table next to piles of twenty-pound notes, all neatly tied together by elastic bands.

Andrea called it in while she kept a close eye on Morrison. As she waited, she noticed a photo amongst the clutter on the old pine Welsh dresser in the kitchen. It was a picture of a smiling Natalie Morrison standing between Mick and his little sister, Kirsty, Sam Kennedy's ex.

This piece of shit was involved in supplying the very drug that had changed Natalie from the smiling, happy girl in that photo into a heroin addict desperate enough to prostitute herself in order to feed her habit. But how was Natalie connected? Another sister? She wondered if Sam had found out who was supplying the girls' drugs. Had he known Natalie was related to Mick? Had Sam arranged to meet Morrison, to have it out with him?

'This is Natalie Morrison,' Andrea pointed out.

'And?' Mick spat.

'Who is she to you?'

'That's my wee cousin, not that it's any of your fucking business.'

He was clearly rattled that his drugs empire had been dismantled. Andrea knew she should bite her tongue.

'It didn't bother you that your wee cousin had resorted to selling her body to feed her habit. A habit that you encouraged.'

'You're wasting your time, I've got nothing to say to you,' he sneered 'You came in here without a warrant. Your boss isn't going to be happy with you. Tut, tut.'

Andrea wished she could slap that smug grin right off his face. A patrol car pulled up outside and Andrea was glad to hand him over to the drug squad, although she imagined Hazel would be keen to talk to him too.

–

Molly Barker saw the police activity from across the street.

'Oh God, oh God, no, no, no,' she exclaimed and paced back and forth. 'No, no, no.' She clutched her stomach because the pains were getting worse.

'Are you alright?' An elderly woman walking a spaniel tugged up her hood against the splashes of rain that had started to come down, with wind whistling around them, clearly alarmed by the state of her.

'Fuck off,' Molly screamed and ran in the opposite direction.

—

Andrea heard a commotion across the street and turned to see an old woman walking her dog.

Chapter Thirty-One

'Well done, Andrea,' Hazel praised her DC. Credit where credit was due. 'That was a great find. He won't be supplying anything to anyone anymore.'

The drugs sitting openly on an ordinary kitchen table in an unremarkable council house had a street value of more than a hundred thousand pounds. The pile of twenty-pound notes added up to almost twenty thousand. Quite a haul indeed. Hazel couldn't have been prouder.

Morrison's connection to the girls was clearer now, as was the reason he'd been hassling Kelly Tate. She'd considered Andrea's suggestion that Sam had discovered Mick was supplying the girls and had arranged to meet him but that didn't account for Sean Cooper's murder. However, she'd not rule it out just yet. She would concentrate on tracking down Molly Barker and Rachel Fox for now.

First stop was Dawn Barker's home after finding details of Molly's mum's address from an arrest report from a few months ago when Molly had been caught shoplifting. She decided she'd take Andrea with her.

—

'Dawn Barker, my name is DCI Hazel Todd, I wonder if I could—' She held up her ID but was immediately interrupted.

'Have you found her?' Dawn asked urgently and grabbed Hazel by the arm, pulling her inside.

Hazel glanced back at a wide-eyed Andrea as she was propelled forward.

'Have we found who?' Hazel asked but had a pretty good idea exactly who Dawn was talking about.

'Molly,' Dawn snapped. 'My daughter Molly, she's not been home and...' Dawn walked away and grabbed her phone from the coffee table. 'I hadn't heard from her for two days and then I got this.' She handed the phone to Hazel who read the text.

> I'm sorry Mum but I think I've done something terrible. I love you x

Hazel held it up so Andrea could read it too.

'So? Have you found her?' Dawn pleaded. 'I tried to call her back after she sent that, but I couldn't get hold of her. I'm going out of my mind.'

'OK why don't we have a seat, Dawn?' Hazel indicated to the sofa. 'Let me take a few details from you.'

Dawn's blank expression made Hazel wonder if she'd heard her. 'Dawn,' she said softly which seemed to snap her back into focus.

'Erm, yes.' Dawn flopped down onto the edge of the black leather sofa and wiped the tea towel she'd been clutching over her wet face.

It was obvious she'd been crying; her eyes were red, and the skin beneath looked puffy and sore. School photos of a smiling Molly hung on almost every wall of the small living room. It was her hair that stuck out to Hazel. Molly had a vibrant, lush, thick head of curly red hair. Something some women paid a lot of money to achieve, and it seemed this pretty girl had it naturally. Her blue eyes twinkled with her smile.

'When did you last see your daughter?'

Dawn seemed to be thinking. 'Erm, two nights ago. I tried to pick her up and we argued so I had no choice but to leave her.'

The CCTV. The driver of the Escort was Dawn Barker.

'How well do you know Rachel Fox?' Hazel asked.

This question seemed to raise hackles. 'What's that got to do with this?' she chirped bitterly.

She was clearly trying to protect her friend's secret. Hazel would have to reassure her.

'We know,' she said bluntly.

Dawn frowned, seemingly trying to figure out what she meant. 'What?'

'I know who Rachel is,' Hazel explained, and it was like a weight had been removed from Dawn's shoulders.

'I suppose, being a detective, you need to know that kind of thing, but you can't tell anyone.'

The worry etched on her face that Hazel might be tempted to share Rachel's secret was admirable. She must care very much for her friend and Hazel wondered if it was more than that.

'I understand,' Hazel agreed. 'I only know because what she was convicted of is similar to the case I'm investigating.'

Dawn gasped and almost fell off the sofa. 'No,' she exclaimed and broke down, tears pouring down her already wet cheeks. 'No, please, it can't be,' she wailed. 'No…'

'Go and put the kettle on,' Hazel whispered to Andrea, realising from the surprise on her face that she wasn't used to the way she did things yet. Sometimes a bit of softly does it over a cup of tea works wonders. Hazel nodded firmly in the direction of the living room door.

'Oh, OK,' Andrea replied and did as she was told.

Hazel moved closer to where Dawn was sobbing her heart out into the tea towel. It was obvious that Dawn suspected Molly had done something, possibly even something unthinkable. Hazel would have to tread lightly with this obviously vulnerable woman.

Hazel patted the back of Dawn's hand and gave her a moment to gather her thoughts and get over the shock as they sat quietly.

'I'm sorry,' Dawn said, wiping her face dry. 'It was just…'

'I know,' Hazel said quietly.

'You asked about Rachel, didn't you?' She composed herself. 'I heard Rachel's story twenty years ago, back home in Belfast, and I wrote to her because…' She hesitated, blowing out a long, slow breath. 'We had similar childhoods,' she said quickly, as if it was the verbal equivalent of ripping off a plaster. 'So Rachel understood what I'd been through. Why I had trouble trusting people.' Her thin smile came and went quickly. 'We helped each other I suppose.'

'I understand,' Hazel said gently.

'We wrote to each other for about six months and then I started to go and visit her,' Dawn explained. 'Once every couple of months at first, then every month until it became every week.' She smiled. 'Molly even ended up calling her Auntie Rachel.'

Hazel knew that already.

'I wasn't in a good marriage,' Dawn said. 'Molly's dad was abusive, from almost the very beginning but it got worse when Molly came along. Rachel got me through it all so when she was relocated to Perth after her release it went without saying that Molly and me would follow her.' Dawn's eyes glistened with tears again. 'Only the move wasn't as good for Molly as it was for me.'

Both women turned to see Andrea bringing in two mugs.

'Thank you,' Dawn said.

'Thanks, Andrea.' Hazel smiled then turned her attention to Dawn, keen to keep her talking.

'Molly was bullied from the minute she started at St John's Academy.' Dawn shook her head and allowed the tears to trickle before pressing her fingers to wipe them clear. 'I could have done more, I *should* have done more…' she added.

'What did the school do about it?' Hazel asked, wishing she could pour the cup of strong coffee that Andrea had handed her into the plant on the window ledge behind her. It was that bad; so strong she could have laid tarmac with it.

Dawn scoffed. 'What do you think? They suggested that Molly was finding it hard to adjust to such a big move, at such a difficult age. When what they were actually doing was pointing the finger at me.' Her head drooped down. 'Maybe they were right.'

'There's nothing anyone can do about the past,' Hazel told her. 'We can only look forward.'

'What kind of life does she have to look forward to now?'

Hazel couldn't answer that because if Molly had done what they all suspected she had, Dawn would not want to hear the answer to that.

'I think the most important thing right now is that we find your daughter,' Hazel explained. 'Would it be OK if my colleague and I take a look in Molly's bedroom?'

'Yes, of course, go ahead,' Dawn replied. 'It's the first door on the right at the top of the stairs. It's in a bit of state, though, I warn you now.'

'Don't worry about that,' Hazel said and followed Andrea upstairs.

–

'She wasn't kidding about the mess,' Andrea muttered.

Hazel couldn't disagree. The smell hit the two detectives like a punch in the face as soon as they opened the door. The stench of stale sweat and food clung to every surface. The bed lay unmade, brown stains marked the greying sheet. The bedside cabinet was covered in plates piled high with old food with mould in various stages of growth. Hazel wondered why Dawn hadn't come in and cleared the place. A half-eaten pizza lay in an open pizza box under the bed. Hazel tightened her latex gloves and opened the top drawer in the white bedside cabinet. She had to turn away at the sight of maggots crawling over a mouldy sandwich.

'Jesus,' she exclaimed and coughed to prevent the nausea clawing any further.

'What the hell is going on with this girl?' Andrea asked. 'When I was eighteen I couldn't have been any cleaner. My room always smelled like perfume and make-up.' She cast her eyes around the room. 'Do you see either of these things here?'

Hazel had to agree. There was nothing feminine about this room. She didn't want to compare it to a teenage boy's room because that wasn't a fair comparison at all. Images of Sam Kennedy's immaculate space sprung to mind. She slid open the door of the fitted wardrobe to find – much like in Sam's dorm room – barely any of the clothes on the hangers, most strewn on top of the accumulated junk that had been stuffed inside. Suitcases, an old TV, several carrier bags filled with clothes and piles and piles of shoes. A shoebox on the shelf above the hanger caught Hazel's attention. She pulled it down, coughing against the dust that shifted when it was moved.

'What have you got?' Andrea asked.

'I'm not sure yet,' Hazel replied as she laid the box in a space she'd cleared on the dresser and flipped the lid off to reveal a collection of letters. 'Mm, interesting,' she muttered and lifted the top one out and opened it.

> *Dear Molly,*
>
> *It was so good to get a letter from you and I'm glad to hear you passed your science exam. It's lovely that you know what you'd like to do when you leave school. Vets do such an important job and from what I've heard they earn a lot of money too.*

Reading the rest of the letter made Hazel think of all the dreams Molly must have had before she came here. Before everything went so wrong in her life. But it was the signature that drew her attention. It was obvious just how close she was to Rachel Fox – or McMahon, as Molly would have known her. Molly must have known exactly what Rachel had done. Hazel was beginning to wonder whether the girl's mind had become so muddled that she was capable of copying what her Auntie Rachel had done.

Hazel turned to see Dawn Barker standing in the bedroom doorway.

'I'm going to flag Molly up a vulnerable adult,' Hazel told her. 'We'll find her, don't worry.'

Chapter Thirty-Two

'Is DC Graham available?' Kelly Tate asked the desk sergeant.

'Take a seat over there and I'll check,' he started to say until Tom appeared behind him. 'Ah Tom, is Andrea around? This girl wants to speak to her.'

Tom looked over and recognised Kelly Tate. 'No, sorry, Andrea is interviewing. Can I help?'

'Could you tell her that I'm sorry I ran away?'

Tom frowned. 'Why did you run away?'

Kelly sighed. 'I panicked, I suppose, she was poking her nose into stuff I didn't want her to and then I panicked but I know she was only doing her job. The two men that were murdered… it's horrible.'

'Do you have any information that could help us?' Tom asked.

'It might be nothing but and I don't like being a grass but…' She stopped and glanced around her.

'Come through.' He nodded to the doorway deeper inside the station.

'Erm…' she hesitated, peering between Tom and the exit.

'Have you eaten?' he asked.

'Erm…'

'I'll get you a sandwich and a cup of tea,' he told her.

Kelly smiled then nodded gently, hitching her rucksack further over her shoulder. 'OK.'

—

'And you're sure about that?' Tom asked. 'Molly put a blood-stained T-shirt into the wheelie bin outside the squat?'

'No, not the one there. The one nearer to the garage.'

Tom narrowed his eyes while he considered her information. 'How do you know it was blood-stained?'

'Because at first I thought it might be red paint but after what's happened I've thought about it again.'

'When did you see her do this?'

'This morning.'

'You saw her this morning,' Tom exclaimed. 'Why wait until now to tell us?'

Kelly shrugged. 'I'm sorry, I just didn't think.'

'Wait here for a minute will you,' Tom said and excused himself from the soft interview suite he'd taken her to. She'd devoured the sandwich and can of Coke quickly, eating as if she'd not eaten in a while but her clothes looked clean so she must be staying somewhere. He called Hazel with this new information and she said she'd get a team to search the bin immediately.

'Sorry about that,' he said when he returned and sat back down opposite her, adjusting his tie as he moved.

'How long have you been a detective?' Kelly asked, smiling at him.

'Almost fifteen years and I've been a police officer for twenty-two,' he told her but thought her question to be a little light-hearted given the seriousness of the situation. To give her the benefit of the doubt he assumed her attitude was a result of being so young and immature.

Kelly's eyes grew wide. 'That's longer than I've been alive.'

'I suppose it is,' Tom agreed. 'What brought you to Perth then?' He asked, knowing her accent was a Glasgow one, like his.

'Och, you know,' she shrugged, avoiding his eyes. 'Stuff.'

'Do your family know you're here, Kelly?'

The girl sighed. 'I don't know,' she said plainly. 'I don't think they care where I am.'

Tom did not give her the usual easy responses to this – empty reassurances that she was being silly, that people would be missing her – because he knew that sadly, she might be right. He'd not spoken to his own dad for almost ten years, after all.

'Sometimes life throws us curve balls, doesn't it?' he suggested instead.

'You got that right,' Kelly agreed firmly. 'But at least I'm not as bad as Molly. God, she's wasted almost permanently now and when she's not, she's rattling something chronic.'

'She has a volatile temper, I believe.'

'You think!' Kelly lifted up her T-shirt to reveal a bruise on her ribs.

'Did Molly do that to you?' Tom grew concerned for Kelly's safety.

'It was my fault,' she said. 'I tried to help her, but she thought I was trying to take something from her. Ironically, she then stole the tenner I had in my pocket.'

'You have a bed in the shelter for tonight, don't you?'

Kelly nodded. 'Yes.'

'Good, I'm glad.'

He passed the information on to Hazel and told Kelly to get in touch if she thought of anything else but especially if she saw Molly. It didn't matter what time of day or night it was. Tom decided he'd nip round to the shelter and talk to the staff in person too. The building was just a five-minute walk from the station, and he could do with the fresh air. They needed to be alerted that they were looking for Molly, that she was unpredictable and potentially dangerous. They should call 999 if she appeared.

–

By the light of the torch on her iPhone Hazel rooted through the crap in one of the two wheelie bins after instructing a gobsmacked Andrea that they'd be searching for the bloody T-shirt themselves. They'd just left Dawn Barker and were on their way back to the station anyway. An official missing person's report would be filed for Molly in light of the fact that the only communication Dawn had from her daughter was in the form of the cryptic text that suggested Molly had done something terrible. Molly wasn't just vulnerable. She was a murder suspect. But she couldn't shake the feeling someone must be helping her. Craig Douglas perhaps. Or Rachel.

'Boss,' Andrea shouted.

Hazel turned to see her holding up a white T-shirt which was covered in a variety of stains, the main one being dried blood.

'So our killer came back once we'd searched the area.' Very clever, Hazel thought.

'Yes, it was definitely not here before.'

How and when it got there would be investigated later.

'Bag it and let's get out of here.'

Chapter Thirty-Three

Rachel yawned as she switched on the eight o'clock news. She turned the television volume up and sprinkled salt over her meal. Fish and chips from the chippy at the end of her street. The place did a roaring trade from residents in her block – she knew that for sure, mainly because there was at least one of her neighbours in the queue every time she went in for her supper. She didn't blame them. The kitchens in the flats weren't built for proper cooking with barely enough worktop space to make a sandwich, a fridge with just a single box for a freezer at the top and a simple cooker. Rachel had been given a box of utensils and a grocery starter pack the day she moved in, containing: two pots, one large, one small; two plates; two bowls; a sieve; two forks; two knives; two dessert spoons and four teaspoons; two tea towels and a washing up brush along with two cloths. Which, Rachel had to admit, was a hundred per cent more than she had owned before her release and she was grateful for any help that was on offer. Her grocery pack had consisted of UHT milk, a bag of sugar, tea bags – Tetley, no less – a loaf of bread and a tub of spreadable butter. Her first meal in her new home had been tea and hot buttered toast which may as well have been steak and chips because it was glorious. Every mouthful was a joy.

The words Rachel heard the news reporter say hit her ears through a mixed bubble of disbelief and terror. She struggled to swallow the mouthful of fish, but she couldn't tear herself away from the shocking news. On the screen was a photo of a young man who couldn't be more than twenty years old. The reporter explained that Sam Kennedy had been stabbed, his body found in his car on Shore Road. She gasped to think that she and Dawn had spoken to Molly not far from there that night.

Rachel moved the food around and around her mouth. Her throat felt tight and she started coughing, spitting out the food into a tissue. Her whole body trembled but she couldn't tear her eyes away. It wasn't until she heard the loud knock on the door that she was able to move away at all, and only then because it had made her almost jump out of her skin. Her legs remained weak underneath her and Rachel feared they might give way any minute. She peered through the spy hole in the door then jumped back just as her doorbell chimed loudly, making her jump again.

Rachel's heart raced dangerously fast. So fast that her chest began to tighten, and her breathing stiffened like she couldn't get the right volume of air into her lungs. She glanced through the hole again. She didn't have a choice. She couldn't hide from this.

'Hello, can I help you?' Rachel said to her visitors. They held identification badges close to her face.

'Rachel Fox? My name is DCI Hazel Todd, and this is my colleague, DI Tom Newton. I wonder if I could have five minutes of your time.'

Rachel thought she might vomit, the nausea biting at her stomach then rising into her throat. She had to take a deep breath to control the sick feeling.

'What's this about?' she lied. Rachel knew exactly why two detectives were standing on her doormat. But how could they know who she was? Had Samiera told them?

'Perhaps it would be better if we chatted inside,' Hazel told her.

'OK, you'd better come in,' Rachel said and held her front door wide open for them. She smiled nervously at the younger of the two detectives. 'Please go right through.'

Rachel followed her visitors along the short hall that led into the living room, which was connected to the small kitchen space.

'Thank you, Rachel, I'm sorry to disturb your dinner.' Hazel pointed to the half-eaten fish supper on the coffee table.

'It's fine,' Rachel replied and hurriedly tidied away the wrapper. 'I wasn't that hungry anyway. What did you say you wanted?'

Hazel lifted a magazine from the two-seater sofa and placed it onto the table then sat down. Tom remained standing. Rachel's nerves were now shredded. Why won't she just hurry up and say it, she thought. Put me out of my misery, she raged silently inside.

'How have things been going?' Hazel asked. 'Since your release,' she added.

'Fine.'

'That's good to hear… and you're volunteering at the soup kitchen down by the Lade, is that right?'

Rachel nodded, becoming irritated by the way the male detective was staring around her small flat. The way he did it made her feel violated, the way she had when she was inside.

'That's right, yes, three days a week usually but I've been doing a bit more recently.'

The detective's eyes bored into Rachel, making her feeling uncomfortable.

Rachel moved the pile of laundry that was on the armchair next to the television and sat down. She reached for the remote control and switched off the television, then rested the remote on the arm of the chair. She couldn't stop the sigh that escaped.

'Is there something specific you want to ask me, detective?' Rachel mustered as much confidence as she dared; she wasn't inside anymore. This was her home. She stared at Hazel as she spoke but didn't feel anywhere near as confident as she wanted to appear.

'The bodies of two men have been found. They were stabbed and suffocated inside their vehicles.'

'I see,' Rachel responded, hoping the trembling inside her wasn't visible to them.

'You know a young woman we are very keen to speak to in connection with those murders,' Hazel said.

'I see,' Rachel repeated.

'Molly Barker.'

'Oh,' Rachel replied.

'You don't sound surprised,' Tom pointed out.

'I'm… erm, I'm…' Rachel stumbled over her words, like English wasn't her first language.

'Do you know where we could find Molly?' Hazel asked, studying the room around her carefully.

'She's not here, if that's what you're thinking.'

Hazel returned her focus to Rachel, staring directly at her, without taking her eyes from hers. 'You won't mind if we take a proper look, will you?'

Rachel knew she had no choice but to let the two detectives traipse through her home. If she refused, they could make her life difficult for her. They hadn't implied that they suspected her of these awful crimes, at least. Not yet.

Hazel nodded for Tom to search the small flat, leaving her alone with Rachel.

'When did you last see or speak to Molly?'

'Two nights ago,' Rachel replied truthfully.

'How did she seem to you?'

'Mixed up,' Rachel sighed. 'The way she always does these days.'

Rachel spotted that Hazel was looking at the unopened envelope on the coffee table and realised she'd forgotten about that. What with everything that had been going on recently, it had completely slipped her mind. She must remember to read it once these detectives had left her alone.

'What does "mixed up" mean, exactly?' Hazel pressed her for clarity.

'Confused, I suppose.'

'Confused about what, exactly?'

'Oh I don't know,' Rachel bit back and instantly regretted it, checking herself immediately. 'I don't know,' she repeated more gently this time, fearing that this detective had seen her rattled.

Tom's reappearance in the doorway, shaking his head, helped defuse the tension. Hazel took a card from her pocket and slid it across the coffee table.

'If Molly gets in touch with you, anytime, day or night, you call this number.' Hazel made to leave. 'In fact, Rachel, dial 999 please.'

Rachel's eyes widened at that. She swallowed hard to hide the shock as best she could. 'Oh OK, I will,' she said, trying to promise, but couldn't guarantee to herself that she would.

Chapter Thirty-Four

Hazel kicked off her shoes and slid them under the coat hooks. She picked up the post and sighed, tossing it aside but not before ripping up the envelopes addressed to Rick. If he hadn't bothered to change his details with the bank by now then tough shit. She yawned and scratched her head. A shower was what she really should do first, but she just couldn't be arsed. Instead, she poured herself a tall glass of white wine from the fridge and scrolled through the Just Eat app on her phone. She was famished but couldn't decide what she wanted.

Hazel read the text from Cara which had chirped in and interrupted her reading the menus. She wanted Hazel to know that a detective had been round to take Rick's details and he was now officially listed as a missing person. *So what?*

Poor Cara. She's deluded if she thinks he's doing anything other than screwing another woman, she thought. Probably someone young and nubile and not menopausal like they both were. Not that the man was even much of a catch, with his receding hairline and increasing middle-aged paunch. Rick's bank balance might actually be his most attractive feature right now. Hazel was so tempted to text back something awful, something cutting and bitchy but she resisted, unsure why she'd stopped herself.

Hazel carried her glass of wine to the sofa and switched on the TV, scrolling through Netflix to see if there was anything that appealed. Plumping for an episode of *Dexter*, she slipped off her socks and stretched out the full length of the sofa, slouching back in the cushions before realising she'd left her phone on the kitchen counter. It had been the ringtone singing to her that caught her attention.

'Bloody hell,' she mumbled and plonked her glass onto the low coffee table and jogged through to catch the call before it rang off. It couldn't be forensics on the bloody shirt yet though, she knew that. It was too quick. It had better not be Cara. She really would get a mouthful if it were.

She pressed 'Accept Call' and said, 'Hello DCI Todd.' This silent call thing was really getting on her nerves. Hadn't she signed up to that telephone preference service? Then she remembered that text and she checked her messages.

> You're getting warm, DCI Todd, but you're not quite there yet.

Her phone rang again, and she answered quickly.

'Hello, is that you?' she said. Silence. *Think, Hazel, think.* 'You must have something to say if you've called me again.' Silence. 'Do you need my help?' Still nothing so Hazel went for it. She had nothing to lose. 'Molly, is that you?'

This time she got more than silence, she got the tone that said the caller had hung up.

'Shit,' she exclaimed. 'Shit, shit, shit.'

It had to be her. The loud buzz from the security door startled her. 'Argh!' she shouted, her nerves frayed. She didn't think Cara would dare turn up again out of the blue and she wasn't expecting anyone else. Another loud buzz. Hazel's heart raced. The phone calls and texts were making her paranoid. It buzzed for a third time, making her jump.

Hazel took her phone out and scrolled through to Tom's number ready to hit the call button, just in case. She hurried to the living room window to see if she could make out who was standing at the front security door and readied herself to deal with whatever was on the other side of that door.

Chapter Thirty-Five

Rachel stood motionless behind the front door once she'd locked it after they left. She closed her eyes tight shut and dabbed at the single tear that she felt gather in the corner of her eye. She couldn't believe this was happening. The thought that someone she cared about could be connected to this horrified her. She prayed that there wasn't someone copying her crimes as some kind of sick homage to her but especially not Molly. She wondered if the police had spoken to Dawn. Poor Dawn was going out of her mind with worry as it was but this on top might push her over the edge.

Rachel lifted a box down from the top shelf in her wardrobe. She flopped down onto her bed with the box next to her and flipped the lid open. She pulled out the photo album on the top, something she hadn't looked through since her move. She gazed at photos of a smiling Molly, who was maybe five or six at most, grinning that toothless grin that children do, the innocence pouring towards her. She couldn't have done those terrible things, no matter how messed up the drugs had made her. Not Molly.

Rachel wasn't prepared for the emotions that spilt out when she flipped through the baby photos of her Steven, the son she'd not seen since he was two years old. He was a beautiful baby, his shock of strawberry-blond curls sticking up in several directions, his big blue eyes twinkling when he giggled. It had been a quick, simple birth which was a relief given that Rachel had given birth to him in the bus station toilets. A member of the public had called an ambulance when she found the pair slumped on the floor in one of the cubicles. His arrival had been the blessing her life had cried out for and had helped her get off the streets, for a short time at least. Eventually, she'd come to realise he was better off living in foster care and hoped he would understand how sorry she was that she couldn't be there for him. Now married with two teenage sons, Rachel couldn't have been prouder of how he'd turned out. A successful architect in the west end of Glasgow.

Rachel dropped the photo album onto her bed and lifted out what she'd been searching for. A second, smaller shoebox contained some of the correspondence Rachel had received in the thirty-plus years she'd been inside. The positive stuff anyway. The hate mail, of which there was a considerable amount, was all destroyed quickly after receiving it. The ones Rachel kept were from people offering support and friendship which for the troubled, addicted, confused person Rachel was at the time had been a lifeline to normality. The woman Rachel had grown closest to was Dawn Barker, Molly's mum, who often wrote to Rachel between visits, which became very regular as a strong friendship developed between the two broken women. She'd kept all of Dawn's letters. Molly had even started writing when she became a teenager which was lovely. It had been refreshing to see the world outside through fresh, young eyes.

Molly was the apple of her mother's eye too. Dawn admitted that on the darkest days of her abusive marriage, it was Molly that had made life worth living. People might ask why she hadn't just left but it wasn't as simple as that, especially living as they had in a predominantly Catholic community in Belfast. Had the damage already been done to Molly, even before the bullying? Was the bullying just what tipped her over the edge?

There was another selection of correspondence that Rachel was compelled to keep but she couldn't explain why. Dawn called these people her groupies and Rachel had laughed at the idea. She lifted the top letter off the pile and began to read.

> *Dear Rachel,*
>
> *I wanted to write to you today to let you know that I came across details of your crimes in the mid-eighties and was fascinated. I want you to know that I think the justice system treated you very unfairly and the abuse you had suffered throughout your life should have been taken into consideration. I think it's a crying shame that you were handed three life sentences. You did not deserve that. I would love us to correspond and have given my address should you choose to do so.*
>
> *Yours sincerely*
> *Laura Samson*

Rachel did start writing to Laura for a while. She had seemed genuinely concerned for Rachel's welfare and the pair became good friends until Laura's tragic death in 2010. Rachel was shocked by the grief she felt at the loss of someone she'd never met. Laura, though, was one of the tame groupies. Rachel lifted the bright pink envelope from the middle of the pile. She took out the sheets of pink paper that had rainbows around the borders.

Dear Rachel,

*I want to thank you on behalf of the sisterhood
for taking out the scumbags who think they can use
and abuse us.*

Rachel tossed the letter back into the box and slammed the lid shut. She'd been wrong to think she could read letters like that. She glanced sideways at her reflection in the mirror on her dressing table. She wasn't the woman that the author of that letter had thought she was. Rachel reached for a hair grip and pushed her long grey hair out of her eyes and held it in place. She looked tired, the dark circles under her eyes evidence of the poor night's sleep she'd had last night. Rachel was about to open the box again when her phone rang in the living room.

She quickly pushed the box back onto the shelf in the wardrobe and hurried to answer it.

'Hello?' she said and frowned when she got no response. 'Hello,' she repeated then sighed, frustrated by the silence. Rachel was about to hang up when a small voice said her name. 'Yes, it's Rachel. Who's this?'

More silence only added to the confusion. 'Hello, who is this?'

'Rachel?' the voice repeated.

'Yes, who's this?' Rachel's eyes widened as she listened to the caller. 'OK, stay where you are. I'm on my way,' she urged.

Rachel's heart broke for the fear in Molly's voice, but she was relieved that the young woman had felt able to reach out for help. Rachel grabbed her jacket from the hook by the front door and tossed her keys into her bag then pulled the door after her, the snib locking it shut as it closed.

Chapter Thirty-Six

'Tom!' Hazel exclaimed at the sight of him standing on her doormat with a pizza and a bottle of white wine in his hand.

'I haven't interrupted anything, have I?' he asked. 'I couldn't stop thinking about the case and I figured you'd be the same so I thought we might as well be thinking about it together.'

'You have no idea how pleased I am to see you.' She grabbed his arm and tugged him inside but before closing the door she peered out and glanced left and right then feared paranoia was getting the better of her.

Tom walked straight through to the kitchen and helped himself to two glasses from the cupboard.

'I've got a little head start on you.' Hazel held up her empty glass then lifted the bottle he'd brought and opened it.

Tom put back one of the glasses and held his out to be filled. Hazel flipped open the pizza box, grateful he'd got an extra-large because she was famished.

'Oh good man, you got a half and half.' She snapped a large slice of bacon and mushroom pizza off, allowing the melted cheese to drip everywhere.

'Well, I know you hate pepperoni,' he said and guzzled a large swig from his glass. 'God, that's good.'

There was something so comfortable about Tom. He seemed to know exactly who he was and was comfortable in his own skin. Hazel loved that about him. Cara had suggested she felt safe with him because he was gay, but that fact never even entered Hazel's head. Still unnerved by the phone call and text, she showed Tom her phone.

'I've got Billy trying to locate the caller ID, but he's not got anything yet.'

'Bloody hell, how many cards do we give out, asking people to call us?' Tom said. 'Who did you give one to since we found Sam Kennedy's body?'

'Lisa Kennedy, Rachel, Dawn Barker, Lynne Cooper,' she said. 'Kelly too, I think and maybe Craig Douglas. What about you?'

'Same, I think. Did you give one to Molly Barker?'

Hazel shook her head. 'I haven't spoken to her. You have.'

'Don't I know it. Shit, I should have held her.'

'Yes but on what charge? At that point Molly was just a witness, albeit an uncooperative one,' Hazel reminded him.

Tom ripped a huge slice of pizza out of the box and laid it onto the piece of kitchen roll he'd placed on the table.

'Have you got any paper?' he asked.

'Aye, hang on,' Hazel replied and opened the drawer next to the fridge then produced an A4 lined pad.

Tom flipped open to the first sheet and frowned at her when he read what was written on it.

'Ignore that, I was just being silly one night when I'd had a couple of glasses of wine.' She reached over and ripped the page off.

'I believe you.' He smiled at the way her face had flushed pink. 'But thousands wouldn't. I mean, writing a list of ways to murder your husband without being caught is quite unusual, especially for a detective.'

Hazel had to agree as she read the first item on the list. *Poisoning with arsenic.*

'Arsenic isn't as easy to get hold of these days,' she teased and screwed the paper up then tossed it into the paper recycling tub.

'Right, let's forget about your creepy to-do list,' Tom said and wrote Sam Kennedy and Sean Cooper's names on the pad.

'What are you thinking?' Hazel asked and devoured another large slice, savouring the way the mushroom melted in her mouth.

'Let's look at the people close to them,' Tom began. 'Starting with Sam.'

Hazel grabbed another pen from the counter behind her. 'Kirsty and her brother Mick. Ex-girlfriend and supplier of drugs to the girls Sam associated with, Natalie Morrison in particular.'

'The only connection between the two men appears to be the sex workers given they come from very different backgrounds. Sexual violence too, do you think?' Tom said and tapped the nib of the pen up and down on the paper.

Hazel frowned at Tom then wrote: *Molly Barker, Craig Douglas and Rachel Fox.*

Tom took the pen from her and scored out the names Craig Douglas and Rachel Fox. 'They alibi each other through phone records, remember?'

'Mm,' Hazel said and pursed her lips as she narrowed her eyes at him. She wrote the names down again. 'But that doesn't rule out them helping *her*.' She drew a large circle around Molly's name.

'Do you really think Rachel would risk being sent back to prison?' Tom asked.

'Molly is like a daughter to her, Tom.'

'Maybe she feels responsible for her,' Tom said. 'Feels guilty that she's caused what Molly is going through.'

'We've all been through stuff, doesn't mean we can go round murdering innocent people.'

'Do we really know how innocent they were?'

Tom's suggestion surprised her. 'That's not what we're talking about here. Let's not cloud the facts.'

Hazel's phone rang before Tom could respond and it was the news she'd been waiting for. The blood on the shirt belonged to Sam Kennedy. Not only that, the blood on one of the knives was his too.

Chapter Thirty-Seven

'Molly, sweetheart,' Rachel exclaimed and reached out to her, drawing her close. She hugged the young girl tight, tears building in the back of her eyes, but she knew she mustn't break down. Molly needed her to be strong.

'I'm sorry, I didn't know what else to do,' Molly said as she winced from the pain of her cut lip and pulled her face out of Rachel's embrace. 'I wasn't sure if you'd come.'

Rachel held Molly's face in her hands and leaned down to kiss her head. 'Of course I was going to come. Can you tell me what happened?' she asked but in truth, Rachel knew exactly what had happened.

'He seemed alright; you know. His car was clean, he seemed OK.'

'I'm so sorry,' Rachel whispered and pulled her close again until Molly whimpered from the pain in her face. 'You have to come home with me, you can't stay here, in this state.'

'Are you sure?'

'Of course, we'll go back to mine, get you cleaned up.' By rights she should take Molly straight to the police station. To make a complaint, as much as anything else. Someone had attacked Molly and should be punished but she couldn't report it, for lots of reasons.

A terrifying memory slammed into Rachel's mind of a particularly brutal rape she'd experienced when she was working as a prostitute.

'I need to report a sexual assault,' Rachel said, her face bruised and her lip bleeding from a large cut.

The officer didn't attempt to hide his irritation.

'Rachel, have you got evidence?'

'Evidence? Look at the state of me!'

'A punter?'

'Yes but…'

'Occupational hazard, love, don't waste my time or I'll arrest you for just that.'

'But look at me…'

'Goodbye, Rachel.'

The memory of his disregard for her safety made her shiver. The taxi ride back to Rachel's place wasn't the most comfortable. Their driver had made his opinions very clear, not in what he said but in the way he looked at the two women and Rachel couldn't wait to get out of his vehicle.

'Here, drink this. I've put some sugar in it, for the shock,' Rachel said when Molly joined her in the kitchen after having a long shower. She knew exactly what the trembling meant.

'I'm so cold,' Molly said, through chattering teeth.

'I know,' Rachel said and wrapped a blanket round Molly's shoulders. 'Here, snuggle in tight and drink your tea, that should warm you up.'

'It's not tea I need,' Molly barked and banged her fist on the table.

Rachel knew that already, but she was determined to help stop Molly taking any more drugs. This had to stop. Too many people had already got hurt. She knew she was taking a huge risk hiding Molly here but what choice did she have?

'Molly, sweetheart,' Rachel spoke softly. 'Drink the tea and then we can talk about—'

'I don't want to talk!' Molly tossed the mug against the wall, almost hitting Rachel's head as it flew past. She stood up and snatched hold of Rachel's bag, ripping open the zip and tipping the contents onto the table before Rachel could stop her. 'I need money.'

Rachel leaned forward, grabbing the bag's long strap. She dragged it away then snatched up her purse before Molly could find it.

'Give me it!' Molly demanded.

Rachel's heart was racing. The hate in Molly's bloodshot eyes was horrible. 'No. Sit down and I'll make you another hot drink.'

Molly screamed in frustration before tearing towards her, pinning her to the wall. The pain from having her back slammed against it surged through Rachel's whole body.

'Give it to me!' Molly screamed in Rachel's ear, squeezing her throat with her fingers so tightly that it became hard to breathe. But this was too important. She held tightly to her purse.

'No,' Rachel tried to say.

Molly pinched a thick fistful of Rachel's hair in her hand and smashed her head against the wall.

From where she'd fallen onto the floor, Rachel stared up, dazed, as Molly was stuffing the contents of her purse into her pocket. She could only look on in horror as every drawer was ransacked and left hanging open. This was like a nightmare. Rachel tried to pull herself onto her knees as the sound of furniture being tipped and cupboards being looted echoed through the flat until the sound of the front door slamming shut preceded the silence, interrupted only by the ringing in Rachel's ears from having her head slammed against the wall.

After managing to get onto one of the kitchen chairs she lifted her purse and saw what was left inside. Two photos. One of Steven and the other of a smiling Molly with ice cream all over her face. Rachel dropped it and sobbed like she hadn't done for many years, grimacing from the pain in her cheek where she'd bumped her face as she fell. She knew she should have called the police as soon as Molly reached out to her but, like an old fool, Rachel thought she could help. All she'd achieved was making things worse. What on earth was she going to tell Dawn?

Chapter Thirty-Eight

Andrea hurried in just before Hazel began her team's morning briefing, sharing where they were at on the case. She lifted a hand in apology and sat next to Billy Flynn.

'Right, as of last night, Molly Barker has become our main suspect. I want to know as soon as possible if the hairs we found belong to her,' Hazel pointed to Molly's photo. 'However, I have a sneaking suspicion that her ability to hide from us so well may be down to help she's receiving from one or both of these two.' She pointed to photos of Rachel Fox and Craig Douglas.

'Surely Rachel wouldn't risk being sent back to prison,' Andrea chipped in. 'Which realistically only leaves Douglas, do you think?'

Hazel shot a glance towards Tom who nodded. 'I am inclined to agree with you to a certain extent but we need to consider how close their relationship is. I mean, Molly calls her Auntie Rachel and when you consider the fact Dawn Barker moved the two of them over here to be closer to Rachel, we can't rule out Rachel helping her out of some kind of loyalty or perhaps even guilt.'

'The blood-stained shirt,' Tom said. 'Our witness says she saw Molly dump it in the wheelie bin.'

'That's right,' Hazel confirmed.

'Do we have a warrant for her arrest yet?' Billy asked.

'On its way as we speak.'

'What about Craig Douglas, boss, are we watching his place?' Andrea asked. 'To see if she shows up there?'

'I'm going to ask an unmarked car to sit outside but what I do want you to do is talk to his neighbours, show them Molly's photo. See if they've seen her coming and going.'

'Good idea,' Andrea nodded.

'Tom, can you go over to the community kitchen again this morning? Take a photo of Molly and show it to everyone again. Talk to Rachel, lean on her a bit, make her uncomfortable. See if that shakes anything loose.'

'Sure,' Tom agreed. 'And if she turns up at the shelter they know to call 999 as well as us.'

'Good, good, come on folks, we can do this,' Hazel clapped her hands twice. 'Molly Barker is out there somewhere, and we need to find her before she hurts someone else.'

A uniformed officer poked her head round the incident room door. 'DCI Todd, there's a woman downstairs asking to talk to you.'

'OK thanks, I'll be right down,' Hazel replied then turned to face her team. 'Billy, get onto the council and get us CCTV from every camera they have. Molly must have left a trail somewhere. I want to see every step that girl takes.'

'Sure,' he said and picked up the handset of his desk phone.

'Andrea, Tom, meet back here in a couple of hours.'

Hazel watched her two detectives shuffle out together, enjoying how well they'd gelled. She grabbed her phone and followed behind.

–

'Hello Lisa,' Hazel said as she joined Lisa Kennedy in one of the interview rooms. 'What can I do for you?'

'Hello,' Lisa replied, immaculately dressed in a matching white skirt and blazer. 'I wanted to let you know that a girl came to the house to say how sorry she was about what happened to Sam.'

'When was this?' Hazel asked.

'Just as I was leaving the house this morning,' Lisa told her. 'She didn't stay long.'

'Did you recognise her as one of your son's friends?'

'No I didn't.' She shuffled uncomfortably on the chair. 'Look I'm not one to judge but she wasn't exactly like someone Sam would associate with, if you know what I mean.'

Clearly Lisa still didn't know Sam's secret.

'In what way?' Hazel asked.

'She seemed…' Lisa screwed up her face. 'Rough.'

'What do you mean by rough?' Hazel wanted her to describe the girl in more detail. Was this Molly?

'Well, you know,' she shrugged. 'Her clothes seemed cheap, and her trainers were dirty.'

If only you knew the sort of girls your son did associate with.

'Can you describe her to me?'

'Oh yes, she was small and thin and pale, very pale.'

'Do you remember her hair or her eye colour?'

'Yes, yes, she had blue eyes and lank, red hair that was long and messy.'

Hazel was annoyed that she'd left the photo of Molly Barker upstairs.

'Can you wait here for five minutes,' Hazel asked. 'So I can run up and get a photo I'd like to show you?'

Lisa checked the time on her phone. 'I'm in a bit of a hurry, actually. I've got an appointment.'

'I'll be as quick as I can,' Hazel pleaded and was starting to walk away when Lisa's phone rang.

'I'm sorry, I have to take this,' she said and got up to walk away.

Hazel headed straight back up while Lisa answered the call. She was disappointed to see Superintendent Daly waiting for her in her office.

'Sir,' she said.

'Ah, DCI Todd, I just wanted to let you know I've made arrangements for the press briefing in two hours.'

It wasn't ideal but Hazel would have to deal with it.

'OK,' she agreed and flicked through the pile of photos on her desk until she found Molly's. 'That's fine.'

'There's something I thought you should know,' Daly chirped. 'Nothing major, just a heads-up.'

'Oh?' Hazel frowned, desperate to get back to Lisa.

'Yes, I should have mentioned this earlier, perhaps, but I'm a friend of the family,' he said without elaborating.

'Whose family?'

'Sam Kennedy's. Or, more accurately, I'm friends with his father.'

Hazel figured it was a masonic connection until he spoke again.

'We play golf together occasionally.'

'Oh OK, thanks for letting me know. I appreciate that,' Hazel acknowledged, before heading straight back down to where she'd left Lisa.

'Where's the woman I was talking to in there?' she asked one of the uniformed officers.

'She left, said it was an emergency.'

Hazel closed her eyes and sighed. Bloody Daly. If he hadn't kept her, she might have caught Lisa before she made her getaway. She scrolled through her contacts to find Lisa's number.

'Come on, come on,' she muttered impatiently as her call went to voicemail. 'Lisa, hi, it's DCI Todd. I wonder, could you please give me a call back as soon as you get this? I want to show you this photo. Thank you.'

Hazel hung up and stuffed her phone into her pocket. She trudged back up to her office because she had a press briefing to prepare for, but a phone call stopped her in her tracks. Hazel had to put everything else on hold for now. She called Tom to let him know where she was going and raced down the station steps, taking them two at a time and out into the pouring, bitingly cold October rain.

Chapter Thirty-Nine

Hazel had sounded terrible, and Tom urged her to let him know when there was any news and if he could do anything to help. She promised she would, of course. From the corner of his eye he was sure that was the back of Craig Douglas he saw, moving away towards where a bus had just pulled away but before he could call out, Kelly Tate came up behind him, her face red as if she'd been running.

'Hello again,' she said, catching her breath and tugging her rucksack tighter up her shoulder.

'Hello, Kelly,' Tom replied as he locked his car. 'How are you doing?'

'Are you coming inside?' Kelly asked and fell in step with him. 'Are you here for Rachel?' she added. 'Your boss was looking for her before. I met her at Rachel's place.'

'Amongst other things, yes,' Tom said honestly as he opened the community kitchen door and allowed her to go on ahead of him. 'Listen, Kelly, have you seen Molly Barker?'

'Not for a bit, no. Did you find that T-shirt I told you about?'

'We did, yes, thank you.' Tom studied the dining area, which was filling up fast. He recognised a few of the faces and was struck by how at ease Kelly was here.

'Here she is,' Kelly announced when Rachel appeared in front of them.

Tom was shocked by the state of her. She had a bruise on her cheek and red marks on her neck, like someone had held their fingers round her throat.

'Rachel, what's happened?' Tom asked, aware that Kelly was still hanging around. He caught Rachel take a sideways glance. 'Is it alright if we go somewhere and have a talk?'

'I'm really busy right now, detective,' Rachel stuttered. 'I've got a full house today.' She pointed to the gathered crowd.

'I'm sure Kelly can help out,' he suggested and gave the girl a wide eyed grin. 'Can't she?'

'Erm, I'm not sure,' Rachel said, seemingly trying to avoid his suggestion.

'Yes, I'd be happy to, I'll even make you both a cup of tea,' Kelly beamed and walked away.

'Is there somewhere we can go that's a bit more private?'

As if resigned to their conversation, Rachel nodded, although her thin smile was not genuine; Tom could tell that right away.

'Follow me,' she said and led Tom into a small room that seemed to double as an office as well as a store cupboard. She shut the door after them and closed the window behind the desk.

'What happened to your face?' Tom wasn't planning on beating around the bush. There was too much at stake.

Rachel instinctively lifted a hand to her bruised cheek. 'I fell getting out the bath.' She shook her head and avoided his eye. 'Stupid old woman that I am.'

'You do know it's not a good idea to lie to the police,' he warned. 'Especially in your circumstances.'

Rachel opened her mouth to protest just as a knock landed on the office door.

'Come in,' Tom shouted.

'I thought you'd like your tea in here,' Kelly smiled and laid a tray with two mugs and a bowl of sugar on the desk. She stared between Tom and Rachel then turned and left them again.

'Such a lovely girl,' Rachel said and dropped a spoonful of sugar into a mug and stirred.

Tom ignored both Rachel's remark and the other mug of tea on the tray.

'I know Molly did that to you,' he pointed to her face. 'And I'm not leaving here until you tell me where she is.'

Rachel's face flushed pink. 'I don't know where Molly is!'

'Come on, Rachel, you and I both know that's not true.' Tom demanded. 'Is she hiding out in your flat?'

'No! I already told you, I don't know where she is!'

'Well then you leave me with no choice.' Tom stood and produced a pair of handcuffs as he walked closer to where Rachel sat, horrified by this development.

'Wait,' she exclaimed. 'Wait, OK, OK, I'll tell you what happened.'

Tom listened with interest as Rachel explained about Molly's explosive outburst last night.

'So you see, I'm not lying, I don't know where she is,' Rachel said.

'Why didn't you call us last night?'

'I don't know. I was pretty shaken up, I suppose.'

'Have you cancelled your debit card yet?' Tom asked.

'No, I haven't got round to it yet.'

Tom imagined that Rachel hadn't done it yet so that Molly could use it for whatever it was she needed.

'Good, perhaps that's good,' he suggested. 'Perhaps we can trace her movements through that.' He pulled out his phone and dialled Billy's number. 'Hi, I'm going to need you to trace a debit card in the name of Rachel Fox.' He gave Billy all the details. 'Let me know as soon as you get anything.' Billy told him he would but so far she'd not surfaced on any of the CCTV he'd been sent.

Tom hung up and returned his focus to a sombre-faced Rachel.

'What's going to happen to me because I didn't call last night?'

By rights, Tom knew he should take Rachel in for obstruction at the very least, but having her outside was more useful to them. If Molly reached out again, he didn't think Rachel would dare keep it secret again.

'Nothing,' he told her. 'For now.'

'Thank you,' Rachel said, genuinely grateful. 'I know I've been an old fool.'

'What did she do to you?' Tom asked. 'That cheek looks nasty.'

Rachel brushed her fingers over the bruise and sighed. 'She was upset, that's all and I suppose I got in her way.'

Tom had heard that before. Hadn't Kelly Tate said the same thing? It seemed it didn't pay to get in Molly Barker's way.

'She took some cash and my debit card. It wasn't much,' she continued. 'Certainly not enough to keep her going for long.'

A text from Billy caught Tom's attention. The debit card had been used in Tesco in South Street ten minutes ago. Tom warned Rachel of the consequences of lying to them again and raced from the building.

'Not now, Kelly,' he urged gently when she tried to talk to him outside. In his rear view mirror he saw her watching his car drive away and was sad that such a pleasant young girl had ended up in her position.

–

Rachel reached into her handbag for a clean tissue to wipe her face. That detective could have, and perhaps should have, arrested her for her stupidity. In the bottom of the bag she found the letter she'd found on the doormat the other night. She ripped it open and read the short note inside.

> *Dear Rachel,*
>   *It gives me no pleasure at all to do this to you but I'm desperate. Finding out your secret has coincided with a huge problem in my life that I have to fix.*

Rachel clasped her hand to her mouth as she read on. This was a blackmail letter. The author said they knew who she was and if she didn't want people to know, she had to meet them to discuss an arrangement to guarantee their silence. They would be reasonable, they said. Rachel's heart hammered as she realised that if she hadn't opened the letter when she did, she would have missed the deadline – which was in three hours.

Chapter Forty

'Dad!' Hazel exclaimed, breathing a huge sigh of relief to see him sitting in the armchair in his room at the nursing home.

She almost fell to her knees as she squeezed him tight in her arms. Tears fell easily. All kinds of terrifying thoughts had swum inside her head as she'd raced towards the home. The place was close enough to the railway line that visions of finding her dad's body on the track had slammed into her as she sped through lights which could technically be described as very late amber rather than red. That phone call had almost stopped Hazel's heart and all thoughts of this case had immediately emptied from her head. Rightly or wrongly; it had happened automatically.

'Hazel, I'm so sorry,' the care home manager had the decency to appear contrite.

'What the hell happened?' Hazel snapped.

'Honestly, we don't know.' The middle-aged woman held her hands up.

'What do you mean, you *don't know*? How can you not know?' Hazel was becoming increasingly irate the longer this woman stood there.

'One of the care assistants went to his room and said he wasn't there. So we checked the bathrooms, the dining room, the sun room but he was nowhere to be found so I called you before activating the protocol.' The woman was rambling, her nerves obvious. 'Just as I was literally about to activate the missing person protocol, a young girl knocked on the front door and said she'd found your father wandering around outside in a pair of slippers and no coat.'

'Jesus Christ, how can something like this happen?' Hazel exclaimed then looked back at her dad who didn't seem to have a clue what any of the fuss and raised voices were about.

'Wasn't the outside door locked?' she asked.

'It should have been but…'

'But what?'

'We found it was unlocked when we went to let your dad in, when the young lady brought him back.'

'Where did she find him? Can I speak to her, is she still here?' Hazel urged.

'I'm sorry, she said she was in a hurry.'

'Did you at least take her name?' Hazel was becoming incredulous at the incompetence.

'No, I'm sorry,' the care home manager apologised again. 'We were more worried about your father.'

'I can't believe this,' Hazel ranted. 'Do you have any idea what could have happened to him out there?' She thrust her finger towards the outside window. 'For a man who doesn't know what day of the week it is? Who can't even remember how to tie his own shoelaces or use a knife and fork!'

Eventually Hazel calmed down when the care home manager had offered the umpteenth apology. It wasn't ideal but she had no choice but to leave her dad where he was. On her way back out she noticed the camera above the entrance and went back inside.

'Can I see the CCTV footage please?'

An awkward silence descended in the office while Hazel was shown footage of a young woman ringing the doorbell to the home, her arm interlinked with Hazel's father's. He was smiling happily at whatever the girl had said. She rubbed his arms to keep him warm while they waited to be let in. She had a hood up but there was enough hair sticking out to see that it was long and red. Hazel felt nausea claw up from her stomach and reach into her throat. It couldn't be, could it?

The sound of a text landing in Hazel's phone made her jump.

> I'm glad he got back safe and sound. It would be a shame to lose your other parent too.

Hazel had to keep her cool. She shouldn't reply but—

> Who is this?

Hazel waited. She stared at her dad's smiling face as he was being helped into the dining room. What if she had lost him? The thought of that made her feel sick.

> Tick Tock. Tick Tock. You're wasting time. The clues are there. You just have to follow the crumbs I've left.

Who the hell was this and how did they get Hazel's number. Her heart pounded as she jogged back to her car while calling Billy.

'Billy, have you had any luck with that unknown number I sent you? I mean,' she stuttered, flustered by the events of the past hour. 'The text from the unknown number.'

While she waited, Hazel watched as two blackbirds pecked at the freshly soaked ground in the flower bed of the home's immaculate garden, tearing chunks up and tossing them aside to get at the juicy worms. What a simple life. Living each day as it came, seeking out your essential needs to survive. For a second she envied them. They wouldn't struggle to sleep tonight because some mad woman was targeting them. They wouldn't wake up tomorrow morning with a sick feeling in the pit of their stomachs because a murderer was taunting them.

Billy's answer wasn't what she wanted to hear.

Chapter Forty-One

Andrea yawned as she climbed the second flight of stairs in Craig's block of flats. It had been a long but, she had to admit, exhilarating couple of days. The excitement of a murder investigation was every bit as thrilling as she'd anticipated it would be before joining DCI Todd's team. The potted plant outside the first of the top floor flats was unexpected – but then she realised it was fake. She prepared her ID and rapped the letterbox loudly.

While she waited for the door to be answered by the occupant, a woman called Sandra, who was a chef at The Holly Bush Hotel just across the Inch, Andrea stared out at the view. From the top floor, the far-reaching views across the river were gorgeous and waking up on a clear day to the sight of the tower on top of Kinnoull Hill must be lovely. Handy too for work, Andrea thought but didn't like the idea of a young woman walking home alone in the dark across the park. Andrea knocked again, this time hammering her fist against the door, hoping to attract Sandra's attention. She checked her watch. Even if she'd been on a night shift, she should be up by now and Andrea's belly rumbled, as she realised she hadn't eaten for ages. The smell of something garlicky wafted into her nostrils as soon as the door swung open.

'Yes?' a middle-aged man scowled. Not what Andrea was expecting. She held her ID closer.

'Hello, my name is DC Andrea Graham, I was wondering if I could come in and ask the occupant of this property some questions in relation to a current investigation.'

That sounded like such a mouthful and not at all as confident as she'd intended.

'Dad, who is it?' A young woman, dressed in a yellow velour robe with a vibrant orange towel wrapped into a turban high on her head, appeared. 'Oh, police, you'd better come in.'

The irate man who'd answered the door gave Andrea a blank stare before kissing Sandra's cheek and walking away.

'Ignore my dad, please come in.' Sandra held out her arm to usher Andrea inside.

Andrea wiped her feet on the doormat which had one of those silly quirky greetings. *Welcome, but only if you've got wine.* The flat was decorated as vibrantly as Sandra. The hallway had been painted a shade of turquoise that hit you, hard, as soon as you walked in.

'Is this about the murder? Everybody's talking about it at work,' Sandra said as she closed and locked the door.

'That's right.'

'Please, go through, don't mind the mess.'

Andrea smiled and walked into a living room painted a gaudy shade of plum. Three cats lay sleeping on various mismatched armchairs. One of them opened their eyes briefly before closing them again, seemingly indifferent to her arrival.

'You're a big cat lover,' Andrea said.

'Yes, the other three are on my bed,' Sandra beamed. 'Let's talk in the kitchen, I've got a stew on.'

Other three!

'Something smells very nice,' Andrea suggested.

'Would you like some?'

However tempted she was, Andrea had to refuse. 'No, it's fine, I just have a couple of questions to ask then I'll leave you in peace.'

'Okay dokey,' Sandra beamed and stirred the huge pot on the stove.

Andrea pulled a photo of Molly Barker from her bag and held it up. 'Have you seen this woman coming and going from this block at all?'

'Yes, her and others like her. They go into Craig's place, you know, downstairs.'

'Yes,' Andrea nodded. 'Have you seen her recently?'

'No, sorry, we've been really short-staffed at the hotel, and I've been doing double shifts.' As if on cue, she yawned. 'It's been work, sleep, repeat for me for the past couple of months so I've hardly seen anyone. It's why dad was here, he was dropping off some shopping for me.'

'When you did last see her, how often would you say she goes into Mr Douglas's flat?'

'Once a week, maybe twice,' Sandra answered without looking up from adding salt to the pot.

'Have you ever spoken to her?'

'Only a couple of times, in passing, like. She's not the talkative type though, barely grunts when you say hello to her.'

Then Sandra's expression changed as if she'd remembered something.

'Actually, there was this one day – I remember it was really sunny – and I came home from a breakfast shift, and they were arguing. Her in the picture,' she pointed to the photo on the table, 'and Craig. His cheek was really red like he'd been slapped. I saw it because he'd come out after her and I bumped into him in the close.'

'How did she seem?'

'Angry, like they'd had a big fight.'

Andrea wrote down everything that Sandra had told her which also included her theory that Craig Douglas might be a pimp – something Andrea knew not to be the case because she'd asked Natalie Morrison and Kelly Tate exactly that question.

Andrea scribbled a short note asking the occupant of the flat next door to call her when she didn't get any response then headed downstairs to talk to Craig Douglas's next door neighbour.

'Hello.' The elderly woman, who could barely be five foot tall, looked up and smiled at Andrea who was showing her the ID badge. 'Come in, detective.'

'Thank you,' Andrea replied and followed the old woman inside.

It was like stepping back in time. The living room could have been something from a 1950s TV drama. Her research had told her that this woman was ninety-one but she barely looked a day over eighty.

'Please sit down, dear,' she said.

Andrea handed the photo of Molly to her. 'Do you recognise this girl?'

The old woman produced a pair of glasses from the drawer in her sideboard. 'Let's see, what have we got here?' She spoke slowly. 'Mm, she does look familiar, yes. Is she missing?'

Technically she was, but Andrea wasn't in a position to give away those details.

'She's a person of interest in an investigation and we're keen to find her.'

'Molly,' the old woman announced. 'That's her name, isn't it?'

'That's right, yes.'

'I know that because I heard him next door shouting after her the other day.'

'What day was that exactly?'

'Monday, I think.' She hesitated. 'Or was it Tuesday? Och, it was one of the two. I'm sorry, sometimes the days all blend into one for me.'

'Could you tell if they were arguing?' Like Sandra had suggested she'd witnessed some months before.

'No, but the poor girl was upset.' The old woman's expression appeared genuinely sympathetic. 'I think he wanted to go after her, but he's got that stookie on his leg, hasn't he?'

'Yes, a car accident, wasn't it?' Andrea said.

The old woman's brown eyes widened until her eyebrows were almost hidden by her silver fringe.

'Is that what he told you?' She pursed her lips knowingly, crossing her arms across her chest.

Andrea frowned. 'Isn't that what happened?'

'It sounds like young Craig next door hasn't been exactly honest with you, dear.'

Chapter Forty-Two

Tom was the only person Hazel had told about the incident with the girl on the care home's CCTV. She'd wait and tell Daly once Billy had something concrete for her because he was having difficulty identifying where the number came from. She was disappointed to hear that despite Tom's speedy arrival at the Tesco on South Street, the person who'd used Rachel's stolen card was long gone. It could only have been Molly but as there had been no video footage she couldn't be one hundred per cent sure. Today had to be the day the cameras were being serviced so were out of action. Typical. Now Hazel had this damn press briefing to deal with. Knowing she'd left strict instructions that her dad was to receive no visitors and wasn't to leave the building under any circumstances, she felt marginally better leaving him there. Once this case was over she'd be reconsidering where his future lay.

The tears had stopped at least but it was the shaking in her hands that troubled Hazel. Stress, she figured, but it was damn inconvenient.

'Are you OK?' Billy Flynn asked.

His look of concern made Hazel blush. 'What? Yes, yes.' She tried to brush it off. 'Long day, that's all. Any updates for me?'

'Sean Cooper's phone has thrown a bit of a curve ball.'

'Oh?' Hazel was intrigued. 'Tell me more,' she said and perched on the corner of Billy's desk.

'Guess whose phone number he called on a regular basis recently?'

Hazel shrugged. 'Enlighten me.'

'Craig Douglas's.'

Her eyes widened at that, and her mouth dropped open at the news. 'Is that right?'

Hazel checked her watch. She had to get to the front door of the station in less than a minute for the press briefing.

'Call Andrea, ask her to talk to Douglas again, she's already over there.' She stopped and turned back. 'In fact, could you nip over there too? Talk to him together.'

'Sure.' Billy grabbed his blazer from the back of his chair and dialled Andrea's number as he walked away.

So Craig Douglas had denied knowing Sean Cooper. Now why would he have done that, Hazel wondered.

The sight of the assembled crowd made Hazel's stomach lurch. It wasn't like she hadn't done lots of these over the years, but it was something she'd never got used to. It went with the senior rank she'd achieved. She looked into the sea of expectant faces, some she recognised, some were new to her. Young and keen.

'Thank you all for coming,' she began then took a long, slow, hopefully calming breath. 'My name is DCI Hazel Todd and I'm the senior investigating officer looking into the murders of Sam Kennedy and Sean Cooper.'

The assembled crowd had fallen silent, hanging on her every word. Hazel held up Molly's photo which caused a wave of clicking to erupt as they snapped photos.

'We're very keen to talk to this young woman in connection with these murders. Her name is Molly

Barker. She is eighteen years old and is known to frequent the Shore Road area as well as the community kitchen down by the lade. If anyone knows Molly or knows where she is then it's vital they get in touch with us. She also has connections to Belfast and we're asking anyone who has seen or spoken with Molly to get in touch with Police Scotland. We're asking members of the public to be vigilant and not to approach her. Instead, dial 999 as soon as possible. Thank you.'

A question chirped from above the noise.

'Is she your main suspect?'

Hazel hated the questions that always inevitably followed.

'At present, she is a person of interest that we are extremely keen to speak to. Thank you. All the details will be available shortly on our website and on social media.'

Hazel headed back up to her office, stopping in the ladies' bathroom on the way. She exhaled a long, slow breath of relief that it was over and splashed her face with cold water in a bid to wake herself up a bit. When she walked out the bathroom door she almost bumped right into a detective she'd worked with two years ago. Hazel and DI Black had never exactly been friends but they'd got on fine.

'Hello,' Hazel said and smiled at her old colleague, unnerved by the serious expression on her face.

'Can we talk?'

'Erm yes, sure,' Hazel replied cautiously. 'We can talk in my office.'

The two had almost made it upstairs when Tom surged towards them.

'A man's been found unconscious on the North Inch. Possible stab wounds to the chest. Ambulance is taking him to PRI now.'

'I'm sorry, this will have to wait,' Hazel said to DI Black and raced out after Tom.

–

'We'll take my car,' Tom said.

'Fine, yes, what do we know about the victim?' Hazel asked as Tom navigated the traffic on Jeanfield Road.

'Fifty-year-old male. ID found on him at the scene says his name is Roy Gallagher. Stab wound to his chest. He was found by a dog walker on the North Inch half an hour ago. It was flagged to us because of the possible link to our stabbings.'

The two detectives were shown into Resus where the man had regained consciousness and was waiting to have his stab wound treated. It turned out the wound was in his shoulder and not his chest, as had been reported. The A and E consultant pulled them both aside.

'Mr Gallagher is in a serious condition. The stab wounds are more superficial than first thought but his lack of consciousness when he was found is my main concern. The stab wound will need stitching but it's not life-threatening.'

'Can we speak to him?' Hazel asked.

'Five minutes. He's going to CT soon to have his head scanned for possible areas of bleeding.' The young doctor was swept away by a nurse before Hazel or Tom could say anything.

Hazel pulled back the curtain to see a thick-built, balding man in his fifties lying slumped on a bed inside the cubicle. His face was ashen, and his eyes looked like a rabbit in headlights. The two detectives exchanged the briefest of glances. They explained who they were and why they were there to see him.

'I don't want the police involved,' he urged, his eyes flitting everywhere round the room except on them. He winced like he was in pain, pressing his fingers to his temple.

'That's quite a bump you've taken to the head, Mr Gallagher,' Hazel suggested.

'Aye, well, I'll be fine. I'd rather just forget about it.'

'I'm afraid it's not quite as simple as that,' she pointed out and pulled one of the black plastic chairs closer to the bed.

As if realising he couldn't escape the inevitable, Roy Gallagher said, 'OK, OK, b-but,' he stammered, 'I'll only talk to you.' He jabbed a finger close to Tom and avoided Hazel's eyes.

'I'll wait outside,' Hazel confirmed and left the cubicle.

Gallagher's shoulders drooped and he stared sideways as he sighed, seemingly comfortable now that it was just the two of them.

'So do you think you're ready to tell me what happened then?' Tom asked and sat down on the chair that Hazel had vacated.

'You have to understand something first.' His eyes pleaded and beads of sweat glistened on Gallagher's forehead. 'I don't make a habit of it but…' he stopped. 'Do you think you could ask if I could get a glass of water? I'm parched.'

Tom glanced up at the notice – *nil by mouth* – written above the bed.

'Sorry,' he pointed. 'You're not allowed.'

Gallagher turned and sighed on seeing the sign himself. 'She seemed alright, you know,' he said.

'Who did?'

'The lassie.' Gallagher avoided Tom's eyes then suddenly stared intently at him. 'You ken what it's like.' He spoke quietly.

'I'm not with you.'

'You're married, right?' Gallagher suggested. 'You ken what it's like.'

Tom shook his head slowly and his answer seemed to disappoint Gallagher, who began to fiddle with the corners of the blanket.

'Aye, well,' he corrected himself. 'I got mugged, plain and simple, alright. She took my wallet and my watch as well as my phone. All she left was my work ID on my lanyard which is how you lot found out who I was. I don't want any fuss. It was my own fault, so I just want to forget about it.'

Tom thought his reluctance had more to do with stopping his wife from finding out his secret. Saying he'd been mugged would elicit more sympathy, Tom imagined.

'Was this the girl that did it?' Tom held up a photo of Molly Barker.

When a look of recognition didn't instantly cross his face, he asked, 'Did she happen to give you a name?'

'Aye, she did. She said her name was Molly.'

Chapter Forty-Three

Andrea's conversation with Craig Douglas's neighbour had been enlightening. He had not been honest about what had happened to his leg and she felt this dishonesty called into question his relationship with the girls who apparently came and went at all hours of the day and night. She was no longer willing to believe his reasons were altruistic as he claimed. He'd not broken his ankle in a car accident at all. He'd got into a fight with some guy that turned up, a man much bigger than Craig who had given him a hiding before leaving him with a warning to leave someone alone. His neighbour hadn't heard who he was supposed to leave alone but the man was angry enough to break Craig's ankle.

She knocked on Craig's door and waited. Billy Flynn had texted to say he was on his way because Hazel wanted them to ask Douglas about his connection to Sean Cooper in light of the phone connection discovery. Andrea wondered if it was Cooper that had left him with the broken ankle. But why? How were the two men connected?

Andrea rapped the letterbox loudly and leaned her ear close to the door. There was definitely movement inside. She hammered her fist on the door, harder this time, leaving him in no doubt she was there.

'Craig, it's DC Andrea Graham, can you open the door please.'

The door behind her squealed open and a concerned face peered out. 'Is everything alright, dear?'

'Yes, yes,' Andrea said. 'You go back inside.'

'OK.' The old woman looked worried but closed the door as she'd been told.

Andrea exhaled loudly and rapped the letterbox as well as hammering on the door.

'Craig,' she called out and lowered her face to the letterbox. She opened it. 'Craig! Could you come to the door?'

A loud crash sounded from inside, like smashing glass.

'Shit,' Andrea exclaimed and hammered again. She tried the handle. The door was unlocked. She knew she should really wait for Billy. 'Hello, Craig,' she shouted out and pushed the door open. 'It's DC Graham.' She swallowed down the fear that was fighting against the exhilaration she was feeling.

There was someone in the living room and it sounded like the place was being trashed. She couldn't wait for Billy.

'Craig, are you alright?' she called out and crept deeper into the hallway.

Noise from behind her made Andrea turn round to see Craig Douglas's elderly neighbour peering out again. As she waved her hand to tell her to go back inside, she saw the old woman's eyes widen and a dark shadow creep up behind her. Andrea turned, then— nothing. The whole world went black.

Craig Douglas had thought he could run from this but staring down at the ancient dog struggling to keep up with him he knew he couldn't leave. So he did the only thing he could do, the right thing, and he turned back. He'd have to face whatever consequences came from the decision.

The sound of Mrs Patel's screams made Craig hobble as best he could up the flight of stairs.

'What happened?' he cried out, horrified to see the detective lying out cold on the floor in his hallway, the little dog frantically jumping up and barking. 'Have you called an ambulance?' he asked and got down awkwardly next to her. He leaned his fingers to her neck, praying he'd find a pulse. 'Yes,' he whispered in relief. He leaned down and rested his ear just above her mouth to make sure she was breathing. 'Thank God.'

The sound of sirens was a beautiful thing. Andrea, he remembered her name was. Craig patted her cheek.

'Andrea, can you hear me?'

Strange moaning grumbles came from her lips and Craig fell to the floor in relief.

'Poor girl was here to ask about you and those girls,' Mrs Patel shouted at him. 'If you hadn't lied to her, she wouldn't be lying there.'

Before Craig could answer, Billy Flynn surged towards them.

'Andrea,' he cried out. 'What's happened to her?' he asked Craig Douglas firmly. 'Go over there, against the wall,' he instructed him and dropped down next to his stricken colleague.

'Wait a minute, I just got back and found her like this,' Craig tried to plead.

'I said, against the wall!' Billy shouted, causing Craig to get up quickly and limp away, leaning his hands against the bedroom door.

'I just got back,' he repeated, 'and she was lying there.' He pointed at Mrs Patel. 'She'll tell you.'

Billy checked to make sure Andrea was breathing. 'Have you called an ambulance?'

'Yes! I mean Mrs Patel called one, didn't you?' Craig snapped in his neighbour's direction, grateful to see her nod her head. 'Now do you want me to go and put the dog in the kitchen out the way or am I still not allowed to move?'

Billy considered his suggestion after pushing the inquisitive poodle away for the umpteenth time.

'Get rid of the dog,' he snarled. 'But put it in there.' He pointed to the bedroom right in front of them. 'Stay where I can see you,' he demanded.

Andrea's eyes blinked a couple of times before they peeled open slowly, and she attempted to get up.

'Woah there,' Billy said and helped her up into a sitting position. He frowned at the confusion on her face. 'Let me help you.'

Craig spotted a smashed vase under the table next to his bedroom door.

'Looks like someone hit her with that.' He nodded to the floor.

Billy turned and glared then focussed on Andrea.

'There's an ambulance on its way,' Billy said. 'How many fingers am I holding up?' He held his hand close to her face.

'What?' Andrea's puzzled expression was concerning. She stared past Billy at Craig then round the room. 'Where am I?' she asked and touched the back of her head before screwing up her face in obvious pain.

'So you're saying you came back and found her like this?' Billy asked.

'Tell him, Mrs Patel,' Craig pleaded.

'Aye, he's just got here, same as you,' the elderly woman said.

Billy shot a glance at Craig then turned to look at the old woman.

'Right, you go back inside, and someone will come and take a proper statement from you soon,' he instructed Mrs Patel.

'But—' she tried to protest.

'Please,' Billy said.

'Don't you want to know who did that to your colleague?' Mrs Patel added.

'Did you see what happened?' Billy urged.

'I did.'

'Do you know who attacked her?'

'Ask him, it was one of his,' the old woman said triumphantly.

'What are you talking about?' Craig interrupted.

'That one with red hair, she came at that lovely detective and whacked her over the head then ran for the hills. She should be locked up.' Mrs Patel tutted. 'Snarling like a mad woman, she was.'

Billy stared at Craig. 'I think you've got some explaining to do, mate.'

Chapter Forty-Four

'I told him already.' Craig nodded to where Billy Flynn had his back to them as he stood in the kitchen doorway talking to Tom. 'I came back and found Mrs Patel in a right state, standing over her. I checked to see if she was breathing then I was told an ambulance was coming.'

'Where were you when DC Graham was attacked then?' Hazel asked, extremely concerned by the confused state she'd seen Andrea in before she was driven off to be assessed in A and E. 'Why was Molly here alone?'

Craig dropped his gaze to the floor and flopped down on the sofa, the sound of high-pitched barking chirping from the bedroom.

'Can I at least let him out? He'll just keep yapping if I don't.'

Hazel considered his request. The dog's racket was irritating the life out of her too. She kept an eye on Craig as he opened the bedroom door. From inside, a tiny black poodle with a silver muzzle ran towards her, leaping and yapping at her leg.

'Spot, get here,' Craig shouted and lifted the tiny dog onto his lap. 'I'm sorry, he'll calm down in a minute.'

'I think you and me need to start again, don't we?' Hazel suggested.

'I guess so.'

'So…'

Craig reached over and slid open the drawer in the coffee table. He pulled out an envelope and pushed it across the table towards Hazel.

'In there. That's why Molly was here and why she gets to come and go whenever she likes.'

Hazel removed the short, scribbled letter out of the stained envelope and started to read the contents.

'Hazel,' Tom yelled. 'Over there, look!'

Hazel dropped the letter as she followed the direction of his gaze.

'Jesus Christ,' she exclaimed. She had to think fast. 'Don't move!' she ordered Craig.

'What is it?' Craig ignored her and raced to the window. The sight that greeted him made his stomach churn. It was a struggle to stop himself from running to the bathroom to throw up. 'My God!' He rubbed his hand roughly back and forth over his cropped hair as he paced. 'Get out of my way, I'm going down there. She'll listen to me,' he snapped and tried to shoulder his way past Billy Flynn.

'No you don't, mate,' Billy told him firmly.

'I'm not your mate,' Craig snapped back and tried again to get past, until Billy had him face-down on an armchair with his arm behind his back. 'Let me talk to her. She won't listen to someone she doesn't know,' he urged.

'Billy, leave it,' Tom shouted. 'Come on.'

Billy glared at Craig then dropped his grip and followed Tom.

Craig couldn't believe this was happening and wasn't able to stop the tears that started to pour down his face.

–

'Molly, my name's Hazel.' Hazel gently pressed a hand against her own chest. 'Why don't you throw down that knife and come with me so we can talk.'

Molly Barker brandished the blade in front of her, her eyes wide and staring.

'One of us should go over there,' Billy Flynn said anxiously.

'Hazel knows what she's doing,' Tom said, trying to sound more confident than he felt. Molly Barker was capable of anything, and Hazel was standing out there all alone.

Behind them, the river thrashed angrily past, currents swirling and spinning at speed. Grey clouds were moving fast, pushed along by the strong autumn winds, dark and threatening. Traffic on Tay Street had been brought to an abrupt stop by the sight of the distraught young girl standing in the middle of the road with a ten-inch blade in her hand. She was pointing it right at Hazel. An armed police team had been called and were en route from Dundee, but Hazel prayed it wouldn't come to that.

'Molly, sweetheart,' Hazel held her hands out so that she could see they were empty. 'It's just you and me.'

Hazel edged forward slowly, moving barely inches then stopping.

'Stay back!' Molly screamed and waved the knife towards her.

'OK, OK,' Hazel held up her hands. 'I won't come any closer.'

Molly lowered the knife slowly. 'Stay there.'

'I will, I promise.'

'You don't get it, do you?' Molly cried. 'How hard it is to be me.' She tapped the blade of the knife against her temple. 'In here.'

'OK, OK,' Hazel said anxiously. 'Be careful, just put the knife down and we can talk about—'

'Talk!' Molly interrupted her. 'What good does that do?'

Hazel had no idea what to say. Her mouth had dried out, from the adrenaline, probably. Her mind had gone blank. The sound of Hazel's phone ringing startled Molly.

'I'm sorry,' Hazel called out. 'I'm sorry, I'll switch it off, see.' She held the phone up before sliding it away from her. 'See, just you and me. I promise.'

Electricity rippled through the atmosphere and the sky above them darkened before huge drops of freezing cold rain started to batter down on them, so hard the thick drops bounced off the concrete. Within minutes they were both soaked to the skin, rain dripping off their eyelashes.

'Come on, Molly, let me take you somewhere to get warm.' Hazel screwed up her face against the deluge. Her teeth chattered in the cold.

'It's too late,' Molly shouted against the noise of the rain slamming against the tarmac.

'It's not too late,' Hazel called back, edging forward slowly, slowly, carefully. One step at a time. 'Come on,' she said. 'Give me the knife.'

The struggle to speak against the deteriorating conditions was painful but Hazel couldn't give up on her. The echoes of flat-footed geese above them caught their attention, seemingly distracting Molly briefly. This was Hazel's chance. She took another step closer. Then another. She was almost there. Almost close enough to take the knife.

'No!' Hazel screamed and raced to Molly as she sliced a huge line into one wrist then the other, blood pouring onto the ground at her feet, joining the puddles of rain as they raced in rivulets towards the drains.

Chapter Forty-Five

'Dawn, what are you doing here?' Rachel said when she spotted her walking in the front door of the community kitchen.

With one eye on the time, she feared she'd miss the meeting that the letter had warned her to attend. Rachel didn't want to find out what consequences would occur if she didn't. She felt the guilt that she'd not told Dawn she'd seen Molly hit her. She feared Dawn would be able to see right through her.

'Is she here?' Dawn asked, her eyes red from crying.

'No she's not,' Rachel told her and guided her away from a group of men who were staring at her. 'Come through to the kitchen. I'll make you a cup of tea.'

'I had a phone call,' Dawn blurted out. 'They said Molly was here.'

Rachel frowned. 'Who told you that? Molly hasn't been here all day.'

'I don't know, she didn't give me her name. She just… oh Rachel, what has she done?' Dawn's face dissolved into floods of tears. 'That detective said…' She couldn't say anything else that made any sense.

All Rachel could do was hug her and listen while she mumbled incoherently between sobs. She ran her fingers over the letter in her trouser pocket. If she didn't hurry she would be late. She would have to think of something, and fast. She handed her keys to Dawn.

'Why don't you go back to my place and make us a pot of tea. I'll go and grab us a fish supper?'

'But—' Dawn began.

'It's alright, I'll not be long.' Rachel smiled. She kissed the top of Dawn's head then watched her head in the direction of Canal Street.

She hated herself for lying to her friend like that, but she had no choice.

'Can I have a taxi just now please?' she said into her phone. 'From the community kitchen at the Lade.' Rachel listened while the operator confirmed her details. 'Where am I going? I'm going to St Magdalene's Hill.'

–

'I'm sorry I took so long,' the taxi driver said as Rachel got into his car. 'Tay Street has been closed because of an incident. Couldn't tell you what's happened. I had to go round the long way.'

'It's fine.' Rachel checked her watch, hoping that it really would be fine. 'Don't worry about it.'

'St Magdalene's Hill, is it?'

Rachel nodded. 'Yes, that's right,' she replied and dropped a quick text to explain to Dawn why she'd be late. Not the real reason, obviously.

'Miserable weather for a walk,' the taxi driver said.

'Mm, yes, I suppose,' Rachel replied, unsure what else she could say.

'Are you meeting friends?'

Rachel wished this nosy old man would shut up.

'Erm, yes, that's right,' she lied and pulled a ten-pound note from her purse. 'Keep the change.'

'Thanks very much.' The driver smiled as he tucked the note into his shirt pocket. 'You take care now' He nodded, then indicated out of the Woodland Walk car park.

Rachel sighed as the feeling that she was being watched swam over her. She spun slowly to check for peering eyes but found none. Her mind was playing tricks on her. It felt like the whole world knew her secret. She'd been so careful, and Rachel knew Dawn would never have told anyone. The only loose cannon in her circle was Molly. But she wouldn't have betrayed Rachel like that, not even during her darkest days. Would she?

Chapter Forty-Six

'Here.' Billy handed Hazel a mug. 'I've put three sugars in it, for the shock.'

'Thanks,' Hazel said quietly with a sigh. 'Are you two OK?' She stared between Billy and Tom.

'We're fine,' Tom told her. 'It's you we're worried about.'

'How is she?' Hazel asked and took a swig before screwing up her face. 'God, that's sweet.'

'I did say,' Billy smiled.

Hazel tapped his arm. 'I love you, Billy Flynn.'

'I know,' Billy grinned before he walked away to answer his phone.

'Are you OK?' Tom asked her.

Hazel nodded. 'Yes, I'm fine, don't worry.'

'Molly's arms are to be stitched but she'll be fine.' Tom informed her.

'She'll be fine physically maybe but...' Hazel was interrupted by Billy calling over.

'There's a man downstairs,' he said. 'Says he needs to speak to the detective from the TV.'

Hazel looked at Tom.

'That sounds like you,' he said. 'Do you want me to go instead? You take a few minutes to get your head together?'

'No, it's fine, I can go,' Hazel assured him. 'Besides, this tea is undrinkable.' She handed the mug to him and headed down to talk to a witness who had come to talk to her following the press briefing he'd seen earlier.

–

'Mr Gillingham, I'm DCI Todd, would you like to follow me?'

The man stood and Hazel was struck immediately by his height. He must be at least six foot four, perhaps even five but he was slim with it, wiry even. She felt like a dwarf standing next to him.

'Please take a seat,' she said as the light blinked on in the interview room.

'Thanks,' Gillingham replied, biting the nails on one hand as he pulled the chair out from the table.

'So, you told my colleague you have information for me.'

The wiry man nodded. 'It's about that girl you're looking for.'

'Mm?' Hazel chose not to tell him they already had Molly in custody. His witness statement would be helpful when they were preparing the case against her. She clicked her pen.

'Yes. I thought she was alright,' he began. 'I've never had any trouble with any of them before. Not that I make a habit of it, you understand,' he corrected himself.

Hazel examined him. The smart suit. The short, neat haircut. A businessman. Probably late thirties.

'I'm not here to judge.'

'Yes, well, she...' He hesitated, seemingly having difficulty in finding the words. He rolled up his shirt sleeve and pointed to a long, red line on his wrist.

238

'Who did that to you?'

'She did, the girl you're looking for,' he admitted as he rolled his sleeve back down, pinching the button on the cuff shut with ease. 'She said her name was Molly. That's who you're looking for, isn't it?'

'When did this happen?'

'About two weeks ago,' he told her. 'For obvious reasons you're the first person I've told.'

She wrote the words *two weeks ago* on her notepad and circled them again and again until the pen almost ripped the paper. How much more damage had Molly done since then? Damage they didn't know about, yet. Who was supposed to be taking care of such a vulnerable young girl? Hazel planned to talk to the drug and alcohol team. They had some explaining to do.

Hazel scribbled down the man's contact details and told him there was a possibility he'd be asked to testify in any future case against Molly Barker.

'Wait a minute, I never said I'd be willing to do that!'

'That could be a long way off yet, but we'll be in touch,' Hazel said and thanked him for his statement then escorted him back towards the exit.

She made her way back to her office where she was intercepted again by DI Black, the detective who'd tried to speak to her earlier.

'Hazel, I realise you're busy, but do you have time to talk now?'

'Hi, yes and listen, I am so sorry about having to bail earlier.' Hazel smiled but was confused by the cool response it received. 'Come on up,' she added, this time without even the hint of a smile.

Chapter Forty-Seven

'Hello,' Kelly Tate beamed.

Puzzled to see the girl standing at the foot of her hospital bed, Andrea frowned.

'Er hello,' she replied.

'Ouch, that looks nasty.' Kelly nodded to the bruise on Andrea's forehead.

Andrea nodded. 'It stings a bit.' She smiled thinly. 'What are you doing here?'

'I had an appointment with the drug team and I over-heard one of them saying Molly had been brought in.'

'Has she?' Andrea said brightly. She seemed to have missed so much since being whacked over the head. 'When? I mean, how?'

Kelly shrugged and tucked her dirty blonde hair behind her ears, the tips skimming her neck. 'They wouldn't let me see her, so I don't know. I should have known they wouldn't let me see her really, though.'

'Pass me my bag, will you?' Andrea pointed to the chair next to the bed.

Kelly laid the leather satchel on the bed and Andrea snatched open the buckles, grabbing her phone. She scrolled and pressed Billy Flynn's number. Disappointed to hear it go to voicemail she texted him a short message.

'Do the police really think it was Molly that killed those men? I know she's got a temper and sure she can be unpredictable, but really?'

'We go where the evidence points us, Kelly,' Andrea informed her.

'What happened to you?' Kelly quizzed her. 'Why are you in A and E?'

Andrea reached up, allowing her fingers to gently skim the back of her head. 'Och, it's nothing,' she said, not keen to tell Kelly too much. Given the girl's inquisitive nature, she figured Kelly would find out for herself at some point.

Andrea's ringtone rang out and she'd answered it before much of the song could be heard.

'Billy,' she chirped, waving to Kelly who was retreating quietly, nodding as Kelly whispered that she hoped she felt better soon. 'What's going on? I've just been told Molly has been brought in.'

-

Kelly Tate headed towards the A and E exit, tugging her rucksack higher over her shoulder. She wondered where she would sleep tonight then heard shouting from a small cubicle nearby. It sounded like Molly's voice above the others. At least Molly didn't have to worry about where she would lay her head tonight.

Grateful that it had stopped raining, Kelly tried to zip up her jacket against the bitter cold evening. She'd have to take her chances with the squat tonight. Staying at the shelter was out of the question. She owed too many people too much money. Rachel would have too much going on to help her either. Molly's mum would be needing her.

'Oh fer God's sake,' she muttered when the zip split right open as she pulled it up.

Kelly's stomach rumbled and she sighed. It seemed she would be popping into Craig Douglas's again. She knew he'd be more than willing to help her.

Chapter Forty-Eight

'I'm investigating Rick's disappearance.'

Hazel almost laughed and if her colleague's expression hadn't been so serious she might have.

'I've told Cara already,' Hazel said plainly. 'He's probably off shagging some new lassie.'

Why was her expression so serious?

'Rick's bank transactions have been checked and there's been no movement on his cards, debit or credit, for three days.'

Hazel frowned. 'So he's been paying cash,' she shrugged. 'To cover his dirty, cheating tracks.' She heard her words exit her mouth with the venom she felt. 'Look, I'm sorry but the truth is, Cara should have known what Rick was like before shacking up with him.'

'His phone has been switched off for the same period of time.'

'Well, he's not going to be wanting interruptions, is he?' Hazel scoffed. 'You seem to be forgetting, I *know* him. I know exactly what Rick's like. This is a pattern he's been following for the past twenty-five years.'

'It broke your heart when your marriage ended, didn't it, Hazel?'

'What's that got to do with this?' Hazel was incredulous.

'You seem angry.'

'What?' Hazel snapped back. 'If I'm irritated it's because Cara has you wasting police time looking for that cheating scumbag.'

'When did you last speak to your ex-husband?'

Hazel knew exactly what was being implied. She curled her fingers into a fist. If she didn't displace the anger that was growing inside her, it would explode from her tongue, spraying volcanic venom into this woman's face.

'The last time I spoke to Rick was when we signed documents for the sale of our home.' She had to focus; remaining calm was imperative.

'When was that?'

'August the sixteenth.'

Her words were noted in the woman's notebook.

'Have you spoken to him on the phone or on social media since? Have there been any emails between the two of you?'

Hazel shook her head, tempted to laugh at the ridiculousness of this. 'Nope.'

'Do you have any idea where your ex-husband might be?'

Hazel took a huge breath. 'Nope.'

If she had said they wanted to search her flat then Hazel would have exploded. As it was, they left it at that, seemingly satisfied with her answers but she was instructed to let them know if she heard from him. Hazel picked up the empty mug on her desk and almost launched it at the office door as it closed behind her unwanted visitor. Enough was enough. It was time to give Rick a piece of her mind. It was one thing to muck Cara about, she deserved it, but it was quite another to bring his bullshit and dump it at Hazel's door. She was done with all that, with him. She dialled his mobile number from memory.

She had deleted it from her contacts weeks ago. When it went straight to voicemail she was tempted to scream obscenities at him but resisted. A text would do.

> You better get your cheating arse back home. You've been reported missing, and Cara is going out of her mind with worry!

There were so many other things she wanted to say but she quickly pressed send instead of adding anything else. She tossed her phone onto the desk and gave in to the tears that were lurking behind her eyes, waiting for their chance to escape. How could he still have this effect on her after all this time?

Chapter Forty-Nine

There it was. The silver BMW. Just like the letter said. Rachel had got to the car park with barely moments to spare. If they wanted money to keep her secret, they'd be out of luck because she didn't have much. Not that she hadn't been offered money over the years for the rights to her biography. Her biography. That wouldn't make pleasant reading. Her phone rang and she stopped to take it out of her pocket. No caller ID. It was probably just some scam call, so she pressed the decline option and stuffed the phone back in her pocket. She walked on, the cold wind biting her face.

The geese overhead startled Rachel momentarily. Her nerves were so on edge, but the birds were a spectacular sight. Rachel was in awe of how they remembered the route, year after year and how each bird seemed to know where they should be. They even seemed to talk to each other as they flew, like they cared about every single member of the flock. Walking in that area was something she'd enjoyed almost immediately on moving to Perth. It was Samiera who'd told her about the place and the views were every bit as spectacular as she'd described. With far-reaching views across Perthshire towards Dundee, it was stunning. But tonight, with the car park at dusk, bathed in the light of the solitary street lamp, it took on a very different, darker atmosphere. With nothing but the sound of the distant geese and the dripping of the rain falling from the soaking wet leaves, heavy from the recent deluge, she felt alone. Alone and vulnerable suddenly. Her phone rang again. This time she answered it.

'Hello.'

'I'm really pleased to see that you decided to come.' The voice on the line came out in a whisper, so quietly Rachel couldn't tell if it was male or female.

'Who is this?' Rachel spun around, scanning the area for someone watching but she saw nobody.

'You'll find out soon enough.'

Then the caller hung up without saying anything else.

'Hello?' Rachel called out. 'Hello!'

Shivers ran down her spine. Who was this person? She should turn back. This wasn't safe.

A text chirped out, making Rachel jump.

> Not far now.

Her heart thudded hard in her chest. She should run. Every fibre of her being was telling her to run but she couldn't. She was being propelled forward towards the BMW by a force she couldn't explain. Another text.

> You're getting warmer.

There was a man in the driver's seat and he was staring straight ahead. Rachel didn't recognise him. She expected him to turn and look at her as she got closer, but he didn't; he remained still and staring towards the orchard

247

in front of the car park. Was he waiting for a sign? Was there someone hiding in the trees?

Rachel glanced to her left and peered, trying to make out a shape, a figure, anything but there was nothing. She got closer, reaching out her hand to knock on the window. Maybe it wasn't him she was meant to be meeting? Maybe she'd got this all wrong.

Before her knuckles could make contact with the glass, Rachel's stomach lurched at the gruesome sight in front of her. The man's lips were blue, and his skin was mottled with pinprick dots in the whites of his eyes. But it was his abdomen that made her turn and vomit on the ground. A gaping hole where his stomach should be was covered with maggots. It was then that she noticed the amount of flies hovering close to the vehicle.

Rachel spat out the last drops of vomit-streaked spit and rubbed her mouth clean. Struggling to catch her breath, she dialled the first number that came to mind.

'Please, you have to come,' Rachel begged as all the strength melted in her legs that now failed to keep her upright. 'Something terrible has happened,' she gasped, falling to her knees, struggling to catch her breath. 'It's all my fault,' she sobbed. 'It's all my fault.'

Chapter Fifty

Hazel pulled into the car park of St Magdalene's Hill woodland park, horrified by what Rachel had called to say she'd discovered. Nobody should have to see that, not even the police. The shock must have been horrendous. She'd arranged for an ambulance to attend to Rachel separately, just to be sure she was OK. Shock did strange things to people. It could even cause heart attacks and strokes to occur hours after the event.

Rachel had told her the victim was a man, sitting bolt upright in a silver BMW with a huge stab wound in his stomach. Hazel had to park a little way back because a large area had been taped off as a crime scene. A crowd had gathered at the edge of the tape and Hazel asked a couple of the uniforms to keep them back. She ducked under the tape and nodded to Tom who looked at her strangely.

Hazel frowned at him then turned to walk up the slight incline towards the parked car. When she caught sight of the vehicle, she noticed the way the assembled officers were staring at her, muttering amongst themselves. Then she could hear Tom's voice behind her. He was calling her name, but it sounded like his words were being batted away by the bubble that had swallowed her up. She was sure she heard someone say. *She shouldn't be here. Why hasn't someone told her?*

Hazel kept walking but something wasn't right. She was running now, but it felt as if she were in a nightmare; her legs propelled her forward painfully slowly, like they were trapped in treacle. No matter how hard she tried, her progress was non-existent.

'Hazel, no, stop!' Tom's voice again. This time his voice was closer.

Then she saw it. Hazel heard a sound. A low, guttural growl, like a dying animal. Her legs gave way beneath her. There was a distant scream that she realised must have been her.

'I'm so sorry,' Tom dropped to his knees and held her, squeezing her close to his body.

Hazel couldn't speak. She looked at Tom's face, at the tears streaming out of his brown eyes, pouring over his dark cheeks and dripping onto the collar of his perfectly pressed white shirt. That'll stain if he doesn't wash it right out, she thought. Her mind was struggling to process the situation, seemingly protecting her from the trauma. It was the bright invasion of the police crime scene flood-lights that reminded her she was present in the moment. Lighting up the scene whether she wanted to see it or not.

'Someone get a paramedic,' Tom called over to a huddle of people standing a few feet away.

'Tom.'

'I'm here,' he told her. 'I'm here.'

Hazel pulled out of his grip and tried to stand. She pushed away Tom's attempts to usher her away from the car. Her body was numb. She couldn't feel her legs.

She stared at the man's face. He was a stranger to her. His expression was blank and motionless. Hazel's eyes drifted to the huge gaping hole in his abdomen where the maggots were squirming and fighting for food, feasting on the contents of his intestines that were protruding from his gut.

'Rick,' she mumbled.

She felt a blanket being swept round her shoulders and when she turned, she held Tom's eyes, still glistening with tears.

'Come on,' he said softly. 'Let's get you out of here.'

'What am I going to say to Cara?' Hazel asked as he helped her away from the car. She took one last look behind her and then repeated the same thing over and over. 'What am I going to tell Cara? What am I going to tell Cara?'

Chapter Fifty-One

'Is she OK? Shouldn't she be sent home after—'

'Shouldn't she be what, Andrea?' Hazel snapped. 'I thought you were in hospital.'

'I, erm, they discharged me, said I didn't need to be admitted.'

Andrea stared at Billy who shrugged gently as he laid a mug of tea in front of Hazel.

'I've put—'

'I know, sugar, for the shock,' Hazel interrupted him.

'Sorry,' Billy said.

Tom nodded towards the incident room door, hoping Andrea and Billy would take the hint, which they did. He watched their backs until they'd disappeared towards the flight of stairs at the end of the corridor, noticing that neither of them uttered a single word as they walked.

'Hey,' he said.

'Hey yourself,' Hazel replied and sipped from the mug of tea Billy had made, wincing at the sweetness.

'Drink it,' Tom ordered.

'It's a glass of bloody wine I need,' Hazel sighed. 'Or a brandy.'

She flopped down on the chair behind her desk.

'You shouldn't be here,' Tom told her. 'Come on, I'll drive you home.'

Hazel waved away his offer. 'No, I'd rather be here.' She sipped again and spat the mouthful back in the mug. 'God, this is shit.'

A wave of exhaustion spread across Hazel's whole body now that the adrenaline had worn off. Her arms and legs felt heavy, and she wanted to curl up and go to sleep. But Rachel was waiting downstairs to give a statement.

'Daly said it's OK for me to stay,' she added. 'In case you're wondering.'

'I wasn't, but OK.' Tom offered her the ghost of a smile. 'That doesn't stop me worrying about you.'

'You get off home, I'll be alright.'

'Indeed I will not!' Tom argued. 'I'm going nowhere, lady!'

That made Hazel smile, if somewhat briefly. 'You're a good kid, Tom.'

Tom laughed gently. 'Thanks. I'll remember you said that when I turn forty-six next month.'

'Did that really just happen, Tom?' Her eyebrows dipped, as she looked intently at him, seeming to search his face for the answer.

He nodded. 'I'm afraid so.'

'Because for a minute there, I thought… I wondered if, maybe…'

'I know,' Tom whispered.

The silence that fell between them was broken abruptly by Hazel's phone. She picked it up from the desk and her heart sank. Cara. She looked at Tom and held up the screen so he could see it.

'Do you want me to—'

Hazel shook her head. 'No,' she replied and pressed the 'Decline Call' button.

'Do you want me to go and tell her about Rick?' he asked.

Hazel did consider his offer momentarily. It was kind of him and probably the most sensible thing under the circumstances.

—

Not only had she declined his offer, but now she found herself standing outside Cara's front door, to deliver the news in person.

Chapter Fifty-Two

Rachel looked up when she heard the interview room door opening. Seeing that man's body had been horrific but the fact it had been a man that DCI Todd knew was awful. She'd told them about the texts and had handed her phone over to be examined by forensics to see if they could get any details from it that might help trace whoever had sent them. The same person who'd done those unspeakable things to that poor man. But Rachel couldn't help thinking she was no different to them. She'd been so stupid. She should have told the police as soon as she'd read that letter. Dawn must be going out of her mind, not knowing where Rachel had got to.

'Sorry to keep you waiting,' Tom said as he closed the door and took a seat opposite. He slid her phone across the table to her. 'We've taken what we need from this so you can have it back.'

'Thank you.'

Rachel snatched it up and was alarmed to see six notifications. Five were missed calls from Dawn and one was a text reminder about an appointment with Samiera the following day. Nothing from whoever it was that had lured her up there to make that gruesome discovery.

'Tell me what happened tonight. In your own words.'

Rachel took a breath. In her own words. Were there even words at all to describe it?

'I shouldn't have gone up there, I know that.' She swallowed hard against the swell of emotion building in her chest. 'If I'd called you first then…'

'Why didn't you call us?' Tom asked plainly.

'Because I'm an old fool.' Rachel sighed, dropping her head into her hands 'I thought I could stop my secret from being exposed if I just went along and met with them, whoever they are.'

'Do you have any idea who they are?'

Rachel's head drooped again and she felt his eyes bore into her, studying her carefully.

'I have a theory.' Her thin smile hid the pain. She allowed herself another deep breath before sharing it with him. 'It was Molly. It had to be. Nobody else knew except me, Dawn, Molly and the probation people.'

Tom realised quickly that Rachel wasn't aware of developments.

'Molly has been in custody for the past three hours. She couldn't have been the one who was texting you,' Tom informed her.

Part of Rachel was relieved. This was proof. It couldn't have been her. She couldn't have done those terrible things.

'Then why is she still in custody?' Rachel asked. 'Surely this proves it couldn't have been her? She can't be your killer.'

Tom felt bad that he had to tell her.

'I'm sorry but Molly is still our most likely suspect.'

'But…' Rachel pleaded.

'The man you found at St Magdalene's Hill has been dead for at least three days.'

'But those texts… she couldn't have sent them.'

'Red hairs have been taken from more than one crime scene.'

'But you know it's possible that she'd had sex with one or more of them at some point.' Rachel felt sick thinking of the depths that Molly had sunk to, to feed her habit. 'Her hair could have been transferred to their bodies then – their living bodies, I mean. You have to admit that's possible, don't you?'

'Molly's fingerprints are in all of the vehicles.'

'But…' Rachel jabbed a finger towards him. 'If they'd picked her up for sex then of course her fingerprints would be there.' She was becoming desperate. Then she thought of something. 'Have you at least got a murder weapon?'

Tom nodded and before he could answer, Rachel persisted.

'Are her prints on that?' she urged.

Tom had to admit that they weren't, and he agreed with Rachel's suggestion that it was strange. He told her about the other witnesses who'd come forward, some more reluctantly than others.

'Have you told Molly's mum yet?' Rachel asked.

'My colleagues are on their way to her now.'

'She's not there,' Rachel admitted. 'She's at my flat. I'll tell her. It would be better coming from me.'

Rachel was grateful that DI Newton had agreed, and he promised that he'd keep them updated with developments once Molly had been examined by the doctors. He alluded to the fact that this might take time, given the state of Molly's mental as well as physical health. Before she left she asked Tom to pass on a message for her.

'Please tell Hazel how sorry I am.'

'I will, I'm sure she'll appreciate that,' Tom replied and closed the station door.

Chapter Fifty-Three

'Hazel!' Cara exclaimed.

'Can I come in?' Hazel asked quietly.

'Yes, yes, of course.' Cara ushered her inside and closed the front door after them. 'DI Black said she'd spoken to you. I'm sorry about that but…'

'Cara, could you sit down a minute?' Hazel asked as gently as she could manage without breaking down.

'What is it?'

Hazel stared at Cara's face. Once she'd said the words there was no going back. Cara's world would crumble.

'Hazel, you're scaring me,' Cara said.

Hazel couldn't do it. She couldn't say the words. Instead, all she could do was allow the tears to trickle out, slowly at first before a torrent was flowing down her face.

'I'm sorry,' she whispered.

'What? But you said he was… he was just…'

'I'm so sorry,' Hazel murmured and reached out to take Cara's hand.

Cara pulled away. 'No, no.' She covered her mouth with her hands. 'No.'

'Cara, I'm—'

'Get out!' Cara yelled.

'Cara…'

'I said get out!'

Standing on the doorstep after having had the front door slammed in her face, Hazel decided to get a couple of night shift uniforms to check on Cara. There was nothing she could do for her now. She didn't blame her for being so angry. Hadn't Hazel told her that she was worrying over nothing? She'd told Cara that Rick was cheating on her, the way he'd done to her. The guilt was cutting her to the bone.

On the drive home it was hard to tell what was rain on the windscreen and what were tears. Everything looked wet.

As she pulled up outside her block she was grateful to see someone standing under the light of the streetlamp.

'Tom.'

'I didn't think you should be alone tonight.' He patted the sports bag slung over his shoulder.

Hazel locked her car and fell into his arms.

'God, Tom, it was awful. She hates me.'

'I'm sure she doesn't hate you,' Tom tried to reassure her as they walked into the building. 'She's hurting, just like you are.'

'But I've said some terrible things to her about him,' Hazel said as she poured the two of them a glass of white wine.

Tom took a sip, then licked spilt wine off his thumb. 'But he hurt you. Betrayed you in the worst way possible. Let's not forget that. Cara, too. She was your best friend, and he was your husband.'

'If only I could,' Hazel scoffed and guzzled her wine. 'What did Rachel have to say for herself?'

'Tried to convince me it couldn't possibly be Molly.'

'She's known the girl since she was a baby,' Hazel shrugged. 'It can't be easy for her.' She sucked a breath of air in through her teeth. 'Can you imagine learning something like that? That someone you've thought of as family, like a daughter even, is a killer?'

'A killer like her,' Tom suggested.

'Do you think she was doing it to impress Rachel in some way?'

'Who knows? I doubt it. I think she was too far gone to think clearly,' Tom said.

Hazel moved to the window and started to pull the curtains shut. Movement in the corner of her eye caught her attention. She screwed up her eyes to see better. It must have been her imagination.

–

The figure that had been watching the two detectives through Hazel's living room window for the past five minutes ducked down behind the white van parked across the street from Hazel's block.

That was close, they decided. They would have to be more careful in future.

Chapter Fifty-Four

Hazel knew that getting in to talk to Molly that morning would be difficult, but this was proving impossible. Didn't they realise what she'd done? Persuading Daly to let her stay on the case had been easier. She wasn't pleased by the response she was getting from the charge nurse on the acute ward Molly had been brought to.

'Dr Kirk has left strict instructions that Molly is not to receive visitors while she goes through detox.'

Hazel would happily have smacked the smug grin off the perky nurse's face, had that been both legal and socially acceptable.

'I'm not sure you understand the seriousness of—'

'Dr Kirk.' The nurse ignored Hazel as a middle-aged woman dressed in a bright blue trouser suit arrived 'This detective says she needs to talk to Molly Barker.'

Dr Kirk stared at Hazel over the top of her red-framed glasses, her silver hair sticking up in more directions than Hazel imagined she'd intended before leaving for work that morning.

'Come through, we can talk in my office,' the plump, middle-aged woman said.

Hazel followed her but not before throwing a sarcastic grin at the young nurse.

'Thanks for seeing me, I appreciate it,' Hazel said and sat down on the chair that was pointed out to her.

'I think all I'm going to be able to do is disappoint you.' Dr Kirk removed her glasses and rubbed the bridge of her nose between her finger and thumb before slipping them back on. She flicked through a brown foolscap folder on her desk. 'Do you see this?' She held up a sheet of paper that had a long list on both the front and back.

'Uh huh.' Hazel wasn't sure what she was getting at.

'This is a list of people in this area waiting for detox treatment.' She took out another two sheets that were stapled together and tapped them with her finger. 'This one is full of people desperate for rehab which I just can't offer them.'

Hazel already knew there was a waiting list for drug and alcohol rehab in Tayside so that wasn't news. She wondered exactly where this conversation was going.

'With all due respect, what does this have to do with me asking to talk to Molly Barker?'

'Ah, yes, Molly.' Dr Kirk almost purred with excitement. 'Very interesting. Do you know she's the first female serial killer I've ever treated?'

Hazel felt sick and considered whether to tell this eccentric woman that one of the victims was her ex-husband but decided against it.

'So can I talk to Molly or not?'

She watched the doctor lift the handset on her desk phone without answering that question. Hazel sighed, resigned that she'd have to wait. Then – was that a glimmer of hope after all?

'OK, Molly has agreed that she will talk to you but I'm going to have to insist a social worker is present.'

Bloody great.

'How soon can that be arranged?'

As the doctor lifted her handset again, Hazel rubbed her forehead and sighed again. It looked like this was going to be a long day. She had arranged a team briefing for ten thirty but feared that would have to be rescheduled.

–

'Anybody fancy a coffee?' Tom asked.

Billy lifted his head up from staring at paperwork. 'No thanks, that stuff is shit. I'll take a tea.'

'Me too if you're making one,' Andrea chirped.

'Tell you what, I'll go across to Tim Hortons and treat us to some decent coffee. I might even throw in some doughnuts.'

'If you're buying, I'm in.' Billy grinned and tapped the pile of paper with the end of his pen. 'An extra-large latte will help me swallow this little lot a bit easier right enough.'

'Andrea, you in?' Tom beamed. 'Do you fancy a coffee? My treat.'

'That would be lovely, but I can go if you'd prefer,' she offered.

Tom smiled and grabbed his jacket from the back of his seat. 'No, you take it easy. I won't be long,' he told them and headed off.

The text from Hazel meant they had extra time to enjoy the coffees. He had offered to go up to Murray Royal to talk to Molly, but Hazel had declined his offer. Tom understood completely and she'd reassured him that she could handle it. But as it turned out, it wasn't going to be as simple as they'd all hoped.

Tom's phone rang but he didn't recognise the number.

'Hello, DI Newton.' Tom frowned, alarmed by the frantic rambling coming down the line at him. 'OK, OK, where are you?'

He listened to the caller tell him her location. He was relieved to discover that she was just a five-minute walk away, so he told her not to worry, he was on his way.

Chapter Fifty-Five

Hazel slung her cardigan across the back of her chair and looked round the office.

'Where's Tom?' she asked.

'He headed across to Hortons for coffees,' Billy told her. 'I thought you were going to be delayed. I'll text him and ask him to get you one.' Billy grabbed his phone.

'Nah it's fine, I'll go and make myself a cup of tea. You know I don't like that fancy barista coffee.' She checked her watch. 'And the interview was a no-go. They couldn't get me a mental health social worker until four o'clock this afternoon.'

'Bloody typical,' Billy said. 'You could always help me file some of this,' he teased.

Hazel smiled and started to walk away. 'Not a chance,' she replied, stopping in the doorway of her office. 'How long has he been gone?'

Billy checked the time on his phone. 'Half an hour, there must be a queue.'

'I'm sure he'll not be long,' Hazel said and closed her office door.

-

'Hey, hey, it's OK,' Tom tried to reassure Kelly when he found her crouched in the corner of the squat.

266

She'd not been able to tell him exactly what had happened on the phone, but Craig Douglas's name was clear in her garbled pleas. Tom was unclear but she was clearly shaken by something Craig had done.

'What's happened?' Tom asked gently and glanced round him. 'Are you hurt?'

Kelly's face was frozen with fear, her eyes wide and staring.

'Is he still here?' he asked, concerned by the state she was in. He was unable to get a coherent answer from her. What the hell had Craig done? As far as Tom knew, Craig only wanted to help the girls.

'I'll go and check upstairs,' Tom said. 'OK, you stay put.'

Tom crept slowly up the stairs, listening for movement in any of the rooms. The first door he came to was wide open but there was nobody in there. He stepped back into the hall. The next door was ajar. He pressed his ear to the chipped wood and listened. With narrowed eyes and his heart racing, he pressed the door open slowly with his finger. The room was dark, the thick grey curtains shut, allowing only a tiny chink of light to peer in at the edge where it didn't quite fit the window.

'Craig, It's DI Tom Newton. Come out so I can see you.'

He listened for movement, straining his ears to pick up even the slightest sound but all that he could hear was a train trundling across the bridge in the distance and the honking of car horns. A dog barked outside, startling Tom momentarily. He stepped inside, all of his senses on high alert. He pressed the light switch, but nothing happened. There was no electricity in the derelict building.

Footsteps in the hallway made him turn on his heels.

'Go back downstairs, Kelly,' he insisted.

Tom turned back into the darkness of the room. He crept deeper and deeper, listening intently for even the slightest of breaths. Behind the door there was a fitted wardrobe with sliding doors. The perfect hiding place. Tom pulled his phone out of his pocket and switched on the torch. He reached forward and slowly slid the door back, shining the torch inside. Nothing but a pile of old duvets and pillows sitting on top of a collection of suitcases. He tugged the duvets out and scattered them. Nothing. He slid the door shut and peeled open the other side, lifting his torch, ready to shine it in when a noise came from behind him.

As Tom turned, a hot, stinging pain spread across his stomach like nothing he'd ever felt before. He pressed his palm tight against the pain that had stolen his breath from him. Quickly realising what had happened to him, he tried to coordinate his fingers enough to dial for help until the handset fell from his grip as he collapsed onto the floor, unable to reach it before footsteps grew closer. A heavy, sick feeling slammed into the pit of his stomach when he recognised the shoes immediately.

He stared up into the face of the person who'd stabbed him, unable to speak.

Chapter Fifty-Six

Rachel was puzzled by the text she'd just read but grabbed her coat anyway. She wondered why Kelly wanted to meet her in the squat of all places. The poor girl must be really upset about Molly. She'd suggest to her that she come and stay at her flat for a few nights. Rachel was glad to see that they seemed to get on OK on the few occasions she'd seen them together in the community kitchen. She had hoped that Kelly would be able to help Molly get her life back to some semblance of normality. Kelly was a good kid at heart. Exactly what had gone wrong with her family Rachel didn't know and hadn't been keen to press her on it, fearing it might push her away.

A text landed on her phone as she was locking her front door.

> They've said I can go and see Molly this afternoon. Will you come with me? Xx

Of course Rachel would go with Dawn. Just let them try and stop her. She quickly typed her reply.

> Pick me up on the way x

She had considered adding 'Try not to worry, they'll take care of her,' but felt she couldn't be entirely sure how true that would be.

Rachel was glad that the sun had finally come out after all the recent autumn rain. The sunlight splitting through the leaves that were now simply glorious showed off a magnificent display of reds, yellows and oranges. She understood exactly why people flocked to Perthshire every autumn.

She watched a couple walking across the South Inch together, holding hands, while a small, curly-haired child threw a ball for an eager Labrador. How nice that must be, she thought. Simple family moments that Rachel had missed out on. One of the many things she'd missed. Steven's entire childhood was another. The first day at school. His first crush. His first broken heart. How she wished he would reply to the volumes of letters she'd sent him. The skate park nearby sounded like it was busy.

A phone call interrupted her musing.

'Hello, yes I'm on my way,' she smiled. 'What's the urgency?' Rachel laughed at the excitement in her voice. 'OK, OK, yes, I do love surprises,' she said as she reached the end of Tay Street. 'I'm less than two minutes away.'

Rachel shook her head, a wide beaming grin on her face as she tucked her phone into her pocket. This was a nice distraction at least.

–

Hazel glanced up at the clock above her office door again. She snatched open the door and poked her head out.

'Is Tom back yet?' she asked, disappointed to see Andrea shake her head.

This wasn't like him. He had been gone almost an hour. Hazel dialled Tom's number and listened to it ring. She was about to hang up just before it went to voicemail but then someone answered.

'Who is this?' Hazel asked, confused on hearing a woman's voice.

'DCI Todd, I'm impressed. You checking up on lovely Tom.'

'Who is this?' Hazel snapped back. 'Why are you answering Tom's phone?'

Clearly Billy had overheard the anxiety in her voice, and he was now standing next to her, wide-eyed and whispering, *'What's going on?'*

Shots of panic burst through her whole body. Waves of nausea threatened to overwhelm her as horrific possibilities swam inside her head. She wondered if the call might be on speakerphone. Maybe Tom could hear this.

'Hello,' she shouted. 'Tom, can you hear me? Where are you?'

'Nice try, DCI Todd.' A sickening laugh came down the line that sounded more like a cackle. 'I suppose it's being a detective that makes you think of that.' The laughter faded before the line went dead.

'Tom!' Hazel cried out. Then, realising her pleas were futile, she begged Billy, 'Can you trace Tom's phone?'

'Sure,' Billy told her and raced to his laptop. It felt like a lifetime while Hazel waited for him to type in Tom's number and the app managed to give a location. All the time images of Rick's body slammed into her mind. God, no, not Tom.

Billy turned the screen to face her. Hazel gasped. 'I thought we'd secured that place.'

'Not well enough, it seems. Come on.'

'Andrea, call for back-up,' Hazel shouted as she and Billy swept out of the office at speed. 'And an ambulance.'

Chapter Fifty-Seven

'Hello?' Rachel struggled to push open the front door to the squat; the wooden frame had swelled in the recent deluge of rain. The police tape left fluttering in the breeze was a ghastly reminder of what had happened. She clutched the carrier bag of clothes she'd brought. Donations that she thought Kelly would appreciate.

The slow *clickety-clack* of the train heading into Perth echoed on the cool morning air. A murder of crows squawked as they took flight.

'Hello,' she called out again.

'You came!' Kelly's excited voice chirped towards her, and footsteps hurried down the stairs.

'Steady,' Rachel beamed, overwhelmed by the huge hug Kelly gave her. 'Here, I thought you'd like these. They're not much but...'

'Oh I love them, thank you so much.' Kelly kissed Rachel's cheek and tipped the rest of the bag out onto the counter in the kitchen. She held a green woollen jumper up next to her body then tossed it down before rummaging through the pile again, this time lifting up a pair of jeans. 'These are amazing,' she beamed, holding them up against herself.

'I'm glad you like them.' Rachel reached into her trouser pocket and held out a ten-pound note. 'Take this too.'

'Rachel, I can't take that as well.'

'Yes, you can,' Rachel insisted and pressed it firmly into Kelly's hand. 'Now, what's this big surprise you're so eager to show me?'

'You're going to love it.'

'Am I?' Rachel smiled.

'Yes! Close your eyes,' Kelly insisted, grabbing Rachel by the hand.

'Don't be silly,' Rachel said. 'Just show me.'

'Please,' Kelly begged. 'Close your eyes. Trust me, you're going to love this surprise.'

Rachel wasn't comfortable walking up a flight of stairs with her eyes shut but Kelly held her hand all the way.

'OK stop here, but don't open your eyes yet,' Kelly insisted.

Rachel couldn't help smiling. Kelly was like an excited child. She covered Rachel's eyes with her hands.

'OK, alright,' Rachel said.

'Walk forward, slowly, not far now...'

Rachel became aware that she'd stepped inside a room that was warmer than the hallway and it smelled different. She could smell men's body spray. She was sure of it, and she got a sense that there was someone else in the room with them.

'When can I open my eyes?' Rachel asked.

'OK,' Kelly beamed. 'You can open them in five... four... three... two...'

'Kelly, come on,' Rachel chastised her.

'One!'

Kelly stepped back and it was a moment or two before Rachel's eyes adjusted to the light in the room. Sunlight beamed in through the open curtains, and it was shining on a person who sat slumped forward with their back leaned up against the wall under the window. It took Rachel time to process what she was seeing. There was a trail of fresh blood across the carpet that led from the wardrobe doors to the window. The man's shirt and jacket were soaked in blood.

Rachel turned to see Kelly's smiling face and saw the large knife in her hand. She was holding it out for Rachel to take.

'Isn't this wonderful?' Kelly laughed. 'I thought you and me could do this one together. Pupil and teacher.'

Rachel couldn't speak. She couldn't feel anything. She was sure her heart had stopped beating and a cold sweat covered her whole body.

'Kelly,' she begged finally. 'What have you done?'

'Nothing that you haven't done.'

'Is he…' Rachel feared the worst, but she had to know. 'Is he…'

'He's still alive.'

Rachel dropped to her knees; the pain of landing so hard jarred her bones painfully. She ripped off her jumper and pressed it against the stab wound in his chest, frantic-ally trying to stop the blood that was leaking slowly.

'It's alright, you're going to be OK,' she told him, desperately hoping she was right and pressing the material hard against the wound.

'What are you doing?' Kelly demanded and grabbed Rachel's arm to pull her back.

'Call an ambulance.' Rachel yanked her arm away and screamed as Tom started to mumble something inaudible. 'It's OK, it's OK, help's coming.' She turned and looked up. 'Kelly, please, it's not too late to fix this.'

The sound of sirens getting closer was a relief. Hazel could hear voices coming from upstairs as she and Billy crept quietly closer. When they reached the top of the stairs, Hazel brushed a finger to her lips then pointed to the room at the end of the hall.

She mouthed the words, '*In there.*'

The horror she felt on hearing just two female voices arguing was awful. What if they were already too late? Heavy footsteps coming through the doorway meant back-up had arrived. It was no longer just the two of them but a team of six, so Hazel gave Billy the go-ahead to go in.

The chaos of voices, all shouting to be heard, was deafening.

As Rachel and Kelly were handcuffed, Hazel fell to the floor next to where Tom was slumped. There was so much blood.

'Tom, can you hear me?' she pleaded with her ear close to his mouth. 'Tom, talk to me.'

'I'm so sorry,' Rachel cried out. 'I didn't—'

'Get her out of here!' Hazel shouted and pushed down on the blood-soaked jumper to stop the bleeding as best she could until she became aware of two people behind her. Paramedics, she realised, when a gentle hand touched her shoulder. She thought she heard them tell her they would take over or something like that. The fear of possibly losing her partner made focussing on what they were saying difficult.

Hazel barely made it outside before she vomited. First Rick, and now Tom. It was then the shaking started, before her legs gave way beneath her.

Chapter Fifty-Eight

'Here.' Billy handed Hazel a mug.

'No thanks, I'm fine.'

'There's no sugar in it, I promise.' Billy's thin smile seemed to wake Hazel out of her trance.

She wanted to smile back but it wouldn't happen. Her lips seemed frozen in fear.

'He's going to be OK,' Billy said and laid her mug on the desk. 'Tom's made of strong stuff, he's a weegie, remember.'

'Did you call his next of kin?' Hazel asked.

Billy shook his head.

'I'll do it,' she told him.

'I don't think he's spoken to his mum for a long time,' Billy reminded her.

Hazel picked up the mug and sipped, relieved not to be hit by a sickly sweet taste. Even if she did understand he'd meant well in the past.

'I know, I'll be gentle. I'll call her once I've seen him.'

'Do you think Rachel has been in on it since the beginning?' Billy suggested.

'Who knows? Has her solicitor arrived yet?'

A figure appeared in her office doorway as a knock sounded.

'Cara,' Hazel exclaimed.

'I'll leave you to it,' Billy whispered and turned to leave, nodding gently at Cara as he passed her.

'I didn't know what else to do with myself.' Cara broke down.

'Here, sit down.' Hazel pulled out a chair and noticed Cara frowning at her, her eyes seemingly focussed on her shirt. She glanced down and realised she'd forgotten to change out of the blood-stained top she'd been wearing.

'What's happened?' Cara asked anxiously.

'Oh, it's nothing,' she replied. 'I don't want to talk about it.'

Apparently happy with her answer, Cara asked, 'What am I going to do?'

Remembering that she'd sent a family liaison officer over, Hazel asked, 'Has it been explained to you what's going to happen next?'

'Erm, I can't remember,' Cara said. 'My head… it's so all over the place.'

'Right, well, a post mortem is taking place today and…' Hazel had to stop because tears were burning at the back of her eyes. The pressure stung. She sipped from her mug, hoping it would interrupt the swell of emotion.

'I heard you've arrested someone,' Cara announced.

'That's right,' Hazel nodded gently.

'Did they say why they did it?'

'I've not been able to talk to her yet, I'm afraid.'

'Her!' Cara exclaimed. 'It's a woman!'

Hazel was grateful to see Superintendent Daly's serious face walking towards the office.

'Listen, I'll call you later,' she said and ushered Cara out the door.

Daly nodded at Cara, his thin smile an attempt to convey his sympathy, Hazel supposed.

'Are you alright?' Daly closed the office door after him. 'Do you want to go home?'

'What? No!' Hazel was appalled at the suggestion.

'Good, good, I'm glad,' Daly replied. 'Because we need you, but I had to ask. I want the t's crossed, and i's dotted as soon as possible on this.'

'And I appreciate your concern,' Hazel tried her best to smile.

Contemplating the interviews that lay ahead of her, she felt her stomach churn with anxiety.

'I came to ask if you'd like me to sit in with you,' Daly added unexpectedly.

'No, if it's OK with you, I'm going to take Billy in. DS Flynn, I mean.'

'Good, good, then I'll handle the press,' he said. 'I'll get a statement together and release it in the next little while.'

'Thank you, sir.'

'Also, Tom is out of surgery,' Daly told her. 'He's in a serious but stable condition.'

Hazel couldn't hold the tears in any longer. 'Oh thank God.' She flopped onto the chair that was behind her. 'Thank God.'

–

Hazel had changed into a clean shirt she'd found in her locker and had spent the last ten minutes in the ladies' bathroom, mentally preparing herself to interview Rachel and Kelly. Seeing Tom slumped there in the squat had been awful. The thought of losing him made her feel physically sick. She was shocked by the level of emotion it had triggered and the fact it cut deeper than when she saw Rick's motionless body. A psychiatrist would have a field day with that, she thought. But Tom was her best friend as well as her partner. Hazel had leaned on him when she'd found out about Rick and Cara, a discovery that had shattered Hazel's whole world. She stared at her reflection, wiping away the last of the tears before splashing her face with cold water.

Once the formalities and introductions were over Hazel sat for a moment just staring at Rachel. The terrified expression on her face betrayed the fear that the woman on the opposite side of the table was feeling. She seemed smaller somehow, like fear had shrunk her. Hazel glanced at her solicitor before opening the brown folder in front of her. She lifted out three photos and slid them closer to Rachel who looked away, seemingly unable to look at them.

'Sam Kennedy, Sean Cooper and Richard Todd.' Hazel tapped her finger on each photo, slowly, one at a time.

'Can you tell me about your involvement in the deaths of these three men?'

Rachel was crying now, and Hazel handed her a tissue from the box on the table. She stared at her solicitor.

'No comment,' she murmured.

'Did you and Kelly Tate plan the murders together?'

'No comment,' Rachel said quietly, sniffing to control the tears.

'Did Kelly lure them with promises of sex while you helped her subdue and murder them?'

Rachel sobbed loudly. 'No…'

'Did you…' Hazel began to ask another question.

'No,' Rachel shouted. 'You've got this all wrong. I had nothing to do with any of this,' she snapped. 'Why would I risk being sent back to prison?'

'Perhaps it's not something you could stop,' Hazel said. 'You were—'

'It wasn't me. I didn't know what I was walking into,' Rachel insisted. 'I was as appalled as you to see him lying there like that!'

Hazel doubted that very much, but the fact still remained that they had no evidence of Rachel's involvement, apart from her presence in the room Tom was found stabbed in. Her fingerprints were not on any of the knives they had found.

'I was trying to save him,' Rachel protested. 'I wasn't trying to kill him.'

'So why were you there?'

'She…' Rachel winced as a sharp pain spread across her chest. 'She, Kelly, she…' Rachel leaned over. The pain was growing stronger, breathing was getting harder. The room was spinning.

Hazel frowned. She was disappointed but acknowledged Rachel needed a break.

'Interview suspended,' she said.

-

'What did you make of that performance?' Billy asked.

'Mm, not sure, what about you?'

'Did you know she suffered from panic attacks?'

Hazel shook her head. 'No, I didn't.'

'She wouldn't be crazy enough to do all that again, would she?' Billy said. 'Surely she just wants to get on with her life?'

'But her fascination with the homeless girls, Billy, that has to mean something. I mean, how well does she know Kelly?'

'And where does Molly fit into all this?' Billy asked.

'Good question. The red hair doesn't fit, does it? Kelly's hair is blonde.'

Andrea walked towards them with a dirty rucksack in her gloved hands.

'I think I can answer that question.' Her wide beaming smile lifted Hazel's mood considerably.

—

Craig Douglas walked away from the station after handing in what she'd hidden in his flat. He was done with all this. It had gone too far. He knew he should have told them the truth long ago but the fear that his secret would be exposed was overwhelming. Now that detective had been hurt. But it ended here. He had to confess what he'd done and accept the consequences. Confess to it all. Something he should have done long ago. Perhaps if he had some of this pain could have been avoided.

Chapter Fifty-Nine

Walking into the interview room that held Kelly Tate couldn't have been more different. The girl oozed with a confidence that made Hazel's skin crawl. She'd duped them all. Even Rachel, it seemed. Listening to her humming a tune from a well-known West End musical – Hazel couldn't remember the name of it – was bizarre.

Kelly was leaning so far back that the front two legs of the chair were completely up off the ground. The humming grew louder as Hazel sat opposite her. Then suddenly she stopped, dropped the two chair legs back down and stared directly at Hazel, her piercing blue eyes boring into her. Hazel started to introduce the interview, appalled by the smirk that was growing on Kelly's face before the girl started to whistle an eerie tune. Hazel could only glare at her in return.

She laid the three photos that had so unnerved Rachel in front of Kelly who seemed unfazed by them.

'Can you tell me about your role in the deaths of these three men please,' she said, pointing to each one individually.

'How's Rachel?' Kelly asked, directing her question at Billy Flynn, ignoring Hazel altogether. 'I had so much I wanted to tell her. So much that would explain everything to her. I know she's confused now but…'

'Answer the question,' Billy replied.

'Nice,' Kelly said. 'Teamwork, I like it.'

'Would you like me to repeat the question for you?' Hazel asked, pushing one of the photos closer.

'Yes please,' Kelly smirked.

Hazel fought the urge to smash Kelly's face into the table. As satisfying as that would be, and as much as the girl deserved it, it would not be worth losing her career over.

'Can you tell me about your role in the deaths of these three men please.'

Kelly lifted up each photo in turn. 'Just to be absolutely clear, you mean these men.'

'Yes Kelly, those men.'

'Erm… let me think.' Kelly tapped her temple. 'I'm sorry, you'll have to remind me, who are they?'

Hazel took each photo from her and laid them back down one at a time.

'Sam Kennedy, Sean Cooper and—'

'Ah yes, Rick,' Kelly interjected. 'Shame… or was it?' she laughed. 'His death did you a favour really, didn't it?'

'How did you know Rick?' Hazel continued.

'Your ex-husband, you mean?'

'That's right.' Hazel faced the question head on. She took a breath. 'Why?' she added simply.

'Would you believe me if I said it wasn't personal?' Kelly's lips curved into a sarcastic sneer.

'So you're admitting that you killed them?' Hazel suggested.

'I didn't say that.'

'Then what are you saying?' Hazel pressed her, appalled by the way Kelly was treating this like it was all a game.

Kelly shrugged. 'You're the detective, Hazel, you figure it out.' Kelly sat right back in the chair and yawned.

Hazel was grateful beyond words that Billy chipped in.

'Did you stab DI Tom Newton?' Billy asked plainly.

'I don't know, did I?' Kelly chuckled. 'Have you asked Rachel?'

'I'm asking you,' Billy pushed her.

They all turned round on hearing a knock on the interview room door. Hazel looked at Billy who was smiling, his eyes wide.

'Come in,' Hazel called out and enjoyed the expression of horror on Kelly's face when the uniformed officer walked past her and handed her rucksack to Hazel. 'You thought you'd hidden this pretty well, didn't you?'

'You can't prove that's mine,' Kelly protested, her cool façade starting to slip.

'If it isn't yours then why are your prints all over the inside and outside of it – handles, zips, the lot?'

'It's not a crime to own a bag anyway, is it?' Kelly turned to face the solicitor who'd been appointed to her. 'Is it?'

'No, it's not, you're right,' Hazel confirmed and started to unzip the rucksack, enjoying the sight of Kelly shuffling uncomfortably opposite her. 'Let's see… ah, yes.' Hazel pulled out a clear plastic evidence bag that held a long, red-haired wig and placed it on the table. She reached in again and laid out a bag with two butcher's knives in it.

'I don't know anything about those things,' Kelly insisted, momentarily shaken. 'You must have put them in there.'

Hazel reached in for a third time and lifted out a pair of black leather gloves. 'We've recovered DNA from sweat inside these. Whose DNA do you think we're going to find it matches?'

Kelly shrugged. 'Whoever has been wearing those gloves, I imagine, isn't that how it works?'

'Do you consent to giving us a sample of your DNA?' Hazel asked.

Kelly squinted at her solicitor. 'Do I have to?'

'They can get a warrant to obtain a sample and the chance of success in applying for one is very high. My advice is to cooperate.'

'Just before I answer that, can I ask you a question?'

'Of course,' Hazel said.

'Where did you find the bag?'

'It was handed in to the station,' Hazel informed her.

Kelly scoffed, the hint of a smile on her lips. 'He has no idea what's going to happen when I expose him.'

'Do you mean Craig Douglas?'

'It was him that handed it in, wasn't it?' Kelly snapped.

'He also told my officer what you did.'

'Oh yes and what was that?'

'You found out his secret and threatened to expose him. You said you'd tell the police and MOD what he did, threatened to ruin his life if he didn't do as you said.'

Kelly smirked. 'It was his own fault, did he tell you that as well? If he hadn't let it slip to Lynne Cooper then Sean wouldn't have found out and blabbed to me.'

'He's told us about his relationship with Lynne Cooper.'

Hazel had been disappointed that Lynne hadn't told her that herself when she'd informed her about Sean's death. If it hadn't been for Craig's recent revelations they wouldn't know a thing. Suddenly it all made sense. Why she'd told Sean Craig's secret was beyond her. Perhaps it was about the hold Sean had over her.

'And that Sean was blackmailing him for money to keep his mouth shut,' Hazel added. The phone calls between the two men all made sense now.

'What did you think about Craig when you found out?' Kelly asked. 'I bet you were shocked to realise he wasn't the saint he painted himself as,' she added smugly.

'How I feel about Craig's past isn't important,' Hazel told her. 'It's in the past.'

But the truth was, she had been shocked to learn he'd got a young girl pregnant while he was a squaddie on a tour of Bosnia. A very young girl, as it turned out. When he discovered she was just fourteen he was devastated. He had been sickened by his own behaviour. He'd explained that he'd spent the past few years trying to help young girls who found themselves desperate enough to become prostitutes. Some of the troops had been known to frequent the prostitutes in one of the devastated towns they'd helped liberate, taking advantage of the women's desperation for money after the devastation by Serbian forces. Not their finest hour.

'The knives were Craig's,' Hazel suggested.

'You'd have to ask him that.' Kelly huffed. 'Another thing, tell me, just out of interest, how many times did you see me with that rucksack?'

'Why does that matter?' Billy chipped in.

'You could have asked any time if you'd wanted to search it.' She pointed down at the bag. 'It was right there.' She glared at them. 'Hiding in plain sight the whole time.' Kelly began to laugh. 'Like I said, the clues were all there.'

'Does this mean you admit murdering these men?' Hazel put the question straight to her. 'All three of them? And attempting to murder Tom Newton?' She'd had enough of this song and dance crap.

Hazel watched Kelly's solicitor whisper something in her ear.

'Do you need time to talk to your solicitor before going any further?' Hazel desperately hoped she'd say no.

'Yes I think a five-minute break would be a good idea at this point,' the solicitor said.

'That won't be necessary,' Kelly laid her hand over his.

'I strongly advise that—'

'Ssh.' Kelly covered his lips with her finger then turned back to face Hazel.

Hazel became aware of her heart beating, not fast but powerfully in her chest. Surely Kelly could see the evidence mounting against her? Witness statements. Fingerprint and potential DNA evidence.

'Did you kill these men?' Hazel asked, almost holding her breath for her answer.

Kelly nodded, her piercing gaze holding Hazel's.

'For the tape please, Kelly. I need you to say it.'

The two women stared silently at each other. Hazel's heart sped up. She was looking into the eyes of the girl who had killed Rick and had almost taken Tom from her.

'Yes,' was all she said. One single, simple word. Hazel had another burning question for her.

'And Molly Barker,' Hazel quizzed her. 'What did she have to do with any of this?'

Kelly scoffed, a smirk growing on her face. '*Molly.*' The venom in her voice was obvious. 'She took what should have been mine,' she spat.

'I don't understand,' Hazel replied.

'No you don't, do you? None of you do.'

'Then explain what you mean,' Billy said calmly.

'Rachel,' Kelly's voice softened. 'It was all for Rachel.'

The two detectives shot a brief glance at each other then watched Kelly's eyes drop down to stare at the floor.

'How was Rachel involved in any of this?' she asked. 'Did you know who she was and what she'd done?'

A wide grin grew on Kelly's lips. 'Dear old Granny, of course I knew what she'd done! I thought it would be nice to do one together.'

Chapter Sixty

To say Kelly's revelations were staggering was an under-statement. She had explained gleefully that she'd not had the chance to tell Rachel the truth. This was something she'd planned to do once they'd murdered Tom, together. Kelly admitted to playing the whole scene over and over in her head hundreds of times. It was going to be so perfect. The family reunion.

'Jesus, I did not see that coming,' Tom gasped and winced from the pain of his stitches. 'She is a messed up kid.'

'And the rest!' Hazel said, worried at seeing him in pain. 'Do you need me to get someone?'

'No, no, it's fine. I'm a bit stiff and sore, that's all.' He held a hand up. 'I'm happy to see you.'

Hazel wanted to scoop him up and squeeze him tight. She was so relieved to see him.

'So she claims her biological father is Rachel's son, Steven, and she found out the family secret when she overheard a couple of her aunties talking.'

'Adopted aunties. Her real mum couldn't cope, it seems, so Kelly was fostered, then adopted. She hinted at some kind of abuse but clammed up when I probed further. Said she stole a letter from Steven's kitchen that had Rachel's address on it. That's how she was able to find her.'

'She had immersed herself in Molly's life of prostitution and homelessness to get close to both Molly and Rachel,' Tom suggested. 'How better to get revenge on the person she saw as having what she should have than to frame her for murder.'

'It seems so, yes.'

'Wow,' Tom exclaimed. 'What's Rachel saying about it? I would love to have been there when you told her.'

'She was as gobsmacked as you.' Hazel struggled to get the image of Rachel's stunned expression out of her mind. An expression that had quickly evolved into sadness and guilt. Guilt that she'd not been there to stop a grand-daughter she knew nothing about from doing those awful things.

'She confirmed that Rachel had nothing to do with it too, did she?'

Hazel nodded. 'Yes, it seemed all she wanted was Rachel's approval. By the sounds of things, Kelly's reunion with Steven didn't go as she'd hoped. He didn't want anything to do with her apparently.'

'Jesus, that's terrible.' Tom sighed. 'Bloody families.'

'Have you…'

Tom raised a hand immediately. 'Don't,' he said. 'I'm not calling them.'

Hazel had to respect his feelings. She privately thought that this was the perfect time to repair the rift in his family but it wasn't her place to insist.

Footsteps came towards his bed. The two detectives were extremely surprised to see who was standing a few feet away.

'Hello, Tom.'

'Hello,' Tom replied.

'I just wanted to come and say…'

'There was no need,' Tom explained. 'DCI Todd has told me everything.'

Rachel looked at Hazel and smiled gently.

'I owe you both an apology.'

'No you don't,' Hazel assured her. 'None of this was your fault.'

'She's right,' Tom agreed. 'You didn't know.'

'Are you going to be OK?' Rachel asked, pointing to the bandage on his abdomen.

'It wasn't as bad as they first thought,' Tom smiled. 'Nothing major has been too badly damaged. I was lucky.'

Rachel cried with relief. 'I'm sorry,' she sobbed, 'ignore me.' She searched her pocket for a tissue and wiped her face. 'I didn't even know she existed or else I would have gladly embraced her into my family. Perhaps I could have prevented all of this. As far as anybody knew, Steven had two sons. Nobody knew about his daughter.'

'Your granddaughter was very good at hiding things,' Hazel admitted. 'I can't believe that Steven could reject her like that.'

'It must have been a shock to find out he had a grown up daughter. I'm sure he has regrets,' Tom said.

'What will happen to her now?'

'All of our evidence against her will be sent to the crown office. They'll decide what happens next,' Hazel explained.

'But they will take care of her, won't they?' Rachel pleaded. 'She wasn't thinking straight, she couldn't have been. Maybe she needs to go to a hospital rather than prison.'

'That's out of our hands, I'm afraid,' Hazel informed her.

'I understand,' Rachel said.

'Try not to worry, Rachel,' Hazel told her. 'I'm heading back to town. Can I give you a lift?'

Hazel had said it before really giving her offer much thought and the expression on Tom's face said he was as surprised as her.

'If you're going that way, that would be nice, thank you.'

'I'll be back to see you tomorrow.' Hazel hugged Tom gently. 'Take it easy.'

'Is that an order?' Tom teased.

'Absolutely.'

Epilogue

Hazel nodded a greeting when she saw Rachel Fox outside the crematorium. She didn't have to come to Rick's funeral, and it must have been a difficult thing to do. Hazel hadn't seen her during the short memorial and assumed she must have slipped in at the back of the packed room.

'Hello,' Rachel smiled gently. 'How are you doing?'

Hazel asked Rachel to move round to the side of the building so that Cara couldn't see. She didn't think she would be as understanding of Rachel's presence.

'I'm good,' Hazel replied.

'Your friend, is she OK?'

Hazel shrugged. 'Cara will be fine. In time.'

'She's lucky, she has you.'

Hazel wasn't entirely sure she agreed with that. Tom passed the two women and nodded without stopping to talk. Rachel opened her mouth to speak but changed her mind.

'Tom will be fine too,' Hazel assured her. 'Stop worrying, Rachel.'

Rachel closed her eyes momentarily while she nodded. She sighed.

'Thank you. I know I don't deserve your kindness, not really.'

Hazel touched Rachel's arm. 'You didn't know. How could you?'

'Kelly told me she's going to be assessed by a forensic psychiatrist.'

'You've seen her then,' Hazel said. Of course she had. Rachel wouldn't abandon her granddaughter.

'Yes, I had to,' Rachel admitted. 'She needs me.'

'What about Steven?'

Rachel sighed. 'He's…' She stumbled over her words, seemingly trying to find the words. 'He's struggling with all this.'

'Have you spoken to him?'

Rachel nodded. 'Yes, a little. It's still early days but he's prepared to try and mend our relationship.'

'That's good.'

'The one good thing to come out of all this horror,' Rachel suggested.

'Quite.'

'He says her sudden arrival took him by surprise, and he panicked. He had no idea she existed. Didn't want his wife to know so he sent Kelly away and told her not to contact him again.'

'Perhaps that's what tipped her over the edge,' Hazel said, wrapping her jacket tighter against her body against the freezing cold air that was biting at her cheeks.

'Perhaps,' Rachel agreed as a gust of cold wind whipped past them.

Winter sunshine lit up the Scot's pine that bordered the garden of remembrance as the first flakes of snow started to fall. The sky was heavy with the first wintry shower of the year.

'Well, I'd better get going. My shift in the kitchen starts soon.'

'How is Molly doing these days?' Hazel was curious and the mention of Molly's name caused a smile to ripple across Rachel's lips.

'She's good. She's been clean for twelve days and has a place in a rehabilitation unit in Edinburgh. She's off there tomorrow, actually.' Rachel held up a hand to show crossed fingers. 'Fingers crossed. She's admitted to mugging a couple of men too. It seems she had a penknife that she stabbed them with as she robbed them.'

The other men. The apparent survivors. Only they weren't, it seemed. They really had been mugged. By Molly.

'That's good, I'm glad she's facing up to it'

'Absolutely. It's going to take time to get back on her feet, but she's got her mum and me to help her.'

Hazel was genuinely pleased to hear that. Molly's life had hit rock bottom. Selling her body for drug money must have been horrible. Being taken advantage of by men like Sean Cooper and Sam Kennedy was awful. Men like Rick. Cara had admitted she knew he'd been visiting a prostitute but had been too ashamed to tell her. Said she didn't want to hear the *I told you so* from her. How had Hazel not known? Had she been too busy with her career to notice he'd been doing it during their marriage? What else didn't she know about him?

'Did you hear about what happened to Craig?' Rachel's words tore into her thoughts.

Hazel had and the news had raised mixed feelings for her. The man had worked hard to make amends for the hurt he'd caused.

'The MOD are opening an investigation into the conduct of the soldiers,' she said. 'Yes, I had heard.'

'What will happen to him?' Rachel asked.

Hazel shrugged. 'That's not my area of expertise, I'm afraid, but I'm sure his evidence will work in his favour.'

'Hazel,' a voice chimed softly behind her. Hazel turned to see Cara standing, watching them.

'I better go,' Rachel told her. 'Take care, DCI Todd,' she said and headed off in the direction of the exit.

'I will. Look after yourself, Rachel,' Hazel replied as Cara joined her.

'What was she doing here?' Cara asked.

'She was paying her respects, that's all.'

'I think it's a bit late for that.'

Hazel slipped her hand into Cara's and squeezed. 'Come on, now isn't the time for that. Let's go and raise a glass to Rick.'

The two old friends got into the back of the black car that had pulled in next to them. Hazel hadn't forgiven Cara or Rick, she didn't think she'd ever be able to do that, but for today at least, they should be there for each other. After all, they'd both lost the man they loved.

A letter from Kerry

Hello!

Thanks for downloading the start of this brand-new Scottish Crime series featuring DCI Hazel Todd. I hope you love it as much as I loved writing it.

Hazel has been living inside my head for a very long time and she's someone I have come to adore. She is so pleased to meet you, to take you with her as she and her colleagues Tom, Billy and Andrea investigate the cruel murders on the streets of Perth. She thinks you'll be as shocked as she was to discover the truth. Hazel doesn't claim to be perfect but always tries her hardest to do what's right. Even if it pains her to do it.

If you have enjoyed reading *Death Rite* then I'd be grateful if you could pop a review on Amazon and Goodreads for me so others can give it a try. Tell your friends, colleagues, the postman, the milk man and anyone who will listen. Your support is extremely appreciated.

I can be found rambling and sharing horseracing videos and more on Twitter where I would love to hear from you. Links to where I can be found are below –

With love and best wishes

Kerry x

@kezzawattsbooks
kerrywatts.simplesite.com

Acknowledgments

Producing a novel from a hint of an idea inside an author's head to the book you are staring at now takes the work of many, many hands. I'd like to take this opportunity to thank some of those hands now.

Firstly, thank you to my family for your continuous support and encouragement.

Flynn for listening to endless paragraphs just so I can see if something sounds right. For his unique acting talent as he brings scenes to life for me.

Thank you to Hannah for always telling me that my work is something she would definitely watch on Netflix.

Mark for listening to endless rambling ideas that make sense in my head but not out loud. Your enthusiasm for my books is truly appreciated.

Thanks, Dad for always asking – how's your book getting on? – it means a lot.

Thank you to my agent Robbie who has had to put up with endless emails since we met in 2019 which he has handled with such patience, he deserves a medal. Thanks. It means a lot.

Thank you to Keshini and everyone at Hera for taking a chance on me as well as DCI Hazel Todd, and for helping me bring her to life with the aid of your amazing team of editors and hawk-eyed proof-readers as well as your

fantastic cover designers. From the bottom of my heart –
Thank you.

To the enthusiastic crime fiction readers of Facebook,
Twitter, Goodreads and beyond – Thank you so much
for your continued support. You make all this hard work
worthwhile.